so shelly

TY ROTH

DELACORTE PRESS

Text copyright © 2011 by Ty Roth
Jacket art copyright © 2011 by Sara Lazzeroni

All rights reserved. Published in the United States by Delacorte Press, an imprint of Random House Children's Books, a division of Random House, Inc., New York.

Delacorte Press is a registered trademark and the colophon is a trademark of Random House, Inc.

Visit us on the Web! www.randomhouse.com/teens

Educators and librarians, for a variety of teaching tools, visit us at www.randomhouse.com/teachers

Library of Congress Cataloging-in-Publication Data is available upon request.
ISBN 978-0-385-73958-0 (hc) — ISBN 978-0-385-90794-1 (lib. bdg.)
ISBN 978-0-375-89792-4 (ebook)

The text of this book is set in 12-point Goudy.

Book design by Kenny Holcomb

Printed in the United States of America

10 9 8 7 6 5 4 3 2 1

First Edition

Random House Children's Books supports the First Amendment and celebrates the right to read.

for bob

PROLOGUE

Most of us like to believe that we are born to do great things, maybe even to be famous. Truth is, we aren't and we won't.

Instead, we are of the anonymous dark energy that accounts for nearly 96 percent of the universe. Sure, in our corners of wherever, we may play relatively significant roles and accomplish important "stuff" like earning good grades and incomes, falling in love, raising families, maybe even advancing worthy social causes, but in the cosmic picture, the vast majority of people—dead, living, or yet to be born—had, have, or will have no freaking clue that we once were, are, or will be.

Sucks. Doesn't it?

"So, what's the point?" you ask.

I can tell you. Better yet, later on, I'll show you. But don't be disappointed when you realize that you've heard it before, and that, deep down, you already knew the answer.

Are you ready?

Love and death.

In the end, that's all there is. Do those two things well, and you may have a chance at something close to a meaningful existence. Screw them up, and life is pretty pathetic.

"Okay," you're thinking. "Love, I understand."

But do you? We throw the word around so much that it is nearly meaningless. We've reduced the experience of "being in love" to that which can be summarized in a pop song or portrayed in a chick flick. Then we're angry and disillusioned when love disappoints. Here's a little secret: love always disappoints. It's the conscious choice to love someone or *not* to love someone, despite the disappointment, that makes it beautiful.

And it *is* beautiful. I know that now.

"Fine," you say. "But isn't this focus on death a little morbid?"

I'll admit, there was a time when I would have said the same thing. Not anymore. Death exists. You can piss and moan about it all you want, but it still exists. And I can guarantee you this: unless you learn to wrap your brain around the fact that you are eventually going to die, you'll never wrap your arms around the less certain fact that you are currently living.

"How do you know these things?" you wonder.

I know because two friends, Gordon Byron and Michelle (Shelly) Shelley, showed me that love and death are far more complicated than your teachers, your priests, and pop culture want you to believe. Until a few months ago, Gordon and Shelly were classmates a year ahead of me in high school. They're the reason I wrote this. They're the ones who showed me that no matter how young or old you are, you'd better start living and loving to the fullest right now. And if, by sharing their stories, I can prove that to you, it might make my having lived worthwhile.

I'm Keats (rhymes with "sheets"). I'm dying. And I don't mean in a someday sort of way, but as in sooner rather than later. I can't tell you exactly when or of what just yet, but trust me, I know. It's the curse of the Keatses. We die young: my paternal grandparents died before I was born, both of my parents died before they reached forty, and my brother is next door wasting away to nothing as I type. The Disease, as Tom likes to call his tuberculosis, is rapidly decelerating his functionality to zero.

That's right, tuberculosis.

I know what you're thinking. "Americans don't die of tuberculosis. That's some third world shit."

Well, they do sometimes, in poor neighborhoods, especially when their immune system, like Tom's, has been weakened by diabetes. Add occasional heroin injections to the mix and the lungs become a breeding ground for the bacterium called *Mycobacterium tuberculosis,* which gives its name to the Disease. If you've never been poor, you'd be surprised at what poor people do . . . or do not do. There are approximately thirteen thousand new cases of tuberculosis reported every year.

Tom's death march follows four years of watching our father waste away from ALS (amyotrophic lateral sclerosis, or Lou Gehrig's disease). (More than five thousand new cases of ALS are diagnosed in America each year. The vast majority of those diagnosed die within four to five years). Shortly after

3

our father died, our mother died from apathy and self-pity (no statistics available).

Prior to the events I'm about to relate, I tried to cocoon myself, to hide from death. However, all I accomplished was to hide from life. Now I've accepted my premature mortality as a matter of fact, and I'll confront whatever assassin God, nature, or chance sends for me.

Yeah, yeah. I know what you're thinking. "Aren't you being a little irrational? Oversensitive? A bit of a hypochondriac?"

Am I? Approximately eighty thousand young people (between the ages of fifteen and thirty) die every year, and that's just in America. I know. I've done the research. (The statistics are a coping mechanism that I've yet to relinquish, but I'm working on it.)

The good news is that in the three months since Gordon and I said goodbye to Shelly, my fatalism has fueled the urgency with which I now try to live, and it has prompted me to record the events of this story while I'm still around and able.

A brief but necessary disclaimer: much of this account is a piecing-together of events that I didn't witness and conversations in which I did not partake. The bulk of my knowledge was gained as I listened to an increasingly inebriated Shelly deliver a monologue spanning nearly ten hours and covering close to eighteen years of her and Gordon's lives. My re-creation is as faithful as possible to the truth as regards the personalities, philosophies, and conversational tendencies of those involved. But after all, who's to say what's truth? Who's to say what's not?

part one

ALAS! THEY WERE SO YOUNG, SO BEAUTIFUL,
SO LONELY, LOVING, HELPLESS, AND THE HOUR
WAS THAT IN WHICH THE HEART IS ALWAYS FULL,
AND, HAVING O'ER ITSELF NO FURTHER POWER,
PROMPTS DEEDS ETERNITY CAN NOT ANNUL.
—GEORGE GORDON,
LORD BYRON, *DON JUAN*

1

It was the last day of school and the first day of summer. One of those limbo days, when you're not quite sure if you're ending or beginning. Either way, my junior year was over, and I hoped I'd never see another one like it. However, there was one more thing Gordon and I had to do before I could put the year fully to rest.

The gym was hotter than hell, but Gordon leaned back, as cool as ever, in one of the ungodly uncomfortable metal folding chairs that were arranged in a semicircle around a makeshift altar on which rested a black marble urn containing the ashes of our mutual best friend, Shelly. Gordon's plan was to steal the urn, drive to Shelly's, break into the pool shed where she'd kept her beloved boom box, shoot over to the island in one of Gordon's powerboats, and then spread her ashes while playing her favorite song from a disc she had bequeathed to me prior to her death. Not much in the way of funeral tributes, but all so Shelly.

According to Gordon, it was what she wanted, which, I know, leads to the question: Why would a healthy eighteen-year-old have thought to share her final wish at all, unless, of course, she knew her death was imminent? And if Gordon knew her demise was coming, why didn't he tell me? It seems obvious now; most things do in retrospect. But since Gordon and Shelly had been friends and neighbors for their entire lives, I figured her final wish had been the product of whimsical childhood speculation, protected by a secretly sworn pact. Shelly was a dreamer like that, full of "What if's" and "If only's."

Even if I had thought to ask the right questions at the appropriate times, the answers would have come too late to change the outcome. Anyway, even knowing what I know now, I probably wouldn't have changed a thing.

In theory, Gordon's plan was simple. In execution, it was not.

Trinity's gymnasium was packed for the early-evening wake with awkward teenage mourners—awkward, of course, because, while most present had flushed a goldfish or two or lost the occasional grandparent, few had attended a wake for someone their own age. Shelly's death was doubly aberrant, considering how extraordinarily *alive* she had always been— so alive that even the memory of her felt more vibrant than the breathing bodies that sat all around me. I, however, felt right at home. In just the past two years, I'd attended funerals for both of my parents, and Tom was, as I've said, not far behind.

Due to Shelly's fall-semester expulsion from Trinity, the school's administrators had hesitated to grant her father's request for the use of the gymnasium, which was the only venue big enough in all of Ogontz, Ohio, to accommodate the large outpouring of young mourners. I've learned that although there is a seemingly endless list of indiscretions that one may perform without being excommunicated from Trinity—including exposing yourself to a junior varsity cheerleader, screwing your English teacher, and stealing and consuming communion wine from the school chapel, all of which Gordon committed with relative impunity—writing a measly five-hundred-word essay on the necessity of atheism that, against all odds, gets published in the "My Turn" section of *Newsweek* is not on it. It was only Mr. Shelley's record of consistent and generous donations that convinced the administration to allow the wake to take place on school grounds.

But his donation, of an amount that only he, God, and Monsignor Moore (the pastor at All Saints Catholic Church) knew, was not an act of selfless grief. The public wake at Trinity was a transparent ploy by Shelly's father to keep her friends (think Gordon) away from the official funeral services. A members-of-the-family-only gathering was planned for the next evening at their home, with a funeral mass at All Saints scheduled for the morning after.

Like Gordon's, Shelly's family lived on a peninsular strip of beach-lined property that juts into Lake Erie, separating the lake from the Ogontz Bay. Locals call that strip the Strand. Seasonal residents from nearby Cleveland and Toledo, and from as far away as Columbus, Cincinnati, and Detroit, populate the majority of the sprawling lakeside mansions during the summer, but a handful of Ogontz's gentry call Acedia, a gated community on the Strand, home. The ultra-exclusive subdivision was intended to be named for Arcadia, the idyllic rural region of southern Greece, but when the wrought iron gate with the subdivision's name artistically rendered across the top arrived misspelled, no one bothered to have it corrected or to look up the meaning of "*acedia*," which is "spiritual or mental sloth."

Most of the "mourners" had hardly known Shelly, but it's hard to resist any chance for drama or dressing up when you're a teenager in Ogontz. And drama there was.

Shelly's disappearance and the subsequent discovery of her body, washed ashore on a small Lake Erie island, had earned her the sort of attention that nothing in her lifetime ever had. Several national cable networks had sent reporters and camera crews, intrigued by what they called Shelly's "socialite" family and her connection to Gordon, but the reporters immediately lost interest when foul play was eliminated and her death was ruled an accidental drowning. (Each year, fewer than 3 percent of all deaths of teenagers between the ages of fifteen and nineteen are caused by accidental drowning.) The cameras immediately moved on to their next fatality, this one having been bled dry. (A Class IV hemorrhage, which involves the loss of more than 40 percent of a person's blood, often results in one's bleeding to death.)

Despite the whirring of my mind and the turning of my stomach, I sat relatively still and looked around me. Even with the ceiling exhaust fan humming, the humidity inside the gymnasium refused to vacate the premises, as if its stultifying presence were necessary for the somber occasion and it felt obligated to fulfill its solemn duty. Oblivious to the heat, like a mannequin in some men's boutique clothing store, Gordon lounged and waited for the opportune moment.

I sweat and bit my nails while I waited for Gordon's cue. In my ill-fitting hand-me-down church clothes—I rarely went to church anymore, but that's what my mother had called any pants other than jeans and any shirts with buttons—I looked like a Geek Squad trainee. Gordon, in contrast, sat unfazed inside a maroon athletic-cut dress shirt open at the collar and tucked into a pair of black designer dress slacks. Unable to subdue my admiration—even on such a somber occasion—I stole sidelong glances at his freakishly good looks. Waves of thick brown, not quite black, hair poured to midway down his ears. The tousled longish locks epitomized the cavalier nature of the mind they concealed. His muted blue eyes peered hawklike over perfectly symmetrical and impossibly high cheekbones curtained by sideburns. I realized then for the first time that it was his mouth to which one was powerlessly drawn. It was almost a girl's mouth: lips full, moist, and ruby red that closed over and guarded the pleasures and words waiting to rise from his tongue.

"Now, Keats." Gordon didn't ask; he commanded and snapped me out of my reverie.

He never called me John.

"Now?" I looked around at the klatches of kids milling about on the gym floor. "There's too many people."

"Exactly. No one's paying attention to Shelly."

Before I could fire a second round of protest, Gordon was up and moving toward the altar. Like a child on parental heels, I followed. En route, I glimpsed Principal Smith with his arms crossed, standing beneath one of the side baskets and engaged in an earnest conversation with Father Fulop. (The puns are obvious and often employed: "Father Fulop Shit," "Father Feel Up." You get the picture.) He is Trinity's youth minister, spiritual counselor, head of the theology department, and first-class douche bag.

We passed a group of pouty-faced senior girls actually bitching about it being "so Shelly" to upstage them on the weekend of graduation.

Without hesitation, in a sweeping three-quarters overhand motion, Gordon grabbed a glass vase filled with red and white (Trinity's colors) roses off of one of the faux marble pedestals arranged on either side of the altar. Dumping the flowers, he continued toward Shelly's remains, scooped the urn from the altar top, replaced it with the completely dissimilar vase, handed the urn to me, and then proceeded toward the receiving line at the gym entrance.

Struggling to match his pace and to hide in his expansive shadow, I shoved the urn beneath my arm, inside my jacket. Thinking back, I should have known better than to fear being anything but invisible next to George Gordon Byron.

With typical nonchalance, Gordon continued toward the Shelley family, who, like most in the Trinity community, had grown to hate his guts. No one, however, disliked Gordon as much as Mr. Shelley, whose loathing was well earned. More on that later.

"Sorry for your loss," Gordon said. His extended hand was immediately rejected with an if-looks-could-kill stare from Shelly's father, who was, as of yet, oblivious to the fact that we had stolen the last of his daughter. "Right. Well, fuck you too."

As Shelly's father lunged for Gordon's throat (after accidental deaths, homicide is the most common cause of death among young adults), I managed to slip, unnoticed, out of the gymnasium with Shelly.

Seconds later, Gordon emerged with shirt tousled and neck scratched, but he smiled with devilish glee.

2

To even begin to understand Shelly, you have to risk knowing Gordon. To know Gordon, you have to consider the Tim Burton movie-in-the-making world that was his childhood.

Most of what I know of Gordon, outside of Shelly's epic monologue, I learned in snippets from Shelly or gleaned from the few-and-far-between conversations I had with him, but I have to believe that much of what he shared was, to say the least, embellished. Anyway, he is not the type of person one *knows* so much as knows *of*. Some things I learned from the publicity that followed the publication of his bestselling fantasy novel. In the spring of his eighth-grade year, Gordon finished his novel and Googled New York City literary agencies until he found the one that was the largest and most prestigious. By June, Gordon and his mother had signed contracts enlisting Martin Literary LLC as Gordon's representative.

With a keen understanding of the marketplace and the particular needs and interests of the various major publishing houses, Ms. Mandy Martin had *Manfred* placed within a week, with a healthy advance and a major—but nonnegotiable—request from Adam Pandroth of Pandroth Publications: "Make Manfred a vampire. That shit sells." (No one has ever died from a vampire bite.) After a quick rewrite, a professional edit, and an unusually high marketing budget for a first-time and teenage novelist, *Manfred* was fast-tracked for release the following summer.

Manfred is the story of an American boy expatriated to the care of distant relatives after the death of the boy's parents in an automobile accident (41 percent of all accidental deaths). Consigned to his ancestral home in the Scottish highlands, he meets and studies under the mentorship of a mountain wizard from whom he learns the secrets of conjuring, shape-shifting, and the controlling of spirits, including those of his mother and father. The novel made an impressive splash in the young-adult market. I was astounded that a boy nearly the same age as me and from my own backwater town had been allowed to swim in the deep end of literature at all. I became not only an ardent but also an envious admirer.

The remainder of my knowledge of Gordon was attained through the grapevine of rumor that sprouted incessantly around him. Regardless of the source, I have no doubt that much of what I'm about to share has been exaggerated, but, I swear, this is how I heard it.

I grew up and still live in a crowded low-class neighborhood of single-dwelling homes on the east end of Ogontz, less than a mile from the entranceway to the Strand but millions of dollars distant. If I walk one block north to the shore on the bay side, I can look northeast across the water to see the palaces rising over their putting-green lawns. These lawns run to backyard beaches from which wooden docks extend, Gatsbyesque, lined with WaveRunners and sailboats and powerboats of varying lengths. The two most prominently visible Georgian monstrosities, at which I still sometimes stare from my cement-footed poverty, belong to Gordon's and Shelly's families. The families are next-door neighbors; although, you could fit ten of *my* neighbors' homes between the two houses.

Prior to the events that followed the stealing of Shelly's ashes, the only intimate connection between Gordon and me, outside of our unrelated friendships with Shelly, had been that we'd both lost our fathers. Gordon's father abandoned him and his mother when Gordon was still an infant. The little that Gordon knows of him was dripped like poison from his mother's vengeful lips.

Gordon is the final bud on his father's Ohio branch of a patrician family of Virginia. The family's sons, all Annapolis-trained, had made their reputations in the United States Navy and their fortunes in the boatbuilding trade in the Chesapeake Bay region and along the Ohio shores of Lake Erie, where for more than a hundred years the Byron brand of cruising and fishing boats have dominated the waters of the Great Lakes.

When he was forced to retire with a less-than-honorable discharge after a female ensign's never-litigated claim of sexual harassment, Gordon's father, the handsome John Byron, still in his midthirties, took his partial pension, returned home, and assumed position on America's inland seas as chief executive officer of the Byron Boatyards. As the incompetent father of a two-year-old daughter, Augusta (the unwanted product of his putting into port with an admiral's not-quite-eighteen-year-old daughter between dinner and dancing at the said admiral's ball), he was desperate to marry. In exchange for John's assuming complete guardianship of the child (meaning the infant, not the teenager), the admiral agreed not to pursue charges.

Not long after his return to Ohio, through mutual friends at the Ogontz Yacht Club, he was introduced to Catherine Gordon, a thirty-year-old never-been-married still-living-at-home only child, and the last bearer of one of Ogontz's most respected family names. Pale, plain-faced, and plump, Catherine was not John's type—or any man's type, for that matter—but she came from good stock, and the pickings were slim in Ogontz for a fast-approaching-middle-age man with a toddler and a penchant for burning through money.

Soon after the tented and trellised backyard wedding at their newly purchased Acedia home, Catherine became pregnant. When Gordon was born on a frigid January day and officially christened, according to his maternal grandfather's insistence, as George Gordon Byron, the Byron and Gordon names were extended into the seemingly forever-rosy future. Rosy, except for one thing. Gordon had been born with a clubfoot and an underdeveloped calf and ankle, an ill-omen that Catherine thought of as the sole mark of imperfection on the otherwise angelic child. As Gordon grew older, Catherine couldn't assuage Gordon's own self-conscious contempt for his deformity. Despite the painful therapeutic manipulations and serial castings endured during his infant and toddler years, and the doctors' claims of success, Gordon developed a slight limp, which he still labors to hide.

Catherine, soon bored by motherhood, joined every social club and service organization that would have her, leaving Gordon and her newly adopted stepdaughter, Augusta, in the full-time care of Missy Fanning, a fresh-from-the-university early-education-major-turned-nanny who boarded in a guest bedroom next to the nursery.

The drudgery of permanent anchorage and the daily mundanities of running a business exacted a wearisome toll on Gordon's father, who, during his navy years, had earned the nickname of "Mad Jack" Byron. One afternoon, Catherine returned home early from her book club to discover her husband, ten toes down on the floor of the nursery, on top of the nanny, whose bare legs were coiled around his frantically thrusting bottom, while Gordon watched, wide eyed, from behind the bars of his crib. Catherine kept the children but sent Mad Jack packing, an exile during which he managed to deplete the remainder of his, and much of her, once-substantial funds. Catherine's remaining resources, though large by my family's standards, barely covered living expenses and the maintenance of the surface appearances required of those living on the Strand. According to Shelly, the interior of the Byron house was sparsely furnished and no one was ever invited in. She once remarked that the mansion was nearly as empty inside as Gordon was.

When Gordon was three, his father died of a massive heart attack in a Washington, D.C., hotel beneath a one-thousand-dollars-an-hour call girl, who, Gordon liked to brag, his father had stiffed three times. ("Although the risk of a heart attack is higher during sexual activity than it is during rest, the risk is still very low."—*The Merck Manual of Medical Information*)

Mad Jack's was a story that Catherine shared—with no detail spared—regularly with Gordon (and anyone else who would listen). It explained her vitriolic hatred of men and Gordon's spiteful admiration for his dissolute dad. She never dated again.

The children received a new nanny named May Gray, a never-been-married Pentecostal Christian in her midthirties who alternately doted on and physically abused Gordon while giving nominal notice to the attention-starved Augusta. May tended to Gordon's body and his soul. His every morning, from the age of two until thirteen, began with prayer followed by a ritualistic cleansing bath, which May administered with a bar of coarse pumice soap, until long after Gordon was capable of washing himself. The inherited wickedness of Mad Jack had polluted Gordon's insides, she believed, and the devil's brand marked the boy's foot. May Gray's divine purpose was to reclaim Gordon for Jesus. If her methods were oddly pedophiliac or abusive, the contradiction was lost on her as she caressed, kneaded, stroked, smote, and ultimately sucked the demon's seed out of him. Gordon never complained.

Gordon's exquisite exorcisms ended when Catherine—she had encouraged her children to call her by her first name—passed his wide-open bedroom door as he stood unashamedly naked, admiring himself in the full-length mirror hung on the inside of his bedroom closet door. Her presence inspired no humility or shame in her son. Suspicious, the next day she installed several "nanny-cams," and that night watched three stomach-turning seconds of a grainy black-and-white video of May masturbating Gordon with her left hand while reciting scripture from a Bible in her right. Only Catherine's embarrassment and desire to spare herself the publicity and spectacle of a trial kept May Gray from prison.

The Byron children were educated at home via an online Montessori school, which Catherine had paid the nanny (she would never refer to May by name again) extra to supervise. Both Augusta and Gordon were intellectually gifted and shared their mother's passion for literature; Catherine's extensive personal library of literally every book she had ever owned was theirs for carte blanche exploration. She made no allowances for age-appropriate texts, trusting that their natural interests and curiosities would either pique or repulse at the proper developmental stages. Her faith in nature was somewhat shaken one winter night, however, when Gordon was ten and Augusta twelve. She stumbled upon Gordon reading, by flashlight, Erica Jong's erotic novel *Fear of Flying* to his half sister as the two of them lay giggling beneath the covers on Augusta's bed.

Still, books were the one extravagance Catherine lavished upon them without guilt or reservation. The first Saturday of every month was set aside for excursions to Cleveland area bookstores, where daylong book hunts bagged armfuls of reading material sufficient to sustain their voracious literary appetites for the next four weeks. Their challenge was always

21

to consume whatever was purchased before the next month's safari.

As neighbors, Shelly and the Byron children were play partners during warm weather months; however, winter on Lake Erie is an inhospitable crone, shooing mortals indoors and out of her frosty company. From early November until late March, Lakers rush from house to car, from car to work, from work to car, and back from car to house, heads down, chins tucked, hands buried in pockets, and eyes, stinging with cold, trained on the nearest portals to warmth and light. A next-door neighbor might as well be the man in the moon, for all the likelihood of any prolonged social intercourse. But during the summer, in the child-starved Acedia, Augusta, Gordon, and Shelly formed a threesome that, according to the ever shortsighted Gordon, "only God or death could destroy," and he dared either one to try.

Their front yard was a Great Lake. The backyard was a shallow bay perfect for every kind of water toy imaginable: Jet Skis, sailboats, wakeboards, paddleboats, Kodiaks, kayaks, and canoes. Between the two families, they owned them all. It was swimming, however, that Gordon did best and loved most. Shelly loved the water as much as Gordon, and, even though she wasn't his match as a swimmer, she'd play with abandon in the shallows, and captain any craft.

If Shelly could be believed—her affection for Gordon sometimes clouded her judgments and remembrances of him—Gordon performed several swimming feats of Beowulfian proportion. One feat included a swim across the Ogontz Bay—congested with boats and Jet Skis—with Shelly, inside her life jacket, rowing alongside in a chop undulating at two to four feet. The two of them went to and around Johnson's Island, which lies off the coast of downtown Ogontz, and on which a Confederate prison had been located during the Civil War, long prior to which an elaborate cave system had been carved underground by the Ottawa Indians who had once populated the area. (It was on Johnson's Island that Gordon unearthed the skull he still uses as a drinking cup.) The distance swam, though great, wasn't as impressive as his avoidance of the propellers of the boats captained by inebriated skippers, who were hard-pressed to see the boat traffic crossing their bows, much less to spot a boy foolhardy enough to be in the water, accompanied by a girl in a dugout canoe (approximately twenty boating-related deaths in Ohio every year). But that was Gordon: taking risks and accepting all challenges, doing anything to prove that, despite his withered foot, he was as good as, if not better than, any "normal" kid.

On many other summer days, the three of them would sail, motor, or paddle to the island, build a camp, tell ghost stories, and conduct séances in the Confederate cemetery, or perform their own reenactments of Gordon's favorite battles from the War of Northern Aggression. Shelly would agree to represent those whom Gordon, true to his paternal Virginia roots, referred to as the "tyrants of the North," as long as he would later return the favor and play the interloping settlers trespassing on the sacred Ottawa grounds. Unlike Gordon's war games, Shelly's play scenarios were usually of peace councils and treaty signings in which she played a fictional female sachem named Me-no au-quay, which she translated as "good woman." She used to carry a small homemade lexicon of handwritten Ottawa words and expressions she'd transcribed from various websites and library books. Her version of the Ottawa language was, in fact, a mishmash hybrid of the Ojibwa tongue from which the various Ottawa tribes derived their own. During their excursions, Gordon and Augusta would randomly point to objects, which Shelly would identify in her particular translation of the Ottawa tongue.

Augusta, though older, responded compliantly to any and all of her half brother's whims and requests, playing whatever role and representing whichever side Gordon designated for her in the reenactments.

Fearful that his mother would improve upon her typically lax supervision should she learn of Gordon's tests of his manhood, he swore Augusta and Shelly to eternal secrecy on a sacred oath, sealed with commingled blood from fingertip pinpricks.

Shortly before her death, on a night when she had drunk too many hard lemonades stolen from her father's pool house refrigerator, Shelly shared much of this history and the secret of her, Augusta's, and Gordon's many midnight skinny-dipping sessions during those innocent summers. She described how the three of them would shamelessly slip out of their clothes on the back beach and walk hand in hand, with Gordon in the middle, to the bay, where they'd languish in the shallow spa-warm waters.

It was two events in the summer before high school that destroyed the innocence and, ultimately, the triad itself. First, Gordon found his life's purpose when he lost his virginity to Annesley Chaworth, a cousin on his father's side from back East. A sophomore marketing major at the University of Virginia, Annesley came to Ogontz partly to complete a mini-internship at the boat works and partly to spy on Catherine for her mother, Mad Jack's sister, who was, at least ostensibly, "concerned for the well-being of her deceased brother's children."

Although Mad Jack had left him little of monetary value, Gordon had at least inherited his father's fitness-model body type. Largely because of the hours spent swimming, he'd also already developed broad shoulders that tapered to a chiseled chest, washboard abs, and an impossibly thin waist. The incessant kicking had produced a rock-hard ass and explosive thigh and calf muscles. He was only fourteen years old, but at six feet and two inches tall, he could have easily passed for a college boy.

His first night with Annesley was less than memorable. Her stimulations were less skillful than May Gray's, but within seconds of entering her, he had spent himself, and Annesley, underestimating what would soon prove to be Gordon's nearly supernatural powers of resurrection, slunk back to the guest room. Over the next two weeks, Annesley performed as his nightly succubus—despite Augusta's jealous snooping and attempts at obstruction. Annesley rounded out Gordon's sexual education, teaching him how to tease and please a girl, and together they nearly exhausted the potentialities of human coupling.

When their respective internships were completed, she limped home with a glowing report regarding the well-being of Augusta and Gordon under the care of Catherine. In fact, she self-servingly reported that while all was well in the Byron home, she might make her visit to Ogontz an annual event, just in case.

For his part and for the first and only time in his life, Gordon made the association of sex with love. In the aftermath of Annesley's departure, Gordon fell into a deep depression during which he rarely exercised; instead, he either ate or slept most of the day.

With summer a month already exhausted, Shelly had been waiting impatiently for Gordon to appear and begin their play, for Augusta, lacking her half brother's vivacity and imagination, had proved an inadequate substitute. Besides, she seemed distracted and angry, though she wouldn't tell Shelly why. Whenever Shelly would inquire about Gordon and why he wouldn't return her texts or calls, Augusta would answer, "He's depressed," with no further explanation.

It was the Fourth of July (typically, seven people die each year in the United States as a result of direct strikes by fireworks) before Shelly saw him for the first time that summer. Augusta had dragged Gordon out to the back beach in order to watch Ogontz's firework display launched from a barge in the middle of the bay. In the sporadic bursts of explosive light, Shelly saw that he had put on a few pounds and that dark circles surrounded his eyes. When she finally approached him, the stench of alcohol, which she recognized from her father's own exhalations and its constant seeping from his pores, poured from Gordon. Shelly was unable to mask her disappointment, which sent Gordon sprinting back into his hermitage.

At around three in the morning, Shelly's cell lit up and

vibrated on her night table, rousing her from a fitful half-sleep in which she'd been wrestling with the possible causes of Gordon's fallen state and the stratagems for rescuing him.

"The dock," Gordon's text read.

When Shelly arrived, barefoot and wearing her summer sleep attire—boys' low-slung cotton boxer shorts and a form-fitting T-shirt that hugged her breasts and left her belly button exposed—he was sitting with his feet swinging limply from the end of the wooden dock. His toes tickled the surface of the bay. A flotilla of clouds blocked the moon. The air was humid, heavy, and wet. In some way not totally comprehensible to the mind of a fourteen-year-old girl, Shelly had come hoping to be desired by him. Though she was still petite, since last summer her body had lost its lean, boyish shape and assumed more womanly proportions; she desperately wanted Gordon to notice. She'd been imagining their night-swimming with great anticipation and with a new-found fascination for their respective bodies.

When Shelly sat down next to him, her long jet-black hair washed over her face and brown calf's eyes. Several strands settled in the corner of her thin-lipped mouth when the rest receded, except for the straight bangs that reposi-tioned themselves in soldierly alignment across her forehead and tickled her fluttering eyelashes. Seated with her hands palms-down beneath the backs of her bare thighs, she was unable to reach the tepid bay water with her feet.

"What's up?" she asked, hoping maybe that night summer would finally begin.

"I'm in love."

It was a punch to the gut that nearly sucked the air right

out of her. In that single declaration, she realized—although she would deny the fact until very near the end of her life— that, in his eyes, she would never be more than a friend, and that the friendship would never be enough, not for her. She considered sharing with him the depth of her own love and even offering herself to him as a measure of her devotion. In-stead she simply asked "With whom?" And she hoped for the miraculous naming of herself.

"You don't know her," he answered. "She's an angel."

"What's this angel's name?" Shelly kept a shoulder against the flimsy door that held back her pent-up emotions.

"Annesley Chaworth. Is that not a name worthy of heaven?"

"You know, Gordon, angels are typically male: Raphael, Gabriel, Michael . . . Satan. Name one angel that's a chick," she challenged him in a simultaneous attempt at humor and avoidance of the notion that he loved someone other than herself.

"Don't be stupid, Shelly. I'm serious."

"I'm sorry. Then who exactly is this Annesley?"

"That's just it. Who she is makes our love impossible."

"I'm not following you, Romeo," Shelly said, still poking fun.

"She's my cousin."

"Oh, *that* Annesley!" she said, bopping herself on the forehead with the heel of her hand as if she should be inti-mately knowledgeable of the Byron family tree. She couldn't hide her relief, and added playfully, "There are laws against that in this state, Gordo. Now, if you want to travel down-state and cross the river into West Virginy, you might be able to pull it off, but that dog won't hunt in these here parts." She had assumed her most hillbilly accent.

Gordon failed to appreciate the levity. He rose to his feet and said, "I thought you'd understand. I guess I was wrong."

"Gordon, wait," Shelly said, grabbing his hand and pulling him back to the wooden boards, still warm with residual heat from the day. "I'm sorry. Is she the girl who stayed with you guys? I saw her a few times coming and going. She's pretty. I thought she was a friend of Augusta's or something. I didn't know. Where is she now?"

"She went home to Virginia. *Not* West Virginia," he said in order to ward off any more smart-ass comments. "We text and call once in a while. I've even offered to move back East, but she insists that I stay in Ohio. I'm pretty sure she's blowing me off."

"It's probably for the best, Gordon," she said, trying not to sound too self-serving. "I mean, she *is* your cousin."

"I know, but I can't help that. She's the one. I love her."

There was a pause. Shelly could sense him sharpening the knife before he laid it bluntly before her. "We did it."

Shelly attempted to organize the ramifications of this unwanted information: (1) she wouldn't be his first, (2) Annesley was a whore, (3) he probably had an STD, (4) he'd have two-headed babies, and (5) Annesley was really a whore.

"We had sex," he added when she failed to respond, as if "We did it" hadn't been obvious enough.

All she could think to say was "I hope you used a condom."

"Condoms," he added.

The plurality made it worse for Shelly, but for Gordon the memories seemed to lift his spirits and to break the spell under which he had languished. He laughed, and the gloom dissipated immediately. He smiled. His confidence returned. He stood up, pulled his T-shirt over his head, dropped his shorts, and dove headfirst into the bay.

"Come on in," he called to her as he rolled over and made several backstrokes with his periscope intermittently breaking the surface.

Shelly knew that she shouldn't. That she mustn't. That there was a snake in the water (five to ten deaths by snakebite in the United States per year). But she never said no to Gordon. No one ever said no to Gordon. In the moonlight that burst through the thinning wisps of clouds, Shelly shimmied out of her shorts and top and stood naked in the spotlight moon, hoping that he would stop and be wowed by her womanly figure, which, in her mind, was every bit as beautiful and deserving of his body as Annesley Chaworth's.

But Gordon was already torpedoing away from her.

Shelly watched as his muscled arms, in a sinuous stroke, carved a path over the surface, and as the rhythmic, gyrating torque of his body intermittently exposed his perfect ass to the moon as he propelled himself away from her until he disappeared in the darkness.

"I love you," she said in a voice that soon tired, plummeted, and drowned like Icarus beneath the waters, long before reaching his ears.

Then she was in the water, a child again, swimming in his wake.

*   *   *

The second event that summer, which more or less divided the threesome forever, occurred on a steamy mid-August night, when Catherine, unable to sleep, and seeking the soothing, somnolent night air, stepped onto the back balcony of the master bedroom, where she heard Gordon's sounding calls of "Marco" being answered by girlish giggles and teasing "Polo." Catherine's storming of the beach revealed the trio, naked in waist-deep water, with Gordon's hands blindly groping for and often finding the welcoming bodies of his glistening sister and "that neighbor girl," as Catherine disdainfully referred to Shelly.

In the aftermath of Catherine's phone call to Mr. Shelley the next day, by his edict his daughter was no longer allowed contact with the Byron children. For her part, Catherine determined that an immediate and long-term separation was needed for Gordon and Augusta. God only knows to what planet Gordon would've been banished had his mother known of his couplings with Annesley.

In early September, she terminated her children's home-schooling and registered Gordon for his freshman year as a boarder at an all-boys prep school, the Brothers of the Holy Rood Academy in Sheffield on Cleveland's west side, while Augusta matriculated as a third-year upper-school student at the Brook School—Catherine's own alma mater—on its sylvan campus in the extreme southeastern suburbs. The Brook School was a secular institution that had been founded nearly one hundred years before by the nouveaux riches barons of Cleveland's industrial renaissance, who'd possessed the progressive vision that the proper education of a young lady should transcend the niceties of Victorian etiquette and social grace. So they'd financed an all-girls boarding and day school for the academic furtherance and social maturation of their urban princesses.

Catherine was completely indifferent to the founding philosophy or the mission of either school. She simply desired to purchase as much separation and containment for the incestuous siblings as her shrinking means could afford.

3

The air-conditioning unit was busting its servile ass to lower the interior temperature of Gordon's new car, a Merino-leathered air-locked, soundproofed black M3 BMW sedan. He calmly commandeered this early graduation gift to himself through the vehicle and pedestrian traffic in the gymnasium parking lot. Shelly rested snugly between my thighs inside the urn. Curious, I removed the lid and examined the contents. I turned momentarily to look through the tinted back window, fully expecting to see Mr. Shelley, with his square jaw set and fists clenched, storming after us through the gymnasium's glass double doors in pursuit of what was left—but being spirited away—of his daughter. But it seemed that Gordon's sleight of hand had yet to be discovered.

As I was still glancing back, without warning I was violently propelled forward. The shoulder belt bit into my neck as my momentum stretched the strap to its protective limits. As if in outer space, Shelly, inside her capsule, took flight.

Miraculously, Gordon's right hand appeared and blocked its path, allowing me to get my own hands beneath the urn before it turned over, plummeted to the floor, and spilled all over the carpet. Just a small puff of Shelly plumed from the urn, only to be immediately scattered by the jet stream of air-conditioning before I replaced the stopper.

The cause of the sudden stop, Claire Clairmont, Shelly's stepsister from her father's remarriage, stood stock-still, with her infant daughter nestled in her arms, less than two feet from the car's front fender. Barely in a little black dress (she was clearly pleased with her decision to nurse her child), Claire was more appropriately attired for clubbing than attending the wake of her stepsister. Another girl, dressed in a waitress's uniform, arrived simultaneously with Claire and stood at Claire's black stiletto heels, casting the evil eye of a gypsy witch at Gordon.

Gordon punched the steering wheel with an open right palm. "Fuck!"

Claire is the daughter of Shelly's father's second wife. His first, Shelly's mother, drowned herself in the midst of postpartum madness mere weeks after Shelly's birth. (About one in a thousand new mothers experience postpartum psychosis, which sometimes causes them to harm, or even kill, themselves or their babies.) During the winter of Shelly's junior year, her father abruptly married Mary Jane Clairmont. Shelly hated her stepmother (to make things worse, Mary had been Shelly's mother's name as well), as she would have hated any woman who wasn't her own sainted one; although, she had no memories of her mother, just photos and imaginings.

For her entire life, Shelly was the ignored princess of the castle, left to her own devices by a distant father who, on some irrational level, blamed the child for his wife's death. He left any and all discipline to a series of nannies, none of whom, for any extended duration, could tolerate Shelly's free spirit or her indifferent father's lack of support for or reinforcement of the disciplinary measures they attempted to administer. It's unsurprising, then, that Shelly didn't take too kindly to her stepmother's usurpation. And with Mary Jane's teenage daughters, Claire and Frances, in tow, Shelly's home was, overnight, transformed into a sorority house.

Shelly tolerated Claire because Shelly had no friends other than Gordon and me. She was pleased to have acquired one who, having no prior knowledge or experience with Shelly's "uniqueness," had few grounds on which to prejudge her.

Frances, on the other hand, was just strange—even by Shelly's liberal standards—a hard-core Goth and, Shelly was fairly certain, a cutter. Whereas Claire had been enrolled at Trinity in the same grade as Shelly and Gordon, Frances had apparently dropped out of school. She stayed out all night, slept all day, and was typically gone from the house by the time anyone returned from work or school.

It was through Shelly that Claire barged into Gordon's life with the misguided assumption that any friend of her new stepsister was a friend of hers. When it turned out that Gordon wasn't going to be Claire's friend, she stalked him. At school in the halls, at lunch, at his locker, at swim practice and meets, she was always there. Texting and emailing messages and pictures she'd taken of him, of her, of him and her; she even sent a picture of her flashing her breasts in a mirror.

Now there she was, too clueless to realize that she was mere inches from being made roadkill.

"It's not my kid," Gordon yelled from inside the air-conditioned BMW. Begrudgingly, he lowered his power window, letting the cool air out and Claire's voice in.

As Claire tottered on her heels toward the driver's-side window, I noticed that the angry gypsy girl's name tag read "Caroline." Shelly had warned me about the infamous Caroline Lamb, but I had never met the girl. Completely bereft of any lamblike qualities, she finally released Gordon from the track of her death stare and made her way toward the gymnasium.

I watched Claire mouth, "Her name is," but I only actually heard "Allegra" as the window completed its descent.

The baby had been born the previous December. Per Trinity's policy, and to Gordon's great relief, Claire hadn't been allowed to attend classes for as long as she was showing, so she had completed her fall semester at home through independent study, before returning during the second half of her senior year and recommencing the torment of her unconfessed baby daddy.

"I don't care what her name is," Gordon said. "She isn't mine."

I don't think even Gordon believed his lie anymore, but he kept insisting upon it, less out of a desire to avoid responsibility for the child than to escape an unimaginable lifelong linkage to Claire and Mr. Shelley.

Leaning nearly into the driver's-side window, she spoke to Allegra in that singsong voice adults use with children and pets, and she waved the baby's disinterested hand at Gordon, saying, "Say hello to daddy, sweetheart."

"It isn't mine," he insisted once more. Then he stomped on the gas pedal, catapulted the BMW into a timely gap in the constant two-way traffic of Madison Street, and, at least temporarily, left three females of his yet-to-be-reckoned-with past in the lurch.

I let a few moments pass in silence before I asked, "Why not just take a paternity test?"

He looked at me like I was the biggest idiot on earth.

4

According to Shelly's intermittent telling of Gordon's biography—any conversation with Shelly eventually wound itself back to Gordon—by the time he was banished to boarding school, he had outgrown his insular box on the Strand anyway, and he took immediately to prep school life. His widely recognized family name and assumed fortune (in fact, Catherine had to secure a second mortgage on the Acedia property in order to finance the children's education) won a warm reception from the faculty and administration, and Gordon immediately asserted himself as a mediocre student, superb athlete, and master prankster, the perfect recipe to expedite ingratiation with the boys of "the Rood."

Gordon won the hearts of the Brothers with his outsider's fascination with all things Catholic. Having been raised in a secular home, he loved the theatricality and sensuality of Catholic rituals, if not so much the "one true God" thing; his basic agnosticism remained sacrosanct. At the Rood, Vatican

II was treated as a malicious rumor; the Brothers remained frozen in 1960. Daily mandatory Mass was still recited in Latin, communicants still knelt at a Communion rail, and no lay hands touched a host. Gordon loved it. Within the first month, he had the Brothers convinced that he was committed to the conversion process. He even teased Brother Lombardy, the vocations director, with the prospect of his seeking a place in the order, despite its mandatory vows of celibacy, poverty, and obedience. There could not be three vows more antithetical to the nature and needs of Gordon Byron.

Within days of his enrollment, Gordon sauntered across campus as if he were already the shit, wearing his navy-blue blazer bearing the gold-braided crest of the Rood on the left breast—a rustic cross over whose horizontal beam a muslin cloth was draped, bearing the words "*Sacrifucium, Sanctimonia,* and *Scientia*"—over a white dress shirt, with blue and gold stripes slanting down the length of the school-issue polyester tie. His first night in the four-story dormitory saw him march onto the first-year students' basement floor, evict one of the boys from the room nearest the communal bathroom and showers, and relocate the poor kid to Gordon's own assigned room at the hallway's end.

The hand-lettered sign outside the desired room bore the names Wildman and Harness.

"Hey, Wild Man, pack up. You're moving," Gordon commanded. He'd eyeballed the single person inside the room and had correctly identified the one to whom the name Wildman belonged.

"Fuck you" was the response of the soon-to-be-expatriated boy, who remained crouched with his back to Gordon while he fidgeted with computer cables.

"Don't flatter yourself, stud," Gordon answered in an exaggerated lisp.

When Wildman rose, he stood two inches taller than Gordon and at least twenty-five pounds heavier. He was a middle linebacker who'd already been promoted to the varsity football team.

Having heard homophobic horror stories of life in an all-boys prep school dormitory, "Wild Man," as Gordon had baptized him, turned around with his fists balled and ready to pummel, but there was something unsettling about Gordon's cocksure stare that set off warning bells in Wild Man's head and emasculated his violent intentions.

After a pause, Wild Man marched from the room toward his new digs in the nether lands of Harrow Hall. Carrying a box of trophies from home, he muttered something about a "faggot for a roommate" and about returning for the rest of his stuff later.

It was then that Gordon spotted a thin, delicate waif of a boy standing timidly in the corner behind the bunk beds. The boy was, apparently, a portion of Gordon's booty of conquest. His name was William Harness.

When Willie emerged from his niche, he did so with a limping gait.

Gordon's eyes opened wide, and Willie intuited the question. "I have a bad leg. I was born with a club—"

"—foot," Gordon finished, and a friendship was born. "What's your name?" he asked, and extended his hand.

"William. I'm new here."

"I'll tell you what, William I'm-new-here. I'll just call you Willie, and if anyone here bullies you, tell me and I'll take care of it."

Despite his personal shame, Gordon's relative wealth, fame, athleticism, and good looks would always be more than enough "cool" currency to compensate for the derision that might have otherwise been directed toward him because of his clubfoot. Willie, however, with his diminutive stature, introverted nature, and tendency toward all things geek, possessed no such bankroll.

Turned out that, like Gordon, Willie was a bit of an artistic prodigy. He had already held gallery showings of his more conservative paintings: still lifes, seascapes, and portraits. For a short time, he had secretly operated his own fantasy art website—filled with rendition after rendition of chiseled heroes, often naked, always male, in throes of various combats with mythical monsters—until his parents discovered his little side project. Appalled by the homoeroticism, but without a sniff of irony, they enrolled William at the Rood. Willie had the Web page up and running under a new URL address and domain name within an hour.

Over the single academic year that Gordon would spend at the Rood, he would discover that a disproportionate number of the boys had been sent there because of parental revulsion for their offspring, not because the boys had been called to an education in "Sacrifice, Virtue, and Knowledge." In his freshman class alone were any number of a variety of deviants, ranging from the simply neurotic to the violent to the perverted, and some who were a little bit of all three.

Gordon had never even seen a game of lacrosse prior to his arrival at the Rood, but he took to the sport as if he had been born with a stick in his hand. Like a stutterer who sings with perfect precision, Gordon lost his limp in the adrenaline rush of athletic competition. He reveled in the fact that Shelly's beloved Ottawa were some of the earliest Native American players of the sport christened "lacrosse" by French missionaries. By midseason near the end of September, Gordon was promoted from the junior varsity, replaced a senior at one of the attackman positions, and quickly became the team's most prolific scorer. By tournament season in late October, the Knights of the Holy Rood were playing with synergistic energy. Inspired play, a good deal of luck, and consistent underestimation by their opponents combined to allow the Knights to blow through both the district and regional tournaments and to qualify for the first time in school history for the state tournament held in Columbus on the turf at the Ohio State University. The Brothers were beside themselves with pride and joy.

Gordon, sensing that the magic had been exhausted, turned his own attention from lacrosse to having as much fun as possible in the state's capitol city. Namely, he was determined to get laid. He had been celibate since Annesley, and other than one exhaustively chaperoned Saturday-afternoon dance with the girls of Ursuline Academy, he hadn't so much as sniffed a girl in more than two months.

In Columbus, Gordon's libido was about to make Holy Rood history.

After a brief "walk-through" practice on the game turf, the Knights' contingent checked into a high-rise Holiday Inn smack-dab in the middle of campus. With hands and faces pressed against the windows of the bus, the boys nearly broke their necks en route as they ogled the smorgasbord of college girls offered up on the campus of the Ohio State University. A literal buffet of dinner entrees had been arranged for them in a hotel conference room, to which they immediately reported after squaring themselves away in their rooms on the seventh floor.

Coach Abbott and Brother Lombardy, team chaplain, conducted a bed check at ten. At eleven, the doorman, after pocketing a twenty-dollar tip/hush money combination, hailed Gordon a taxi. Gordon was dressed in his school uniform, minus the patch, which he had carefully detached with nail clippers thread by thread, sans the tie, and with his white shirt unbuttoned to his sternum. The cabbie drove to a nearby ATM, where Gordon emptied the account of the entire two-hundred-dollar allowance his mother sacrificed to deposit each month for his expenses.

"Where now?" the cabbie asked.

"Strip club."

After a protracted dubious look in the rearview mirror, the cabbie asked, "Which one, Sherlock?"

"The best one," Gordon answered without hesitation.

"That would be Xanadu."

*   *   *

The blond behemoth of a bouncer/ID checker with a buzz cut and biceps the size of Gordon's thighs wasn't stupid. He'd watched Gordon exit the taxi and attempt to lose himself inside a just-arriving group of preppy college-aged fools. But it was a Thursday night; business was slow. The kid was by himself and clearly not looking for trouble, just ass. Bouncer guy admired the kid's moxie and pretended not to notice as the boy slipped past him to the cashier, where Gordon forked over a twenty-dollar cover charge. Including the twenty-dollar cab ride with a five-dollar tip, and now the cover, Gordon's wad had taken some serious hits, and he had yet to see a single pair of tits.

After he stepped through a set of red velvet curtains, it took a few seconds for his eyes to adjust to the darkness and the garish motley-colored lighting lining the stage, which was shaped like a giant phallus—a long thrust stage with a mushroom top and two semicircular stages at the bottom. One girl worked the runway while two others performed circus feats on brass poles, inside cages, on top of the base stages.

Gordon stood statue-like, stiffened to paralysis and overwhelmed by his good fortune.

"Can I get you something?" The voice came from the darkness, barely rising above the thumping dance music and the DJ's imploring, "Let's give a Xanadu welcome to Brittany, now performing on the main stage."

Slowly, he realized that he was the target of the inquiry rising from the murky depths beneath him.

"Can I get you something?" a pixie of a girl repeated

patiently, if not slightly exasperatedly. She was holding a cocktail tray and was dressed in a version of a Catholic schoolgirl's uniform, with a white button-down blouse tied in a halter over an impossibly small plaid skirt and white kneesocks.

"Do you go to Ursuline?" Gordon asked.

The uniform was an exact match.

"What? No. What are you talking about?"

"The uniform."

"No, stupid. Look around."

Scanning the club, Gordon saw a bevy of Ursuline girls. Some carrying drinks, some bent over, whispering in men's ears, some actually sitting on laps. All smoking hot.

"But Xanadu is an oriental fantasy," he said, explaining his confusion. "I expected harem girls, belly dancers, genies, that sort of thing."

"What?"

He wasn't sure if she was befuddled by his observation or sincerely unable to hear him.

Gordon raised his voice to a low shout, "You know, Coleridge. The poet. 'Kubla Khan.' 'In Xanadu did Kubla Khan / A stately pleasure-dome decree . . .'"

"Look," she said, made unhappy by the delay but also mildly intrigued by the poetry-spouting kid, "I'm no English major, and the owner is a moron. Tonight is Catholic Schoolgirl Night." She actually made air quotes with the fingers of her free hand.

"What *are* you studying, then?"

"How do you know I'm studying anything?"

"Well, you said, 'I'm no English major.' The implication is that you must have some other major."

She hesitated, uncertain how much she should reveal beyond what the ridiculously tiny uniform already advertised.

By boss's orders and economic necessity, she insincerely smiled and teased and flirted with her customers; although, in the three months that she'd been waitressing at the club, she'd grown secretly to loathe the men whose tips were making her attendance at the university possible. But there was something different, really attractive, about this guy. He wasn't exactly sweet, but he was interesting, and impossibly good-looking. She knew better, and she hated herself for liking him.

"Marketing," she finally answered.

Gordon studied her through the thick miasmic mix of light and sound and shadow. She was in a completely different category of girl from Annesley, who was red-haired, fair-skinned, nearly six feet tall, and big-boned. This girl was dark, tiny, and taut. His appetite was whetted.

"What's your name?" he asked.

Before she could stop herself, she answered, "Caroline." It was the first time she'd used her real name with a customer. She usually ran down the roster of Pussycat Dolls: Monday, Nicole; Tuesday, Ashley; Wednesday, Kimberly; Thursday, Melody; Friday, Jessica; Saturday, Carmit; off Sundays.

"What time you get off, Caroline?"

"We close at two."

"How about coffee?"

Caroline hesitated. "Coffee?"

"Yeah, coffee. I like you, and I haven't been with a girl in a very long time."

"And why's that?"

"Business," Gordon answered without hesitation.

"Business? What kind of business?"

"Mine," he said almost too brusquely, "but I'll tell you all about it over a cup of coffee."

"Exactly how old are you?" Caroline asked.

"You want the truth?"

"Sure."

"Nineteen." Gordon knew she'd seen enough underage guys con their way into the club so that she was most likely suspicious, but he also knew that his actual fourteen and three quarters years would cause an immediate rejection from Caroline and an ejection from the club.

"Me too," she said. "Look. Sit here in my section. I'll take care of your drinks and keep the managers away. If you're still here at two and able to walk out, I'll take you up on that cup of coffee. If not, I'll call you a cab."

"Deal," he answered, and sat down at a square-topped table, a safe distance from the cash vacuums writhing about onstage.

For two hours Gordon threw back mixed drinks at an alarming rate, but they were weak, and he and Augusta had been helping themselves to their father's well-stocked liquor cabinet since Gordon was ten years old, building the alcoholic tolerance of veteran barflies. To his great disappointment, he quickly grew bored with the equally anesthetized strippers onstage and turned his full attention to admiring Caroline as she worked the floor and the pathetic losers populating it.

*   *   *

Caroline's "You win. Let's go" pulled him from the fog of fatigue and slight inebriation that had settled around him.

Gordon followed her out through the front entrance, earning a disbelieving yet congratulatory gaze from the bouncer, who had seen most of the girls exit with customers at one time or another, but those men were almost always dressed in tailored suits and expensive jewelry, and they tipped him and the valets generously, obnoxious in their blasé disregard for their money, and they almost always sped away in foreign sports cars. This kid's apparent conquest of Caroline, the Ice Queen, was an upset of historic dimensions: 1980 U.S. Olympic hockey team proportions.

Her hair was down now, flowing freely past her shoulders, with occasional wisps falling over her blue-gray eyes. She had wiped away her makeup and had changed into an oversized red hoodie and a pair of tight-fitting gray fleece sweatpants with "Buckeyes" emblazoned in an arch across her ass. The sway of her breasts and the pistonlike pumping of her butt cheeks against the fabric betrayed that she wore nothing underneath. Despite all the flesh he had just seen paraded, Caroline was, by far, at that moment, the sexiest girl Gordon had ever laid eyes on.

"Everything all right, Melody?" the bouncer asked. He knew her naming system.

"Fine, Tim. He's an old friend from high school. I'll see you tomorrow night."

Walking awkwardly, and battling the dragon suddenly roused inside his pants, Gordon followed Caroline across the

paved parking lot to the farthest corner, where the employ-
ees parked.

Caroline threw her bag into the back of a girlish pastel
purple Geo Tracker, one of those half-ass two-door minijeeps
that only a chick could drive with even a modicum of dignity.

An Indian summer day had given way to an early autumn
night that was clear and crisply cold. Gordon's breaths rose
in puffs of expiration until they were taken away as she sped
south toward campus through the northern suburban streets
of Columbus. Whatever residual buzz he had left the club with
was blown away by the fast-flowing and bracing air, which
somehow seemed to leave Caroline completely unfazed.

Without a heads-up of any kind, she whipped the
Tracker left into an open-all-night Denny's, then right into
a vacant parking space, before pressing purposely too heavily on the brake, abruptly engaging Gordon's seat belt, which
pressed hard into his collarbone. He was shaken, stirred, and
sufficiently warned that she was not to be fucked with, but
she had no idea of the depth of Gordon's own mad, bad, and
dangerous personality or that she was actually the lamb leading itself to slaughter.

Coffee became a full meal once the laminated menus appeared in front of them. Neither read a word. For the waitress, they simply pointed at the photographs of the stack of
pancakes, the waffles covered with strawberries and whipped
cream, dip-worthy sunny-side eggs, grease-smeared bacon
and sausage, and piles of home fries. They weren't a bit

disappointed when the actual items failed to live up to the promise of the photographs. Despite her no more than one hundred and five pounds, Caroline ate like a long-haul trucker. Their sparse conversation never strayed from the goodness of the food until Gordon swiped the bill off the table.

"I'll pay for my own," she insisted with a stone-cold seriousness.

"It's no big deal," Gordon said, and laughed. "I got it."

"I don't want to owe you anything," she said.

"You won't owe me. It's just breakfast."

As she would later tell Shelly, and Shelly would share with me, Caroline gave in, surrendering absolute control of all things Caroline, which she had been struggling so hard to maintain ever since she and a longtime boyfriend, high school crush actually, had decided to "take a break" and "see other people." She hadn't "seen" anyone since and had no plans other than to reunite with him once he came to his senses. Yet here she sat with this stranger, a boy more beautiful than handsome, beautiful in what she thought was a safe, almost kidlike way.

"So, what's your name?" Caroline asked.

Without hesitation, he said, "Will Parry," and hoped she wasn't a fan of Pullman. Gordon had a Huck Finn–like capacity to lie on the fly.

"You go to the university, Will Parry?"

"No. I mean, yes," he stumbled purposefully. He'd discovered a long time ago that to make a lie believable, it's helpful to allow the person being deceived to think you're lying at first, then to lure him or her in with half-truths and crumbs of information. And, usually, the more ridiculous the story, the more believable it becomes.

As he had hoped, Caroline bit. Thinking that she had uncovered his dissembling, she raised her right eyebrow in consternation.

"I mean," Gordon recovered, "I don't go to *the* Ohio State University, if that was what you meant. I go part-time back home."

"Where is that?"

"Cleveland. I go to Cleveland State. I wanted to go to Ohio State. I was actually accepted, but I had to change plans when I was elected mayor."

Caroline laughed into her cup, nearly blowing coffee out of her nose. "You expect me to believe you're the mayor of Cleveland?"

"No! Not Cleveland. Pepper Pike. It's a suburb." Pepper Pike was Willie's hometown.

"And you're the mayor?" Her tone betrayed her disbelief.

"Yes. I was still a senior in high school when I was elected. At the time, I was the second-youngest elected official in the state. Some kid from the Toledo area had me beat by twenty-three days."

That was the kind of shit that hooked them. Although he was freestyling his story, the Toledo kid was real. Gordon had read about it on the Internet.

Caroline hesitated. Holding her coffee cup in two hands, she brought it to her lips and stared through the rising steam into Gordon's eyes, searching for any sign that would unravel his unlikely story. It was almost too silly to be true—yet was almost too silly to be a lie.

"So, how's the mayor business going?" She continued her cross-examination.

"It sucks." Gordon had also learned that people are more willing, more likely, and happier to believe the negative rather than the positive.

"Why's that?"

"Well," he said, continuing his ad lib, "Cleveland State sucks. And being mayor of a small town is a lot more difficult and a lot more boring than you'd think. I only ran on a dare from my government teacher anyway, but when I won, I was stuck."

"What's his name?"

"Whose?"

"The teacher?"

"Kohler. Mr. Kohler." It was his fallback name. He'd gotten it off a urinal.

Again, she paused and studied his face.

"Why are you in Columbus?"

"A city planning convention." There actually was such a convention taking place at Gordon's Holiday Inn. He'd read "Welcome, City Planners!" in white letters on a black placard on top of a gold stand inside the lobby of the hotel. He had a way of unconsciously recording almost everything he saw, even things only in the periphery. It was likely that that little sign had prompted the entire "I was a teenage mayor" story, even if at the time of its inception he hadn't made the connection himself.

"Uh-huh," she said.

"Seriously. Come back to my hotel and I'll prove it."

"How?"

"When I checked in, they gave me an identification badge on one of those dorky lanyards that you wear around your neck, and a bunch of crappy swag."

Caroline performed a prolonged lie-detection scan of his retinas.

He didn't blink.

A pregnant silence settled between them over the table. The tipping point.

She took a drink of water. Wiped the glass's condensation from her hand with her napkin. Looked into his eyes once more. Weighed the implications of hooking up with this guy. Weighed the implications of not. Decided that at least this one time in what had become her lonely life, she would take a chance, live a little. She must have thought, "Fuck it."

"Okay," she said. "Let's go."

Caroline watched as he slid out from beneath the table, stood up, and walked to the cashier. She liked what she saw.

She drove toward campus with her left hand death-gripping the steering wheel and her right index finger poised over and periodically punching her presets. (Traffic fatalities caused by distracted driving have doubled in recent years.) Gordon gave up on holding a conversation over the alternating Top Forty and rap music blaring, and the wind rushing past his ears. Instead he concentrated on keeping his pancakes down while surreptitiously texting his assigned roommate for the weekend, Pauly Dadeno, a senior second-string defenseman.

He attempted to text "Get out. Got a girl," but typing

blindly with his cell wedged between his seat and the door, he spelled "Gnt nvt. Gnt d girl."

Apparently, Dadeno had decoded the message, for after an "I told you so" moment when Gordon and Caroline passed the welcoming placard in the lobby, Gordon found his seventh-floor room unoccupied. However, in the shaft of hallway light that rushed like a playful puppy ahead of him into the room, he spied his large equipment bag, labeled "Knights Lacrosse," lying at the base of Dadeno's double bed near the windows. He spun toward Caroline, clutched her wrist, and pulled her into the room and him as he closed the door behind them.

Before their eyes had even adjusted to the semidarkness or she'd had a chance to consider playing coy, Gordon's lips found hers, which he gently parted with his tongue. Caroline sighed appreciatively as a dam of pent-up desire broke deep within her. Without disengaging, Gordon slid downward, cupped his hands beneath her bottom, and lifted her to his eye level. Caroline placed a hand over each of his cheeks and opened her mouth wider. Later, she would remember the too-youthful smoothness of his face and curse herself for her stupidity, but in that moment, she instinctively wrapped her legs around his hips and thrust her body upward, as if she were shinnying up a pole. Her face above his, she fooled herself into thinking that she had assumed control of the situation.

With Caroline grafted onto him, Gordon spun toward the room's interior and walked to the foot of the near bed, where he seated Caroline in front of him.

With her ex-boyfriend—the only boy with whom Caroline had ever been naked—Caroline, like most high school

55

lovers, would undress hurriedly in the dark or beneath blankets. One can only imagine her titillation when Gordon confidently and arrogantly teased her by slowly sliding out of his jacket and unbuttoning the sleeves and front of his dress shirt. In the moonlight that squeezed through the narrow gap in the otherwise drawn curtains, his shaded torso appeared sculpted. She compulsively reached between her legs when, at a painstakingly slow pace, he slipped his belt from its loops, unbuttoned, and unzipped his pants without averting his gaze. Gordon turned his back to her and inch by agonizing inch tugged his khakis past his bare hips and ass (he never wore underwear) and let them drop and puddle at his ankles and cover his deformed foot, pausing to allow her to drink him in. When he turned full frontal toward Caroline, she gasped, fell flat on her back, and watched him approach through her widespread knees.

Later, she wouldn't remember the sequence of movements that left her lying naked. The only experience she could compare it with was the time when she volunteered to be hypnotized during an assembly at her high school. Her friends had accused her of acting when she'd claimed that she couldn't remember what she'd done under the hypnotist's sway, but she knew she'd succumbed to a force beyond her control, and it happened again with Gordon. She would, however, never forget and forevermore seek to repeat the sexual awakening that she experienced in that Holiday Inn, and she would forever love, hate, and haunt the man who unleashed and then left her.

Caroline was not a virgin, but sex had been rough, brief, and disappointing on those previous occasions. She had never experienced an orgasm. With Gordon, she had one before he entered her. Then another before he carelessly finished inside her.

In the half-light of the next morning, Gordon woke with Caroline already straddling him. With her in the final throes of a transcendent screw, applause and calls of "Bravo!" and "Encore!" burst from somewhere in the room. The shock of which launched Caroline off of Gordon and sent her sprawling in terror across the room, where she tripped backward over the lacrosse bag and landed flat on her pretty little ass. Legs akimbo, she lay staring into the leering faces of Dadeno, Justin Terlander, and David Thurston, who were recording the entire performance on Dadeno's phone.

As she rose to her feet and stripped Dadeno's bed of its duvet in order to cover her nakedness, Caroline read "Knights Lacrosse" on the equipment bag that lay at her feet, from which the taped handle of a stick extended. Shamelessly, Caroline dropped the duvet, extricated the stick, and started swinging at the boys, who, despite repeated slashes against their shielding forearms, laughed hysterically and gladly suffered blows in exchange for the view of the hot naked chick.

Only the arrival of Brother Lombardy in full collar and Coach Abbott, in boxer shorts and more body hair than an evolved man should be expected to bear, brought the burlesque to a close. One by one, Coach Abbott grabbed each boy by the nape of the neck and peeled him from the room. Brother Lombardy advanced until he spotted Gordon, naked and propped up on his elbows, bemusedly watching the bad vaudevillian skit that he'd initiated.

Caroline dropped the stick (there have been only three substantiated lacrosse-related deaths in the United States in nearly twenty years) and wrapped the duvet around her.

"Young lady, do you need help?" Brother Lombardy asked in a despair-filled voice, his eyes averted.

"No. I just want to go home."

"That's fine. Gordon, we'll need to talk as soon as you're dressed," Brother Lombardy said, before turning and exiting, leaving behind all his dreams of adding Gordon to the brotherhood, dreams mingled and lost in the intoxicating smell of sex that still permeated the room.

"Gordon? You told me your name was Will!" Caroline said.

Gordon lay unmoved and silent.

"You're no mayor either, are you?"

No response.

"Are you even in college?"

The evidence was beginning to pile up: the bag, the boys, the chaperones.

"What are you? In high school?" Her voice rose several octaves. "Don't tell me you're in high school! How old are you?"

"Fifteen," Gordon finally spoke.

"Fifteen! I just fucked a fifteen-year-old!"

"Well," Gordon corrected himself, "actually, I won't be fifteen until January." He grinned.

"That's statutory rape! I could go to jail!"

"Don't worry. I'll cover for you," Gordon promised without sarcasm.

"I don't believe this. I don't believe this. I don't believe this." She must have said it a hundred times as she gathered her scattered clothes with one arm while the other insufficiently covered her swaying breasts.

Bedraggled, one shoe on and one shoe in her opposite hand, she slunk toward the door.

"Caroline," Gordon called.

"What?"

"Thanks."

"Fuck you," she said, flipped him off, and then exited, slamming the door behind her.

The boys were all suspended for the semifinal match. Without them, the Knights got smoked by a team of waspish blue bloods from suburban Cincinnati. By Monday night, Caroline's naked tantrum was posted on several juvenile and sleazy, yet tremendously popular, file-sharing sites under the title "Crazy Naked Lacrosse Chick." It had already received more than a thousand hits.

Among the student body at the Rood, Gordon was instantly deified.

Within six months, Gordon was expelled from the Rood. When rumors began to fly around campus regarding Gordon's relationship with Willie, Wildman seized his opportunity to exact revenge for his room eviction. He alerted one of the Brothers to Willie's website, where it was discovered that all of Willie's most recent homoerotic drawings of heroes bore a striking resemblance to Gordon. They were both called into the office of the dean of students, Brother Randolph, where Gordon freely admitted to posing for and being flattered by Willie's representations. Willie was forced to move to a single room on another floor, and further punishment and scandal were avoided.

Three months later, however, when Gordon was discovered in the athletic director's office, midcoitus with the athletics secretary, Mrs. Guiccioli, there was no saving him. The incident was covered up to save Mrs. Guiccioli her job, her husband and children, and the Rood's reputation. Gordon was allowed to finish the term but was told that he would not be welcomed back in the fall.

On his last day at the Rood, as he marched toward the limousine that Catherine had sent to chariot him home to the Strand, Willie, Mrs. Guiccioli, and Brother Lombardy wept. But the vast majority of the jealous crabs in the bucket were glad to see him go. Gordon was too much of a reminder of their own boring choices and limited potentials.

When the janitors cleaned Harrow Hall that summer, they found, "The meek shall inherit the sloppy seconds of the BOLD!" spray-painted in red on the walls of Gordon's room.

After the initial anger and shame wore off, Caroline found that she couldn't get Gordon out of her mind. The following summer, she quit her job and dropped out of Ohio State. With the image of Gordon's equipment bag seared into her memory, Caroline Googled all things related to Ohio high school lacrosse until she found and visited the Brothers of the Holy Rood's Cleveland campus. A surprisingly empathetic Brother Lombardy informed her of Gordon's real identity and of his return to Ogontz. She followed him, enrolled in community college, waited tables at a Denny's (I guess she felt closest to Gordon there), and stalked him like it was her job.

One evening that summer, after spotting Caroline's Tracker parked outside the gates of Acedia for a third consecutive night, Shelly approached Caroline and introduced herself. They sat for hours drinking Red Bulls and eating pork rinds while they traded stories of their mutual object of addiction, including the story I just shared. In commiseration, they enjoyed one another's company well enough, but, ultimately, each was a poor substitute for Gordon.

I know this all sounds crazy. Don't believe it if you don't want to. I didn't believe it myself until I had my first Caroline sighting on the day of Shelly's wake. But be careful not to judge. There was just something about Gordon. He was the drug you hated yourself for using, but you smoked, snorted, or injected it anyway, because you loved his magic circle even more. Ultimately, he was the drug that killed Shelly, but he was also the drug that had allowed her to live—at least for a while.

5

We drove eastward through the half-light of the early summer evening and through the failing heart of Ogontz. At every turn, I half-expected a roadblock.

"You have the disc?" Gordon asked.

I performed one of those lame self-pat-downs people do when they've been caught empty-handed and know it but want to delay the admission of their screwup.

"Shelly said she gave it to you," Gordon insisted.

"I know she gave it to me," I said. I could feel a panic attack mustering in my chest. "I must have left it at home."

"Where do you live?"

There it was. The real source of my mounting terror. Gordon Byron of literary, athletic, and erotic greatness was about to journey inside my miserable excuse for a life. This wasn't part of the plan.

* * *

Ogontz, Ohio, is a worn-out notch on the rust belt that stretches beneath the bloated-from-economic-famine belly of the Great Lakes, from Detroit in the northwest to Buffalo in the northeast. It's a onetime blue-collar city—too large to be quaint and too small to be worthy of note—full of American dream–believing suckers, the middle-class beneficiaries of the post–World War II manufacturing boom, especially in the auto industry. The past few decades, however, have seen that golden teat dry to a trickle. In desperation, Ogontz has chosen to prostitute its lakefront and transform itself into a resort town that caters to tourists, fishermen, boaters, and especially condo dwellers—who are willing to mortgage their futures for a killer view and are willing to drop an occasional dollar on the community nightstand.

Before he died, my dad would sometimes recall the "old days" growing up in our east end neighborhood. "It was a fine part of town then, John. Working people [think white people]. Everybody knew everybody else and looked out for each other. Not like it is today. Hell, half these people don't even own these homes around here anymore; they're renters [think African Americans]. Renters don't give a damn about their property or neighbors. It ain't theirs and they don't plan to stay. They invest nothing but want everything, like the world owes them a living."

It's a good thing our home *was* bought and paid for, or I don't know where Tom and I would live. It's the one good turn the folks did us before dying.

* * *

"Fifth Street and Elm," I answered Gordon, seeing no escape.

Ogontz is laid out in an almost perfect grid. East to west streets are numbered, and north to south streets are named. West side streets are named for the array of Native American tribes who once occupied the area, downtown streets in the central city are named for presidents, and east side streets are named for indigenous trees. Gordon's deceleration as we entered my neighborhood suggested what I assumed to be his unfamiliarity with my side of town. Or perhaps, I thought, it was a genuine sociological curiosity with how the other 95 percent lived. Or maybe it was concern for the attention his BMW was attracting as we passed porches and front yards crowded with "renters" driven from their non–air-conditioned homes into the still tropical night air.

"The next corner," I said. "The last driveway. You wait in the car. I'll run in and get it. It'll only take a minute." It felt odd to be giving Gordon orders, but there was no way I was letting him inside that house of death.

I handed Shelly to Gordon, then ducked hurriedly from under the automatically retracting shoulder belt. Climbing the cracked concrete steps two at a time, I bounded onto the porch in two strides. As I removed from my pants pocket the three keys necessary to unbolt all of the locks, I saw Gordon climbing out of the BMW.

"Fuck," I muttered. "Just perfect."

The disc that we were so desperate to retrieve was an R.E.M. mix that Shelly had burned; she called it the sound track of her life and had assigned a song from the R.E.M.

catalog to every important person and significant event she'd experienced. She had entrusted it to me at the end—which I know pissed off Gordon—and we couldn't go forward without it because it was central to fulfilling her final wish, which she had imparted to Gordon and placed him in charge of planning—which, trust me, pissed me off.

My bedroom was upstairs, overlooking the street, and now overlooking Gordon, below. Tom's was to the left of mine, but soon he would be too weak to climb the stairs, and, like Dad before him, he'd require a rented wheelchair and hospital bed placed in the first-floor living room. His world would rapidly shrink: first to the wheelchair, that room, the kitchen, and the bathroom; next, to those four walls of peeling wallpaper, worn carpet, and the stench of bedpans and atrophying flesh; finally, just to the decreasingly burdened mattress. For now, at least, when I peeked in, he was fast asleep, still in his own bed and recognizable skin.

The disc, inside the clear plastic lid of its dust-covered case, lay on top of my dresser. I had set it there a little more than a week ago, a few days before her body washed up on the shore of North Bass Island. Seeing the letters "R.E.M." scrawled in Shelly's handwriting in black Sharpie across the silver face of the disc stopped me cold. More than the wake, more than actually holding the urn in my own hands, I felt the reality of her absence, and, for the first time, I felt its permanence.

I was summoned from my private pity party by the sound of a multitude of voices filtering up through the screens in the bedroom windows. The cacophony itself wasn't unusual. In my neighborhood, cars constantly cruised with stereos cranked, and legitimate east-siders regularly gathered in groups and always moved in numbers, and at all hours. So it wasn't the noise itself that had caught my attention. It was the incongruous sound of Gordon's refined pronunciations intermingled with the street talk.

Unsure of how long I had left him abandoned, I tore from my room and down the interior steps at a breakneck speed. If it was trouble brewing, I had no idea what my scrawny ass could do to end it, but I actually felt that Gordon was in need of my protection.

As I burst onto the porch, Gordon's expansive back was to me. He was surrounded by a half-dozen shirtless and ripped black dudes. T-shirts were slung over shoulders, wrapped around heads as makeshift do-rags, or half-stuffed into the waistbands of their shorts that sagged halfway down their butts. The largest one, whom the others called T and who had a body that looked like a photographic negative of Gordon's, was clearly wearing nothing under his shorts. The rounded top of the two loaves of his muscled ass, where it met the small of his back, showed itself proudly.

There were also two girls, one on either side of Gordon, who stood slightly bent at the waist with his cupped hands to his mouth. Each of the girls leaned heavily on an arm, as if they were holding him up, preventing his escape, or engaging in a tug-of-war for his attention.

"Hey!" I yelled. "Get away from him!"

All eyes, with the exception of Gordon's, turned immediately and menacingly in my direction. I'd never felt so exposed, or white, in my life.

"Leave him alone," I said with diminishing conviction.

They exchanged looks with one another, then stared at me and back to the circle before they broke out in laughter.

"Relax, White." That's what T called me. "White." Not whitey, not white boy, just "White."

Finally, Gordon turned around with a face that looked like an imitation of a constipated Sean Penn sucking the juice out of the most tart lemon in the history of citrus. I wasn't sure if he was in pain or angry until he let go a cough, and a tiny cloud of smoke passed his previously pursed lips.

Pot. He was smoking pot with these guys! I didn't know—still don't—if Gordon somehow had known them previously or if he had just met them that day, but they were calling him G. There he was, already more a part of the neighborhood than I was, and I had lived there my entire life. That's just Gordon. Most people fell in love with him right away. There'd be a glorious honeymoon period, and then, given any length of opportunity, he would wear his welcome out.

"S'up, Keats?" Gordon turned to me before turning back to his circle.

Soon they were inspecting his car. The girls crawled inside and began fidgeting with the radio station, until one slid out of the driver's side, holding Shelly.

"What's this?" she said.

"That's our friend," Gordon answered with a smirk and a quick glance in my direction.

"Whatchu mean your *friend?*" The others stopped making their imaginary upgrades to Gordon's car and began to gather around the girl holding the urn. The whole thing was making me increasingly uncomfortable, but Gordon didn't seem a bit bothered. Actually, he looked amused.

"Those are her ashes," he said.

"Ashes? What ashes? She dead?" Her voice rose at least an octave as she reached the end of her verbless questions, and once again Shelly was airborne. It was as if a creepy bomb were about to explode. Bodies catapulted in all directions among the sound of half-terrified, half-hysterical laughter and cries of horror, except for Gordon, who effortlessly caught Shelly before she mixed her dust with the dirt. That would have been an abomination; Shelly hated dirt. She'd been a complete slob, but that had been an organizational issue, not an elemental one.

My spell of incredulity and Gordon's amusement were broken when, still standing on the porch, I saw in my peripheral vision the familiar navy blue of an Ogontz Police car turn onto my street from Maple, one block west.

"Cops," I warned matter-of-factly. The presence of the police was certainly no oddity on my street. My neighbors' ears had been finely conditioned to that word; it commanded their attention and put an immediate end to the levity. The Ogontz PD patrolled my end of town with near-obsessive diligence, so I had no need for unnecessary concern regarding my and Gordon's outlaw status; although, Gordon's face showed a small degree of unfamiliar alarm.

It's hard to say who's the greater cause of the high crime rate on the east end. Are the omnipresent cops a justifiable and necessary response to criminal behavior, or is the criminal behavior simply a spiteful and equally justifiable "fuck you" to the cops and their assumed necessity, a sort of self-fulfilling prophecy?

By the cop car's leisurely speed, I knew Gordon and I had yet to be targeted; there was no APB out on us. It was a cruising pace, not a pursuit; however, a well-dressed white kid with a BMW surrounded by neighborhood kids would most certainly raise the hackles of even the most novice of officers.

Gordon nonchalantly dropped the joint he cupped in his hand and ground it into my scraggly lawn.

"Marks," T spit the name out.

Patrolman Marks had been the bane of my neighbors' existence since the moment they'd been born, and he would go on in his sheriff of Nottingham way until the day he finally started collecting on his patrolman's pension, a day that couldn't come soon enough as far as my incessantly hassled neighbors were concerned. Sadly, they also knew that another Officer Marks would be coming up the ranks to fill his racist shoes.

Marks pulled to the curb, shifted into park, and turned on his overhead flashers just to be a dick. He leaned toward and spoke through the open passenger-side window. "There a problem here, boys? You know there's a loitering law."

He referred to a law that limited the number and length of time that juveniles, unattended by adults, could gather in public places. The law had been passed in the fifties, long before the mall to the south of town had been built, when downtown Ogontz had still been a thriving business and shopping district. The law had been passed by the urging of merchants, whose storefronts had been being inundated by penniless teenagers just hanging out but supposedly scaring away potential paying customers. Today, that law was used primarily by cops pulling a shift on the east end. There wasn't a store in the sixteen-block area. The police claimed to be disrupting drug deals and gang activity, but all they were really doing was harassing people and furthering the alienation of the black community.

"I live here, Officer. These are my friends," I called from the porch.

"Uh-huh," he said, nearly choking on his skepticism before dismissing me. "How about you?" He was talking to Gordon.

"Me?" Gordon touched his chest with both hands.

"Yeah, you and your Beamer. Don't see your kind around here unless your party planning came up a little short and you need to make an immediate"—he hesitated, then said—"purchase" as he took a long toke from an imaginary joint.

"Purchase, Officer? Why, I have no idea what you're talking about. I'm just visiting a few friends, soaking up a little of the local color, if you know what I mean." He gave Marks a quick wink and made a subtle nod toward the girls.

I stared in disbelief. In an instant, Marks believed that he and Gordon were on the same team. The interrogation was over. He waved Gordon to the squad car.

"You know what they say," Marks began in a hushed voice. "Once you go black, you never go back." He laughed at his own cleverness.

"Yeah, but it's all pink inside," Gordon said, tapping the roof of the Crown Victoria, signaling it was time for Marks to move on, which he did, but not before doing that dorky thing of pointing to his own eyes and then at T and his friends in my yard.

"What'd he say?" one of the girls asked.

"Nothing. Don't worry about him," Gordon said. "He's an asshole."

Gordon looked to me on the porch. The temporary diversion had ended, and an earnest look had returned to his face. "Keats, we need to go."

He was right. It was only a matter of time before Shelly's disappearance would be discovered. Her father would know exactly who took her, and Claire could identify the car we were driving. Whenever the inevitable call came out over the radio, even Officer Marks would be able to do the simple math and pin us to an exact place and time with a fairly good fix on the direction we were heading.

"We need a different car," I said.

"Absolutely," Gordon agreed. "Any ideas?"

"Hold on," I said before disappearing into the house. Within minutes I was reversing out of our detached one-car garage in the back of the house. I was sitting behind the leather-covered steering wheel of a black '78 Trans Am with a gold eagle, wings spread, emblazoned on the hood, my dad's onetime prized possession. Inconspicuous it wasn't, but it didn't need to be. The cops and Shelly's father would be looking for a black BMW.

"Genius," Gordon muttered. "Fucking genius."

Without a word, a warning, or a worry, Gordon tossed his keys to T, who, with as many others as could fit, was out the driveway and into the slowly descending Ogontz night, playing the wild goose.

Inside the Trannie and heading toward Gordon's once again, I pointed toward the fuel gauge, where the red needle was nearly flatlined.

"No problem," Gordon said. "We're running on karma."

"Right," I said, and actually believed it.

I asked him, "How'd you know those guys?"

In typical Gordon fashion, he answered, "Just do."

We left it at that.

6

For Gordon, the month after his expulsion from the Rood began the summer of *Manfred*. His debut novel made the "Must-Read" lists of several national magazines and was picked as one of *USA Today*'s Hot Summer Reads for Young Adults. Reporters from a variety of teen-oriented magazines and websites interviewed Gordon and featured his photograph in their articles. His stock quip was "I awoke one morning and found myself famous."

Gordon spent much of those months driving with Catherine from one bookstore to the next for signings and meets and greets. She was the mother of all cock blocks; Catherine intercepted or fished from his pockets every phone number slipped to him by members of his largely female fan base.

In the fall, Catherine enrolled him for his sophomore year at Trinity Catholic, a school primarily populated by the children of Ogontz's shrinking middle class, who were desperate to avoid the blacks and Hispanics now constituting the majority of students in the Ogontz public school system. At Trinity, based upon his filial heritage, Acedia address, and burgeoning celebrity, Gordon was immediately welcomed as a member of the noblesse oblige.

I'm sure that secretly Catherine was relieved by the reduction in tuition costs afforded by Gordon's departure from the Rood. The cost of maintaining two children in private boarding schools had depleted her cash reserves and she had nearly exhausted the generosity of her parents, who actually still blamed her for the demise of her marriage and, therefore, her current financial shortfall. As a result of her divorce settlement, she'd received substantial shares in the Byron Boatyards. However, consumers' discretionary spending on luxury purchases is often the first to be cut in tough economic times; therefore, her dividends fluctuated wildly. Lately, cash flow had been tight. Despite Catherine's legitimate legal access to his earnings, Gordon maintained tight control over the advance he'd received for *Manfred,* and since his homecoming, he had taken to intellectually bullying his emotionally fragile mother, and saw no good reason why he, as a minor, should be expected to reduce her financial responsibility to raise and educate him.

After his termination from the Rood, Gordon possessed even less regard for formalized schools and the fascists who administer them. To his mind, he'd done nothing wrong; each so-called offense had been victimless. Caroline? Mrs. Guiccioli? He'd liberated them. He'd given them what they wanted. If anything, he was the victim.

Therefore, Gordon was relatively indifferent to his enrollment at Trinity. He would never conform his intellectual or existential pursuits to their narrow-minded curriculums or reading lists, anyway. His interest *was* piqued, however, by a photograph in a full-color Trinity brochure, which his mother left conspicuously open on the island in the kitchen, of a fully extended swimmer diving off starting blocks. Beneath the photograph the caption read "Twelve State Swimming Championships!" Browsing a list of extracurricular sports offered at Trinity, Gordon was disappointed to find lacrosse absent, but he was impressed by their athletic success in general and was especially intrigued by the swim program. His aquatic prowess was entirely natural and, even worse, unheralded. Despite his stubborn independence and aversion to authority, Gordon wondered what he might accomplish as a swimmer if he only had a little coaching.

When she heard the news of Gordon's enrollment, Shelly was nothing short of euphoric. She had attended Trinity's schools since kindergarten. Her father was a product of the school himself and a staunch supporter of All Saints, tithing ten percent of his income to the church since his first paper route; however, despite her father's wealth and standing in the community, or maybe because of it, she had never fit in with the other kids at Trinity. She'd always been picked on, always been alienated, nicknamed Psycho Shelly.

Though bright, Shelly had the focus of a gnat, and was almost entirely uneducable. She hated the indoors; her attention was always directed out the classroom window, and like Gordon, she had little respect for or fear of authority. She could have been the poster child for ADHD, if she could have sat still long enough for the photograph. Having grown up in the relative isolation of Acedia, with only the equally eccentric Byron children as playmates, Shelly was already socially dysfunctional when she was thrown into the survival-of-the-fittest world of elementary school.

She did herself no favors, however, when in first grade she liberated the class gerbil, Brownie; or, when in second grade she convinced her classmates of the implausibility of Santa Claus; or, when in third grade she was caught with a consecrated communion host under a microscope, searching for evidence of the transubstantiation; or, when in fourth grade she temporarily earned the nickname Lorax by climbing a tree in a field adjacent to the playground and refusing to come down because it had been marked for removal for the expansion of the jungle gym; or, when in the fifth grade she became a proselytizing vegan; or, when in the sixth grade she shamelessly explained the process of tampon insertion (complete with visual aids) to a group of mortified boys; or, when in the seventh grade she was thrown into the boys' locker room after gym class by some of the "cool" girls, and she laughed at all the tiny peckers; or, when in the eighth grade she attempted to form a FLAG (Friends of Lesbians and Gays) Club; or, when as a freshman she contributed an article to the school literary magazine critical of the "obscene expenditures" earmarked by the school for the state power-house football program and the award-winning cheerleading and dance squads in comparison with the paltry amount spent in support of Trinity's service organizations or in the actual "feeding of the hungry, clothing of the naked, or housing of the homeless."

But now, with Gordon about to join her at Trinity, she wouldn't be so alone—or so she thought.

*   *   *

The truth turned out to be that Gordon had little time for Shelly, her causes, or her peculiarities once he stormed into Trinity. A summertime friendship in the relative anonymity of Acedia was one thing. The real world was something else. It didn't take him long to understand that an affiliation with Shelly would keep his hands out from under more skirts and from inside more blouses than he cared to miss, for he was immediately impressed by the Amazonian bodies of the daughters of Ogontz's plebeian class, and he longed to sample as many as possible.

By the first day of school, Gordon had earned his driver's permit, which, by Ohio law, enabled him to operate a car at fifteen, as long as he was accompanied by an adult licensed driver. With Catherine's promise to make the subsequent monthly car payments herself, he used part of his advance to make a down payment to lease a black Hummer H3, in which he pulled into the student parking lot at the nearby All Saints Catholic Church.

According to Shelly, he made his mother slouch in the backseat under cover of the tinted windows in order to save him the embarrassment of her accompaniment. She waited until well past the opening eight a.m. bell to climb into the front seat and drive home, only to return to the same location before the final bell at three, or at whatever time Gordon assigned, when she would resume her crouched position in the backseat. This routine they continued until Gordon earned his actual license on his sixteenth birthday in January. I don't know why she tolerated it. Something about

Gordon made women want to please him, protect him, save him, and, in general, do for him. If you could have bottled Gordon's charisma, you could have made a fortune doing creepy late-night infomercials in between the even sadder ones for *Girls Gone Wild* and for male "enhancement" pills.

You know, it's ironic. Shelly's mother killed herself before Shelly's baptism and left her in the care of a disinterested father, yet Shelly loved her. My mother couldn't put her smokes down long enough to make me a toasted cheese sandwich, yet I loved her. There was nothing Gordon's mother wouldn't do for the boy who'd grown into the spitting image of the man who'd nearly destroyed her, yet Gordon loathed her very being. I don't know. Just saying.

Gordon's body rocked the school-mandated white polo shirt with the Trinity crest and the khaki uniform pants like they had never before been rocked. Word of his enrollment had preceded him. Even I, then the lowliest of freshmen, had overheard the news of his arrival. On the first day of school, I stood, rising to tiptoe and peering between bodies, to get a peek as packs of his less-than-peers parted from his path and then re-formed in his wake as he entered the building and walked the main hallway of Trinity in search of the guidance office and his schedule of classes. The girls parted their lips and dropped their chins while the boys either did the same or clenched their fists according to their respective unconsciously inspired first desires.

"Jesus" was the ambiguous reaction of one unidentified voice nearby.

Gordon was especially surprised and disappointed by the rampant homogeneity of the male members of Ogontz's chapter of the Benedict Youth. The school uniforms certainly contributed to their sameness, but it was more than that. There had been a dress code at the Rood, but the boys had been somehow able to rebel and to resist the school's attempt to dehumanize, whitewash, and control them, primarily through constant, even if ineffectual, complaints and small bits of civil disobedience: low-hanging ties, untucked shirts, sockless feet, and hair grown beyond the established parameters. All petty but clear "fuck you's" directed at the administration and the slavery of institutionalized conformity. The mannequins of Trinity, however, appeared happily anesthetized, except for Shelly, of course, who Gordon passed in the main hall that first day. She was wearing a black "Save the Planet" T-shirt over her white blouse, an offense for which she was summarily sent to the office by her homeroom teacher.

Trinity was a jock factory, one that would have done cold war East Germany proud. Ironically, a large percentage of Ogontz's population are descendents of German immigrants, who came too late to the American party and were forced to leapfrog the already immigrant-saturated East Coast and settle in Ohio in order to pursue their dreams of New World prosperity. Every parent in the four-county area, Catholic or not, sent his or her child to Trinity—if the parent had even the slightest hope that his or her son or daughter had college athletic scholarship potential.

The halls were yearly stocked with long, lean, broad-shouldered, and graceful demigods. To the contrary, most of the kids at the Rood had been rather anemic, bookish, and soft—absolute pussies by comparison with these Warriors, which just so happened to be the name of Trinity's sports teams. Gordon must have immediately determined that it would be impossible to impress these roboteens by mere physicality; nor could they be intimidated by intellectualism. For they were the most unquestioning party-line-swallowing irony-deprived adult-pleasing collection of kiss-asses Gordon could have ever imagined, and their Teflon-coated psyches were angst resistant and oblivious to both his superior erudition and his sarcasm.

The purchase of the Hummer, however, had been a stroke of accidental genius. He would soon discover that the lever that would move these lumps of clay and undo many a button, zipper, and Velcro strap was good old-fashioned American materialism and class envy.

It was common in those first days at Trinity for Gordon to be regularly asked—exclusively by girls—to sign copies of *Manfred* or one of the various magazines in which he had been featured. His cell phone fast filled with girls' numbers that he couldn't match to faces, so he took to taking a photo with his cell and loading it with the girl's corresponding phone number. By the end of his first two weeks at Trinity, he'd compiled a sheik's harem's worth of available ladies. All of which was fine, since he was finding the girls of Trinity to be nearly his equal in their concupiscence.

On the second Monday in September, Gordon stuffed himself confidently inside his first Speedo, joined the swim team for its preseason conditioning sessions, and made a Vesuvius-sized splash. He was a raw but powerful swimmer, who, compared with the technique-driven swim team members, bludgeoned the water's surface rather than carved his way through it. Regardless of his lack of technique, he was a tsunami-like force in the water. (The chances of dying as the result of a tsunami while on the American mainland is more than half a million to one.) Coach Mancini saw the *David* inside the Gordon block of granite and went to work immediately to streamline what he could only classify as a gift from Poseidon himself.

As word spread of Gordon's physique, his talent, and the coach's obsessive attention to him, the number of participants at the voluntary workouts swelled with both prospective female swimmers and suddenly expendable returning lettermen.

Gordon quickly grew indifferent regarding the idol worship of his countless nereids and found his divining rod pointed in the direction of Ms. Yancey, a second-year sophomore English teacher and the advisor to Trinity's literary magazine, *The Beacon*. I'm sure that among any gaggle of twentysomething girls, Jennifer Yancey would have been nearly invisible, but at Trinity, in opposition to the just-out-of-the-wrapper freshness of her students, at twenty-three she seemed damn near world-weary and exotic, which were vestigial attributes from her short-lived Gothic stage during her own sophomore year of high school. That dark period also accounted for her continuing penchant for black outfits and silver crosses.

Despite Ms. Yancey's professional devotion to serious literature, her guilty reading pleasure remained young adult fiction, especially anything to do with vampires, evidenced by the occasional novel she carelessly let lie exposed on her desk or let slip from her bag. I imagined that her typical Friday nights for the past eight to ten years had been spent inside the pages of those stories, fantasizing herself the object of vampire seduction, rather than teasing and tempting the attention of flesh-and-blood real boys. I'm sure she gasped when she discovered that the "Byron, George" listed on her third-period class roster was *the* Gordon Byron of still-growing *Manfred* fame.

For his part, Gordon knew on the first day of class that Ms. Yancey would belong to him. She tried so hard not to appear impressed, not to make him aware that she more than knew who he was and what he had accomplished. She tried so hard not to look too long into his eyes (she knew better than most not to look deeply into the soul-stealing eyes of a vampire) that Gordon knew she was already his. It was simply a matter of opportunity, surrender, and sinking in the fangs.

I was a freshman that year. I'd been allowed to skip what should have been my final year at Trinity Middle School by virtue of my off-the-top-of-the-charts test scores and my obvious boredom with the facile nature of the middle-school curriculum. My folks balked at the placement, fearing my diminutive stature, and questioning my ability to socialize with the older students, but they were too absorbed in my father's dying to put up much of a protest. I was actually pleased with the advancement; it wasn't as if I would be leaving behind many friends my own age. Even then I sensed the urgency of putting my life on fast-forward, for fear of never accomplishing anything of significance.

In the diminishing number of conversations I held with my mom, she continually pushed me toward becoming a doctor. After watching my father's humanity corralled, prodded through the chutes, clubbed over the back of the head, and processed into ground beef by the butchers of the modern American health care system, she had grown disillusioned with the medical establishment. Having been blessed with an intellectually gifted son, she thought that she might offer me as that establishment's savior.

My entire life I'd dealt with the typically unspoken assumption of my parents, and of career-disaffected school guidance counselors, that because I was smart, I owed it to them to become a doctor or lawyer or engineer or something else with a "promising financial future." So I humored their vicarious medical aspirations by joining Trinity's Future Professionals in Medicine (FPM) club and by serving as a volunteer wheelchair valet at the hospital, but my own fast-crystallizing dream was to write—Novels? Movie scripts? Plays? Poems?—what, I didn't know yet, but definitely not the fantasies of Gordon and Ms. Yancey. I knew then, and I still plan—if death doesn't intervene too soon—to write the kind of literature that wins awards and will be read and taught hundreds of years after I'm dead. I knew that whatever form it was going to take, however, I needed to decide soon. Hell, I was nearly fourteen and one book behind Gordon. I didn't share my plan with my mother, but I did join Ms. Yancey's staff on the *Beacon*, where my path first intertwined with Shelly's and Gordon's.

Fifteen minutes late, Gordon sauntered into the second-floor corner "media center," which housed Trinity's literary magazine, *The Beacon*; the school's newspaper, *The Warpath*;

and its yearbook, *The Yearbook*. He came as a favor to Shelly, who believed, once the word got out of his participation, that his celebrity presence might inspire others to join. On one arm, he had a blonde; on the other hung a redhead. They seemed to be competing for the title of Miss Most Put out by Actually Having to Make a Brief Stop at the Lame Media Center Before Proceeding to Do the Cool Things That Cool Kids Do.

Despite Shelly's plastering of the school with posters that advertised the organizational meeting, she, I, and now Gordon and his playmates were the only attendees.

Without greeting or introduction, Gordon asked, "What's that?" He nodded toward the rear of the room, where a red light spilled from beneath a closed door.

"That," Ms. Yancey answered, "is a darkroom. At least, it was once. We no longer use it. At least, not to develop film."

"What *do* you use it for?" Gordon asked.

Flummoxed, yet flattered by his come-on, Ms. Yancey could only manage, "Uh . . . Well . . . We, um . . ."

The red lights within the erstwhile darkroom had been turned on and left for no apparent reason, an experience with which Gordon's bookend hotties, whom he abruptly dismissed, could probably have identified.

"Ms. Yancey." Gordon flirted and lied as he squeezed himself into a front-facing first-row desk immediately beneath her podium. "I didn't know you were coming."

"I'm the advisor, Gordon, and we're"—she paused to indicate Shelly and me with a Vanna White wave of her hand—"glad you joined us."

"The pleasure's all mine . . . for now," he said, causing Ms. Yancey to blush and Shelly to roll her eyes.

"Well, like I said." Ms. Yancey, for Gordon's benefit, proceeded to summarize the discussion points he had missed. "Our goal this year is to increase involvement and expand readership."

Gordon interrupted her once more, as he surveyed the nearly empty room with a slow roll of his head over each shoulder. "Looks like you're off to a good start."

His eyes landed on me. "Who are you?"

"John." I answered in a mousy prepubescent voice that quavered with awe. Over the summer, I had read *Manfred* and followed its trajectory up the bestsellers charts, and had followed Gordon's increasing celebrity.

"Do you have a last name, John?"

"Keats," I said.

"Keats," Gordon repeated. "I like that better. It's . . ." He settled on "Poetic."

I blushed.

"Anyway." Ms. Yancey reclaimed the floor. "So far, we've discussed adding visual pieces, such as photographs, political cartoons, and/or a comic strip; someone mentioned an advice column; Shelly thinks we should address more 'socially relevant' topics; and I've shared that I intend to write reviews of current young adult fiction in order to encourage students to read independently of their assigned classroom texts."

"Maybe you could review me, Ms. Yancey. Or, at least my book," Gordon said.

Knocked off guard, Ms. Yancey stammered while searching for an appropriate response.

"Good luck with that," I said to Ms. Yancey, saving her. Although I was new to the high school, I wasn't new to the culture, nor did it take supersensitivity to sense the lowly position of the arts in Trinity's pecking order. For one thing, the whole place smelled vaguely of a locker room, and within the first fifteen minutes of the meeting, Shelly had referred to the school's artistically challenged masses as Neanderthals, Spartans, cretins, and as having shit for brains. That last one had earned her a detention from Ms. Yancey.

In Shelly's defense, the literati of Trinity *were* few. Ms. Yancey recounted for our benefit that when Mr. Preston, the *Beacon*'s longtime advisor, retired the previous spring, the magazine was nearly disbanded. In fact, it would have been if Ms. Yancey, with her youthful idealism and Shelly in tow, hadn't marched into Principal Smith's office and pleaded with him to give them one last chance to pump some fresh blood into the near corpse. Mr. Smith relented and agreed to its continuation on a probationary basis. Increased student involvement and the meeting of expenses would mean the maintaining of its charter as a school-sponsored organization. The failure to meet those goals would mean extinction.

"What about," Gordon suggested without recognition from the chair, "an online edition linked to Trinity's Web page? Keep it always a semester behind so as not to interfere with current sales. It could be linked to Trinity's main page and also generate advertising revenue."

It was the first really good idea anyone had offered. Shelly immediately seconded the proposal, and it was passed as our first order of business for the new and improved *Beacon*.

With his contribution far transcending the original

purpose of his attendance, Gordon rose to leave as abruptly as he had arrived. As a boy-wonder author, I'm sure he considered himself to be above our amateurish production. Who could blame him? But I had the feeling that he would be back, if only for the number of opportunities that participating on the *Beacon* would provide him for working intimately with Ms. Yancey.

With Gordon gone, business and hormonal levels returned to normal. Though slightly discouraged by the sparse turnout, we charged forward. Inspired by Ms. Yancey's romantic optimism, we divided among us the responsibilities of soliciting advertisers, vetting submissions, procuring the printing at the *Ogontz Reporter*, and marketing and selling the finished product to a student body of reluctant aesthetes.

By October, we'd all settled into our separate routines. In addition to serving as the student editor in chief of the *Beacon*, Shelly had been elected president (she ran unopposed, despite the faculty advisor's repeated begging for additional nominations) of Trinity's Key Club, a Kiwanis-sponsored service organization full of college résumé builders and those in need of the service hours mandated for graduation. She had also begun secretly volunteering after school at Ogontz's Planned Parenthood, where she gave several of Trinity's (one of Gordon's) deflowered coeds quite the shock when they walked through the door to find her answering phones or collating literature or doing mailings.

I didn't have much of a life other than school, my for-appearance's-sake-only involvement in FPM, and the few hours I spent pushing wheelchairs at the hospital. I did play flag football in the Catholic Youth Organization (CYO)—for kids not involved in interscholastic athletics—and I wasn't too bad, considering my age and size, but most of my time was spent helping Shelly with the *Beacon* or in my upstairs bedroom rereading *Manfred*—I was searching for the formula—and writing poems and stories of my own.

Gordon had begun a regimen of private workouts before school with Coach Mancini, followed by seven hours of classes, and finishing with team practice after school. Occasionally, if Shelly and I were putting in a late night at the *Beacon*'s office, he'd swing by, but he would spend most of his time leering at Ms. Yancey or flirting with the five of Trinity's hotties (Shelly referred to them as the Gordonettes) who, she believed, had bit on her Gordon-as-bait trick and joined the staff. The truth is, concerned for Shelly's success, Gordon had secretly recruited all five of them. If nothing else, they did take over some of the more tedious work, allowing Shelly, Ms. Yancey, and me to focus our collective attention on reviewing the occasional submissions and writing and revising our own. When he did show up, Gordon fell immediately under the intoxicating sway of the pheromonal effervescence of the fully stocked chick bar and, in general, didn't seem to notice that I existed.

I remember only a single conversation with Gordon during that entire year. On a night when Shelly was "vegging" on a cot in the darkroom, not a single Gordonette had shown up at the office, and he sat sullenly studying Ms. Yancey.

I approached him.

"So, I really loved *Manfred*," I said.

"It was easy," he answered, which really pissed me off, since I'd agonized over every word I'd ever written. None of it was easy, and most of it sucked. Unlike for Shelly or me, writing was not something Gordon seemed to enjoy, or something he felt particularly inspired to do. He was simply good at it, and he would use his talent, not because it was his calling but in order to earn the spoils of fortune and fame.

Dismissing me, Gordon rose and walked to where Ms. Yancey sat at her desk. It was the first time I had really noticed his limp. I mean, I'd seen it, but I had always thought the slight hesitation in his step was part of his "cool." I think, having grown somewhat comfortable at Trinity, Gordon was beginning to let down his guard, to ease the intensely focused micromanagement of his every movement.

Gordon stood at Ms. Yancey's side, so that if she had turned her head to look over her left shoulder, she would have been staring directly at his crotch. I was unable to hear their conversation, but I watched as she grew increasingly discomfited, adjusting her glasses and pulling together the top of her blouse. All the while, she kept her attention glued to whatever she had been reading on her desk, but she was unable to hide the warm red blush that ran up her chest and neck into her face, like heated mercury. Beneath her desk, only one foot, inside an open-toed flat, reached the tiled floor of the classroom; the other bounced nervously at the end of her crossed leg.

Gordon eased over a pile of papers on the corner of the desk and sat down so that he was facing Ms. Yancey with his arms crossed and legs extended in a relaxed manner that penned her in the corner. He continued whatever small talk he had begun. Eventually, she let go of the top of her blouse and lifted her eyes to make contact with his. I noticed that she had uncrossed her legs and that both of her feet were planted flat and hard against the floor. Whatever Gordon said, it slowly transformed Ms. Yancey's face until she was smiling, brushing back loose strands of hair from over her rectangular rimless glasses, laughing, and looking more like one of the Gordonettes than the teacher.

"What was that all about?" I asked when Gordon returned.

"Turning over the soil," he answered as he slid into one of the desk/chair torture devices the school still used to rack their students. Somehow, as he situated himself by slouching his upper body and elongating his lower, he still managed to look Abercrombie cool.

"But how do you do that?" I asked, sincerely befuddled, amazed, and curious to know the secret. "I mean, how can you just walk up to all these girls—and Ms. Yancey!—and be so cool and know just what to say and how to act?"

"It's cake," he said.

I wanted to punch him. I wondered what, if anything other than walking without a limp, came hard for Gordon Byron.

Then he explained his philosophy. "You see, Keats, your problem, like almost everyone else's, is that you think you're in control, that what you say or do in an instant actually has some impact on what happens in that instant and the ones that follow. That kind of thinking puts way too much pressure on a person. It's paralyzing." He took his eyes off of Ms. Yancey, still glowing from across the room, and directed his blue-eyed gaze at me.

"Now, me, I don't think like that. I believe that whatever is going to happen is going to happen whether I do or say anything at all. I'm just playing my part in a cosmic drama that I didn't write and in which there is little room for ad-lib. So, if I fuck up, it doesn't get me down. I was going to fuck up no matter what I did. You see, it isn't my fault. I'm just reading my lines. You, on the other hand—again, like most people—overthink everything; you place the weight of the whole world on your shoulders, believing what you do or say actually matters, actually changes things and determines outcomes. Which, I think, is pretty fucking arrogant of you and your kind. Don't you think?"

"Let me ask you this," I said. "Who wrote this 'script'? God?"

"If that helps you to sleep at night, that's fine. You call it God. I don't waste time thinking about it; I just know the script exists."

"That's fate. You believe in *fate*?" I was incredulous. Although I'd known him for less than two full months, it seemed too romantic for a guy like Gordon.

"Whatever. My point is that I don't worry because I believe the future is already past. We just don't know it yet. Kind of like . . . Here, come with me." Gordon slid out from beneath the desk, walked to the window, leaned his head against the cool glass, and gazed up into the cloudless night sky. "Look up. What do you see?"

"I don't know," I said, afraid of saying the stupidly obvious. "Stars?"

"Correct!" Gordon said as if I'd answered a double bonus question on some television game show. "Stars. But do you realize that some of those stars may already be extinguished, and we're just now being washed in the light that took . . . who knows how long to reach us?"

My confused expression betrayed that I understood the physics but not the point.

"Some of those stars are dead—in what we mistakenly think is the future because of our perspective but is actually the past—but as far as we can tell in the present, they are still putting off gas and heat and light. Do you get it?"

"Sort of," I lied.

"You see, if astronomers just knew what the signs were inside of the particles of starlight we're currently looking at, maybe they could identify which ones have been long dead, which ones are still pumping, and which ones still have eons to burn. You following?"

"I guess. But what does all this have to do with talking to girls?"

"Oh, Keats." He actually draped his arm around my shoulders. "You just aren't paying attention."

"No. I am," I said, a little too enthusiastically, for fear of Gordon's cutting the lesson short.

"With girls, I can read the signs. I don't know how, from where, or why I can, but I can. It's kind of like, why can one person sing so prettily or jump so high or solve complicated math problems in ways that most people can't, when they don't look any different from anybody else?

"When I meet a girl, I know instantly whether or not she's doable. What I don't know is whether or not I will do her. That's in the yet-to-be-read pages of the script and out-side of my control. My role is simply to show up every day and play my part. But either way, it isn't to my credit or fault."

My head spun as he walked me back to my desk next to Shelly's. "What about Ms. Yancey? Is she?"

"What? Doable?"

Gordon didn't answer. Instead, he smiled, grabbed his denim jacket, walked to Ms. Yancey's desk, leaned over and whispered something, and then left the room.

After a few moments of hard thinking, I got up to go, but was stopped by Shelly's ambiguous comment. "He's good." She said it with just a tiny hint of jealous longing clinging to her voice. I hadn't noticed her return from the darkroom cot, but she must have been watching.

"You really believe that?"

"Yeah. I mean . . . Gordon can be shallow, narcissistic, even destructive, and he tends to eventually piss everybody off, but . . . I don't know . . . there's just something . . . necessary about him. He makes things . . . interesting. You know what I mean?"

"No," I lied. "I don't, and you shouldn't make excuses for him."

She shook her head. "Don't you see? He's a kind of measuring stick. He's a guardrail, a Mr. Bad Example. He's a flashing red light, a siren, a warning bell . . . the scarecrow." She threw up her arms to pantomime a scarecrow in cruciform position as she finished her exercise in metaphorical free association. "We need Gordon. Without him we couldn't fantasize or define ourselves or know when to stop or when to seek shelter. He's the stove on which we burn our hands. He's the almost that counts."

"I have no clue what you're talking about."

"Hang around long enough, and you will."

"What I really don't get is the way he treats you. He completely ignores you, when you're clearly the most interesting girl in the room." My previously unspoken—hell, unthought—thoughts completed an end run around the filter separating my brain from my mouth.

Shelly took her eyes from Gordon's exit stage right in order to look at me for the first time in the conversation. Her unkempt long black hair spilled from underneath the rainbow-colored horizontally striped toboggan that she slipped over her head the minute the final bell rang each day, along with the matching fingerless gloves. The look in her eyes couldn't have been more different from the longing one I'd watched her give Gordon a thousand times; it wasn't condescending so much as it was appreciative.

It sucked.

I wanted to puke.

"He ignores me because he loves me."

I paused to consider that unwanted pearl of wisdom before I said, "That makes a lot of sense."

Ms. Yancey was gone by Thanksgiving and was replaced by the reluctant Mr. Robbins, a senior English teacher already overburdened by club advisory positions. It left Shelly with the job of putting out the fall semester's edition of the *Beacon* almost entirely on her own. Apparently— at least according to the rumors that ran amok in the Trinity community—a night janitor, who, unbeknownst to his bosses, occasionally used the darkroom cot for napping, was an unobserved spectator one night when Gordon turned on the lurid red light and led a coy Ms. Yancey into the darkroom. The janitor wasn't discovered until Ms. Yancey and Gordon, both shirtless, tumbled onto the cot and on top of him.

After much pleading from Ms. Yancey and "good old buddying" by Byron, the janitor compromised—largely for fear of losing his unsanctioned napping privileges and station. His conscience and state law demanded that he report the incident, but he'd swear that all that he had seen was the two of them kissing if they'd say nothing of his napping.

Ms. Yancey's contract with Trinity was immediately terminated—something about a morality clause. A criminal complaint was never filed nor a report made to the state board of education (of course, to avoid the publicity and the embarrassment for Trinity).

Gordon and his mother were called to Mr. Smith's office, where the principal apologized profusely for Ms. Yancey's having "taken advantage" of Gordon. Mr. Smith pleaded with them (for Gordon's sake) not to seek litigation or in any way go public with the incident. Coincidentally, they were told, Gordon had just recently been chosen as the recipient of the newly instituted Novitiate Scholarship to be given annually to the most promising transfer student of the year. It would cover full tuition and fees for the entire duration of the recipient's years at Trinity.

Mrs. Byron hemmed, hawed, and made a good show of righteous indignation, but in the end, she more than gladly took the scholarship and ran.

7

"Nice ride," Gordon said, checking out the red interior of the Trans Am. I wasn't sure if he was being sincere or sarcastic. With Gordon, it could be nearly impossible to tell.

"You know, I never would have guessed," he said.

"It's not mine. It was my dad's car. I think he loved it more than me." I should have known my whining would fall on unsympathetic ears.

"I don't mean about the car. I never understood why Shelly liked you, but I'm starting to get it. You're all right, Keats. Nowhere near as much of a loser as I thought."

"Is that supposed to be a compliment?"

"It is."

"Then, thanks."

"Put the disc in," Gordon said.

I laughed and pointed to the dash, where the original eight-track player mocked us.

"You've got to be shitting me," he said. "What is that?"

"An eight-track player. The car's more than thirty years old. What'd you expect? Look in the glove compartment."

Gordon reached inside and pulled out a handful of eight-track tapes, holding them as if he were handling recently unearthed dinosaur bones.

"Got them five for a dollar at a garage sale. Put one in."

"Which one?" Gordon asked. He read the titles: "Foghat? REO Speedwagon? Styx? Lynyrd Skynyrd? Or Journey? Dude, I know Journey."

"Put it in."

"How?" He took a few stabs and flipped the case over a few times before it took.

"'Just a small-town girl,'" the song began, and we joined in singing what may be the most cheesy yet somehow poignant song ever written, yelling as much as we were singing—"'living in a lonely world'"—while bobbing our heads in rhythm. I couldn't help but think of Shelly as that lonely small-town girl, and I wondered what, if anything, I could have done differently.

The song played through. The lyrics' incongruous mixture of despair and hopefulness washed over and soaked us through in one of those moments that two people share, each knowing that he is experiencing the same thing as the other guy without having to say a word.

As I turned left onto Sand Road, aptly named for the fine layer of the stuff that perpetually coats it, and the small dunes that form sporadically along it, we entered the Strand. I pretended to be transfixed by the bay waters on my side, which lay as flat as I'd ever seen them, but I was actually hiding my reddened eyes and muffling occasional sniffles that, thankfully, were drowned out by the nervous drumming of Gordon's fingers on the passenger side of the dashboard.

Finally, I decided to break the tension. "What's your favorite Shelly story?"

"Oh, man." A smile broke across Gordon's face. "There are so many." He hesitated. I imagined him pressing the Main Menu button in his brain and scanning the scene selections. "You know about the skinny-dipping?" he asked, followed by a sidelong glance and a stifled laugh into his balled right fist.

"Yeah. Shelly told me."

"What about Johnson's Island when we were kids?"

"She talked about that too," I said.

Gordon hadn't noticed, but Shelly and I had grown close during our countless hours of compiling editions of the *Beacon*. Maybe it was the two-year difference in age (teen years are like dog years: seven teen years to one human year), or maybe it was the difference in social classes—if so, it was my problem not hers—but we never hung out anywhere else or at any other times. We were friendly and all in the hallways, but we never stopped to talk. In a way, it made our time in the media center special.

The best times were the nights when we'd stay late and order pizza delivered. She always paid, and I always apologized and promised to get the next one. We'd get sodas from the machines in the cafeteria, sit cross-legged on the floor with the pizza box between us, and play "What If? Past, Present, and Future." It was a stupid game we'd made up. We each had to answer the three questions in a series.

For example, Shelly would ask, "What if? Past."

I'd answer with something like, "What if I'd been born to different parents?"

Then she'd say, "What if? Present."

"What if . . . I lived next door to you instead of Gordon?"

"What if? Future."

"What if . . . I die before I do anything that matters?"

You know, she didn't patronize me as if I were being irrational when I hit her with that one. She knew I meant it, and she respected my intuition. I really appreciated that. I guess it's kind of ironic now.

Then it was my turn to ask the questions. "What if? Past."

She'd begin "what if" riffing about her childhood with Gordon and Augusta. Before long the pizza would be cold and the soda warm. That game is another reason why I know as much as I do about when they were kids. Now that I think about it, I never got to ask her the "present" and "future" questions.

Gordon was continuing his internal probing of his catalog of Shelly stories. "How about, do you remember at the beginning of my and Shelly's junior year, your sophomore, when she went all sixties, protesting Trinity's sports team names?"

*   *   *

That incident occurred shortly after my father's funeral. My mom had gone off the deep end, beginning the process of willing herself to death. Tom and I were taking turns staying home from school, babysitting her for fear of what she might do. (That was when Tom was still relatively healthy and taking classes in radiology at a nearby branch campus of the Ohio State University.) My father had died in September. Nothing dramatic. One morning, he just didn't wake up.

I remember calling goodbye to my parents from outside their closed bedroom door as I did every morning before leaving for school, even though, typically, I'd receive no response. By then, my dad had already lost his ability to speak, and my mother—well, let's just say that she'd never been the communicative type. That day, however, she returned my goodbye. It struck me as odd, and I sensed that something was wrong. But I immediately dismissed it and went on about my day.

By the time I got home from school, he was gone, both body and soul.

"Your father's dead" was the extent of the explanation my mother offered through the exhaled smoke that rose from the lowered right corner of her bottom lip as she pressed a half-finished cigarette against the metal ashtray on the kitchen table. "Tell your brother. I have to go and meet with the man at the cemetery. I don't know how we're going to pay for this," she mumbled without once looking me in the eyes. Life insurance, by the way, is one of those things I mentioned at the beginning that many poor people don't do.

And then she left.

I stood frozen in the kitchen while she ignited the tired engine in the rust-covered piece of shit we called our "family" car and backed it out of the driveway. Alone, I aimlessly toured the entire house: downstairs and upstairs. Nothing had changed; he was just not there anymore. I peeked through the opening in my parents' nearly closed bedroom door, but I didn't go inside the room. Instead, I went to my own, lay on my bed, and waited for Tom to come home.

No obituary was placed in the *Reporter*, just a listing under "Death Announcements." There was no wake or showing of the body. No funeral mass.

A Trinity school van was parked on the winding drive when my mother, Tom, and I arrived at the Ogontz City Cemetery (think permanent public housing). I had imagined that there'd be trees and tombstones. There was neither, just row after row of bronze-colored grave markers lying flat against the earth. The hearse parked behind the van. Through the tinted windows of the hearse, I saw Principal Smith; Father Fulop; six senior football players, all dressed in school-issued black sport coats; and Shelly. They stood in a solemn row near the canopy over the green-tarp-covered hole that was to be my father's grave. I was both moved and mortified.

The football players were members of Trinity's Joseph of Arimathea Society, a prestigious service organization that provided pallbearers and a touch of dignity for the homeless or for those who die without able-bodied friends or relatives to serve in that role. Joseph was the man in the New Testament who surrendered his own tomb for the burial of Jesus after the Crucifixion.

When the hearse stopped, the Joeys, as they're called at

school, moved in practiced precision to the rear of the hearse, where they met the funeral director and extricated the coffin as we walked to the graveside accompanied by Father Fulop and Mr. Smith. Shelly met me there, took my hand, and stood silently by my side throughout the brief prayer service.

I felt oddly happy.

I walked Shelly to the van as Mr. Smith and Father Fulop paid final condolences to my catatonic mother. Inside, the Joeys had turned on the radio and were roughhousing, the way guys like that do.

I stopped about ten feet away from the van. "I don't want to die," I confessed to Shelly. It was the second time I'd shared my grim, irrational obsession with death with her.

Shelly didn't laugh dismissively or tell me I was being silly. She simply said, "Write something." She squeezed my hand, then squeezed herself inside the van among the Joeys, who, in their continued horseplay, remained indifferent to her company.

Afterward, not much, if anything, changed. Tom returned to his college classes, Mom kept to her cigarettes, and I kept to my anonymity with a greater resolve to make some mark of my existence, which, along with Shelly's urging, prompted me to compose the following poem. It appeared in that semester's edition of the *Beacon*.

WHEN I CONSIDER TIME
When I consider time and its short lease,
I wonder why I'm granted life at all.
So little time to snatch the Golden Fleece

Before answering Death's unerring call.
Considering the mark I want to make,
Poetry seems to be my only course.
The magic, rhyme, and rhythm it creates
Lives only in the wonder world of verse.
And what of love? Don't I deserve its charms?
To possess someone and be possessed myself.
To lie and love in sympathetic arms—
Only a day—for me would be enough.
Fully to live, to write, to love will be
Priceless pleasures not provided me.

I didn't tell Gordon any of that; I just shook my head and said, "No." But, of course, I'd heard about Shelly's protest. She had even asked me to be part of it, but I'd turned her down for fear of . . . well . . . for fear of lots of things. Instead, I made sure I wasn't in school that day. Telling the story, however, seemed like it would be somehow therapeutic for Gordon, so I played ignorant and let him tell it.

"Aw, man," he began. "You know how she loved Indians, right? Even when we were kids, if you asked her what she wanted to be when she grew up, she'd say an Indian."

I nodded.

"I mean, the Warriors makes no fucking sense for a god-damned Catholic school anyway. We should be the Peace-makers or the Apostles or at least the Crusaders or something like that. Anyway, Shelly had already collected signatures on a petition, written that article for the *Beacon* about the persecution of Indians and the bigoted use of tribal names by athletic teams, and took her cause to a board meeting.

Because of her dad, the school board humored her, allowed her to make a proposal, and politely listened to her demand for a name change. But, in the end, all she got was ignored."

Gordon lost himself in the retelling.

"Then one day, during lunch, she walks into the cafeteria carrying her book bag. Without saying a word to anyone, she pulls her shirt off over her head and steps out of her uniform skirt, which gets all the guys screaming shit like 'Take it off!' Shelly ignores them like only Shelly could. So, she's standing there in a one-piece buckskin Pocahontas costume or something—I think she wore it for Halloween in, like, the seventh grade. It barely covered her ass. Anyway, she pulls out of her bag a white bedsheet on which she's written in black paint 'Down with Bigotry' and starts to walk up and down the center aisle of the cafeteria with her arms spread wide, holding that sheet like a goddamned ring girl, making sure everyone gets a good look, but all anybody is really looking at is her in that outfit. I don't mind telling you, dude, although Shelly is—I mean, *was*—like a sister to me, she looked good. She got a whole new type of respect from the boys that day, even if it wasn't exactly the kind she was hoping for.

"Now, there's only one teacher, Father Fulop, in the whole place. And, at first, he seems to be enjoying it as much as anybody. But he eventually senses that he's in over his head, right? He goes running for help. The next thing you know, Shelly returns to her bag, spreads out the sheet like a picnic blanket in front of one of those big, square load-bearing columns in the cafeteria. She pulls out a can of blood-red paint and pours it all over the top of her head. Finally, she

removes a heavy chain from the bag and motions for someone to wrap it around her and the column and to secure the
chain with the biggest fucking lock I've ever seen. Trust
me, there was no shortage of volunteers. Man, it was so
Shelly. Fulop returned with Mr. Smith. Everyone was sent
back to class. Even though some people hadn't even touched
their lunches. On my way, I saw the janitor heading toward
the cafeteria with the most massive set of bolt cutters I've
ever seen." Gordon laughed out loud at the memory.

"I wish I had been there."

"I can't imagine what that stunt cost her old man in donations," Gordon said.

"Yeah, for all the good it did."

Gordon stopped laughing. Most of Shelly's good deeds
somehow ended in disaster—like her last one.

Talk about killing the mood.

"I guess you're right," Gordon said.

To the east, the horizon had begun to darken. Massive
boulders, which had long ago been placed along the lake
side of Sand Road, blocked my view of what I knew to be a
strip of soft brown sand on the private beaches that ran the
length of that side of the peninsula.

When I was a little boy and my dad was still in good
health, he took Tom and me out on a fishing charter. Other
than puking my guts up, the only thing I remember about
that day was when my father pointed toward the miles of
brown sugar-fine sand along the Strand, where I could make
out only a few privileged and scattered beachgoers. He said,
"Get a good look at it, boys. This is as close as either of you
will ever get."

*   *   *

Now that I was on the Strand for the first time, I was surprised to see that it actually contained a diverse assortment of homes, ranging from simple A-frames and one-room bungalows—most of which had been in the possession of people of modest means for generations—to the villas and two-story mansions of Ogontz's gentry and its seasonal nouveaux riches. It reminded me a lot of Gatsby's West Egg. All the homes were situated on the west, bay side of the road, which had to be crossed by the residents or renters to get to the private lakeside beaches.

"It's right here," Gordon said abruptly, pointing with his left arm extended through my line of vision.

I pressed heavily on the brake pedal and slid to a stop on the sandy surface. I shifted the Trans Am into reverse and returned to the wrought iron security gate between two large redbrick pillars that marked the only land entrance to Acedia.

"Five-eight-two-six," Gordon said.

"What's that?"

"The code for the gate. Press five-eight-two-six, then star."

I did as instructed and watched the right side of the gate, topped with the "dia," rise like prison bars against the orange-red gloaming of the western sky. Even intermingled with the magic colors of early twilight, the expansive, verdant cul-de-sac containing the cloistered inhabitants of Acedia dominated the scene and my senses.

The massive and many-windowed homes lorded over a veritable orchard of Babylon willow trees. Buried sprinkler heads popped out of lush lawns and from among the manicured landscaping in a synchronized greeting in honor of our arrival. They began their frenetic oscillation, launching arched streams of water to battle the life-choking nature of the sandy and windswept soil. I instinctively turned right and followed the rotary around a centralized miniature English garden, replete with benches, a circuitous walkway, a dog park, and a fountain of three leaping dolphins spewing water from their mouths.

"That one's mine," Gordon said, pointing toward a massive Georgian colonial.

Beyond the horseshoe driveway, like sentinels, six bone-white columns rose from the front porch to a steeply pitched corniced portico high above. Paired redbrick chimneys rose from opposite ends of the roof on top of the gray-brown wide-planked wood-sided mansion. The weatherworn home was in desperate need of a refacing. Five second-story multi-paned, rectangular windows encased in black shutters watched our approach in symmetrical perfection above four matching first-floor windows and centered French doors. The grounds were the only ones in the neighborhood not professionally maintained or washed in ambient landscape lighting.

I must have looked like I'd seen a ghost or something, because Gordon said, "It's okay, dude; they're just houses."

I brought the Trans Am to a complete stop at the foot of the driveway, somehow feeling unworthy of advancing farther. I'm not sure how long I had been idling and staring, but a flood of shame washed over me as I considered Gordon's unplanned visit to my neighborhood and home, precipitated by my dim-witted forgetting of Shelly's disc.

"It's that one," he said. "Shelly lived there." He pointed at the monstrosity to the immediate right of his house.

"I know," I said. "I've just never seen it from the front or this close."

It was even bigger than Gordon's and in much better repair. There were no signs of life in or around the house, even though the wake at Trinity should have ended by then.

"Let's go," Gordon announced. "We can't have much time. Grab the disc and Shelly. I've got to get into Shelly's pool shed and grab the boom box. I'll meet you out back."

I snickered.

"What?" Gordon asked.

"Boom box?" I said. "It sounds so eighties."

"Says the guy with the Trans Am. What do you want me to call it? That's what she called it. Do you want me to get it or not?"

"Sorry," I said, stifling my amusement and shifting into park. "What should I do with the Trannie?"

"Leave it. My mother won't notice or care, and by the time anyone connects it to us, we'll be on the water."

I took Shelly from the Trans Am and hurried around the side of Gordon's house to the backyard, which I had viewed from my side, across the bay, so many times. On those occasions, I never could have imagined the events that would lead to my crossing his backyard at that moment.

Gordon reappeared from Shelly's property carrying the boom box, and we headed directly toward the wooden docks that extended into the bay from the thin strip of beach behind the houses.

"No trouble getting into the shed?" I asked as we reached the horizontally slotted planks.

He unclenched his hand. Resting in his palm was a key. "I know where they hide it," he said, before carelessly whipping it, sidearm, far out into the water. "That ought to piss off her old man a bit."

I gasped as if he were Sir Bedivere returning King Arthur's sword to the Lady of the Lake.

We both tried not to notice the vacant space along Shelly's dock, where her sailboat, *Ariel,* used to be tied off. Gordon jumped down into his sixteen-foot fiberglass Byron-brand Corsair-model outboard, powered by twin Mercury motors, and placed the boom box beneath the captain's chair. I handed him Shelly in exchange for one of those puffy orange life jackets, double-checked that Shelly's disc was still in my pocket, and cautiously lowered myself into the boat.

"Where's yours?" I asked, meaning a life preserver.

For the second time that evening, Gordon looked at me like I was the biggest idiot in the world.

I undid the lines and tossed them into the boat while he started the engines.

When I joined Gordon beneath a hard plastic canopy behind the steering console, where he half-sat, half-stood in the captain's chair near the dead center of the hull, we paused, perhaps each waiting for the other to change his mind. A moment passed before Gordon said, "Let's go, then," and he reversed the boat out into the bay.

After reorienting the bow, he set the GPS headings for North Bass Island and slowly pressed forward the dual throttles until they reached a three-quarter speed position. The Corsair gently skimmed the surface of the bay on a due north course toward the shipping channel that runs past Johnson's Island and Marblehead Point on the left and the tip of the Strand peninsula on the right.

The open waters of Lake Erie proved to be only slightly less accommodating than those of the protected Ogontz Bay had been. One-to-two-footers rolled in the South Passage that separates the Ohio mainland from the smattering of islands that lie in Erie's western basin. Unimpressive wave heights for a regular Laker, but I hadn't been on the water since that fishing charter with my dad and brother that had left me green and vomiting. As Gordon navigated through the west-to-east-running rollers, I felt the nausea beginning to percolate and rise.

"Stare into the horizon; it'll help," Gordon advised, sensing my discomfort. "And eat these." He reached beneath the stainless steel steering wheel into a bin and pulled out a bag of pretzels and a warm can of Sprite.

Holding fast to Shelly, pressed between my left arm and side, I nibbled on the pretzel rods with my right hand and tried to maintain my balance on my landlubber's legs. Beyond the bobbing red bow light, I watched the last vestiges of the day surrender to a translucent night. In the middle of the lake, the canopy of stars shone in a number and with a brilliance I had never before seen from land. Remembering Gordon's lecture of several years past, I wondered which stars were already dead and which were still pulsating, and into what already-plotted future I was currently heading. Gordon steered the Corsair according to the path on the blue-lit screen of the GPS, but the moon hanging over us from the stern graciously projected its reflected light before us and illuminated a path that ran straight to the Bass Islands.

part two

BYRON! HOW SWEETLY SAD THY MELODY!
ATTUNING STILL THE SOUL TO TENDERNESS,
AS IF SOFT PITY, WITH UNUSUAL STRESS,
HAD TOUCH'D HER PLAINTIVE LUTE, AND THOU, BEING BY,
HADST CAUGHT THE TONES, NOR SUFFER'D THEM TO DIE.
O'ERSHADOWING SORROW DOTH NOT MAKE THEE LESS
DELIGHTFUL: THOU THY GRIEFS DOST DRESS
WITH A BRIGHT HALO, SHINING BEAMILY,
AS WHEN A CLOUD THE GOLDEN MOON DOTH VEIL,
ITS SIDES ARE TING'D WITH A RESPLENDENT GLOW,
THROUGH THE DARK ROBE OFT AMBER RAYS PREVAIL,
AND LIKE FAIR VEINS IN SABLE MARBLE FLOW;
STILL WARBLE, DYING SWAN! STILL TELL THE TALE,
THE ENCHANTING TALE, THE TALE OF PLEASING WOE.
—JOHN KEATS, "TO BYRON"

8

Looking back at the first half of Shelly and Gordon's junior—my sophomore—year, it's easy to pinpoint the signs of Shelly's unraveling, which at that time, absorbed in the aftermath of my father's death, I missed.

By then, a full year into their time together at Trinity, Shelly and Gordon's relationship had been mostly relegated to his hot and cold involvement with the *Beacon*. No amount of her less-than-subtle worship was capable of causing him to reimagine her as anything more than a childhood friend. No matter how much more she wanted, Gordon would always be Gordon. He was a lot of things, but a white knight was not one of them. Without friends her own age or boyfriends, Shelly felt freer to devote herself to her causes (thus, the red paint protest) and the *Beacon*.

Then, as the universe continually proves itself ironic, Shelly made the first non-Byron friend of her entire life other than me.

"Hey, Shelly," I said, as she entered the media center. "You're late again."

"One more week of detentions to go," she explained.

In addition to the one-week in-school suspension Shelly had earned and already served for her little act of cafeteria civil disobedience, she'd been assigned two weeks of after-school detentions and ten service hours working with the maintenance crew.

"I missed you at Mass today," I said slyly.

"Oh, yeah? I was there," she answered, but I knew she wasn't. Shelly may have been the worst liar in history.

That year, for extra credit in sophomore theology, I had volunteered to film the daily Masses, from the rear balcony of All Saints. The Masses were replayed for the kids who were serving in-school suspensions. (I'm pretty sure that is some form of double jeopardy or, at least, cruel and unusual punishment.) I didn't need the extra points, but it saved me the humiliation of, morning after morning, having to find a pew where I would be welcomed. Skipping a grade had left me a man without a class.

The camera was stationary. Once I pressed the record button, there was little actual "filming" required, so I'd spend most of my time voyeuristically watching Trinity's mortals below. You'd be surprised by the unholy goings-on that I regularly witnessed, such as surreptitious gaming on all sorts of handheld devices, constant text messaging, and even the occasional hand job or "stinky pinky" beneath a varsity jacket placed across a lap.

To pass the time, I'd play "Where's Shelly?" Since, like me, she didn't belong to any of Trinity's cliques, she lacked their vital membership privileges—one of which was the communally understood and enforced provision that members of said cliques were not only guaranteed but also expected to sit with fellow group members at all school gatherings, such as assemblies, pep rallies, lunch, athletic events, and school Masses. During any given Mass, I'd eventually locate Shelly anywhere from parked among the freshmen, to mixed in with the faculty, to sitting unwelcome and alone among the upperclassmen—usually with the width of a full body free on either side of her. Once, I even caught her sneaking in to hide inside a confessional. But I always found her. That day, I hadn't.

"Okay," Shelly finally admitted under my accusing stare and the prolonged silence. "I ditched. But I made a friend."

"Who might that be?" I asked.

"Hogg."

The unfortunately but aptly named Tammy Jo Hogg was a fellow outcast and survivor. She possessed the cruel combination of a beautiful face and, let's just say, "full" figure. Everyone at Trinity called her Hogg. (According to the National Institutes of Health, an estimated three hundred thousand deaths a year in the United States are the result of obesity.)

The contrasts in the two misfits couldn't have been more pronounced. Shelly was slim and her hair long, black, and unruly; her face was not beautiful, but she was far from unattractive. Hogg was, obviously, overweight, blond, and had a ruddy skin tone. Shelly was deep-thinking and artsy, whereas Hogg's next profound thought would be her first. Shelly's fashion sense, like her retro taste in music and movies, veered toward vintage consignment shop pieces, and she loved bright colors and stripes at any and all angles. Hogg chose classic cuts, patterns, and colors that complemented rather than advertised. Shelly grew up bereft of family and largely ignored by her disinterested father, who thought her at first odd and then, later, crazy. He actually threatened to make her see a shrink after the red paint stunt in the cafeteria. Hogg, in contrast to the constant cruelty she endured from the fitness Nazis at Trinity, had a family of similarly oversized parents and siblings who loved every inch and pound of her. She was never happier than when at home in her neighborhood of modest, mostly ranch-style homes on Ogontz's west side, watching movies, playing board games, and eating junk and fried foods at a suicidal pace.

As Shelly explained it to me, their friendship began in the girls' lavatory.

Separately, they had each decided to skip the mandatory Thursday-morning Mass and were sitting—each unbeknownst to the other—on toilets in adjoining stalls, with their feet scrunched up on their respective seats—not an easy piece of contortion for a girl of nearly two hundred and fifty pounds. A female faculty member, typically Sister Margaret, the last remaining nun at Trinity, would perform a pre-Mass sweep of the girls' restrooms and locker room, taking a quick peek under the stall walls, looking for ditchers before moving on to nearby All Saints Church. The girls had both figured out how to outmaneuver her long ago.

No sooner had Sister Margaret completed her casing of the restroom and closed the door than Shelly heard the unmistakable sound of a lighter being torched, followed by the smell of a cigarette burning.

Shelly delicately slid the latch to the door, lightly placed her feet on the ground, and snuck out of the stall. Turning past the bank of stalls toward the exit, she nearly fainted when she spotted Hogg leaning heavily against a sink—cigarette to her mouth and eyes squinting hard through the rising smoke. (According to current trends, 6.4 percent of teen smokers will die from a smoking-related disease.)

"Hi, Hogg," Shelly said.

Ignoring Shelly's greeting, Hogg said, "Psycho Shelly," while doing that trying-to-talk-and-inhale-simultaneously thing that smokers do so that their words, like firefighters in a burning high-rise, have to ascend the esophageal stairwell through clouds of toxic smoke, only to emerge spent and nearly unrecognizable in the fresh air. Hogg exhaled and offered Shelly a cigarette. Although she'd never smoked one before, Shelly took it. The cigarette felt uncomfortable in her hand, like a sixth finger, and she wasn't quite sure what to do with it in her mouth, but she definitely liked the way she looked in the mirrors while holding it and placing it between her lips. She felt bad, and bad felt good.

Shelly looked up and caught sight of the smoke detector, then looked back at Hogg.

"Relax," Hogg said, reading her mind and recalling Shelly's infamous red-paint-induced probation. Between her thumb and forefinger, Hogg showed Shelly the nine-volt battery she'd removed from the smoke detector. (In approximately 60 percent of all home fire deaths in the United

States, there is either no smoke detector in the home or a malfunctioning one.)

Shelly's eyes ran another quick relay from Hogg to the top-of-the-wall location of the smoke detector and back.

"I know," Hogg said, "pretty impressive for a fat girl."

"You're not so fat, Hogg," Shelly lied.

"And you're not so psycho, Shelly." Shelly wasn't sure whether that was a lie or not.

"Why aren't you at Mass?" Shelly asked.

"Don't feel like it, and I had a serious craving for one of these."

"I didn't know you smoked."

"You didn't know anything about me until a couple of minutes ago. And now, besides my being fat, the fact that I smoke is the only thing you know." She hesitated, smiled, and then looked with kindness into Shelly's eyes. "But it's a start." Hogg stuck out her arm—it reminded Shelly of a baby's—and said, "I'm Tammy Jo, but you can call me Hogg. Everyone does."

With something less than enthusiasm, Shelly took Hogg's amply padded palm and shook it lightly. "Shelly," she said.

"Why aren't *you* at church?" Hogg asked.

Shelly vacillated, unsure if she should risk going nuclear on what might be a budding friendship, but, being Shelly and relatively lacking in tact or subtlety, she said, "I'm an atheist."

Without responding, Hogg took a final drag of her cigarette, waddled toward the stalls, dropped the butt into the toilet, and flushed. Shelly imagined the short-lived cigarette and Hogg's mime show to be symbolic of their own brief friendship. Feeling claustrophobic, she awkwardly imitated Hogg's process of evidence removal and began once more to make her way to the door.

"What does that mean? Atheist? You don't believe in God or something?"

"Or *nothing*, actually," Shelly said.

"What?"

Shelly's attempt at humor had cleared Hogg's head by a good foot.

"It was a joke. Anyway, atheism for me means I don't believe in *believing* in a god." She could almost smell the wires crossing and burning behind Hogg's gray eyes beneath her knitted brow, so she attempted to expound on her anti-credo. "What I mean is I don't believe in some grandfatherly man sitting on a cloud somewhere beyond outer space making ridiculous laws and passing arbitrary judgments but not caring how we treat one another or the planet as long as we do our weekly Catholic calisthenics. You know." Shelly broke into a mock fitness routine as she performed the actions accompanied by the voice of an aerobics instructor. "Genuflect! Cross yourself! Sit down! Stand up! Kneel! And again. Genuflect. . . ." She paused to catch her breath. "If there is a god, I can't believe she cares what you call yourself: Catholic, Lutheran, Methodist, Muslim, Jew, or atheist. It's the churches that cause the divisions and the hatred and the wars. It's the belief *system* I don't believe in."

Shelly could see that Hogg was reconsidering her "You're not so psycho, Shelly" comment from earlier.

"So you *don't* believe in God, then?" Hogg asked from square one.

"No. I mean, not really. Maybe. There might be some force or energy or something beyond my knowing, and the way everyone talks about God is just some metaphor. You know what I mean?"

By the look on Hogg's face, metaphor was a bad strategy.

"Okay. Let's say I'm more of an agnostic," Shelly tried.

"Agnostic?"

"Yeah, agnostic. You know. I don't commit either way. There might be a god; there might not be a god. There's just no way of knowing. So why bother wasting so much time, energy, and effort on what might be, when there is so much curable pain and injustice around us that definitely is and that we can definitely do something about?"

Serious contemplation of Shelly's pontification caused Hogg's eyes to narrow and her face to pinch with genuine concern. "What about heaven?" she asked. "What happens when you die?"

The tone of Hogg's voice had changed, as if she had conferred expert status on Shelly in regards to all things ontological, and Shelly's answer to this question could completely discombobulate Hogg's perception of her present and future in the universal space-time continuum.

Shelly's pathological honesty demanded that she renounce that which she considered nonsense, such as the resurrection of the soul in some realm beyond the material, and she was about to do so when Hogg extended her upturned left forearm and said, "Look."

Unsure of what she was supposed to look at, Shelly stared

in stupefied silence until Hogg pointed to a tiny horizontal scar across her wrist. "I did that in the sixth grade. I wanted to die and go to heaven, where everyone is thin, but I couldn't cut through enough of the fat to really bleed much, and it hurt real bad, so I didn't even bother with the other one."

Shelley looked at Hogg's wrist and weighed her own intellectual integrity against Hogg's hope for a skinny afterlife, and compromised. There was no way she could bring herself to agree with the gibberish she'd been taught in school, but she couldn't see the benefit of crushing Hogg's hopes either. So she told a story of half-truths.

"I'm going to tell you something I've never told anyone," she began. "A couple of years ago, my friend Gordon was sent away to prep school. I thought I'd never be allowed to see him again. I was crushed and sadder than I'd ever been. I didn't want to live without him. So I snuck into my father's bathroom when he was at work and swallowed half of a bottle of the Vicodin he took for his arthritis. I went back to my room and lay down to die. I actually thought I did die because it seemed as if I'd gone to heaven." ("Pharmaceutical suicide" is the trendy name for it.)

"How'd you know it was heaven?" Hogg interrupted, fully engrossed in the story.

"Well, I didn't see a god or angels or my mom or anything like that, but there was a sweet and peaceful feeling that came over me."

"What did it look like?"

"I don't remember many details. Like I said, it was more a feeling than a place, but it was really bright and warm."

"Who was there?"

"I can't remember specific people, but everyone there spoke in rhyme." Shelly smiled in the telling. "Even I did; it just poured out of me!"

"You mean like poems?"

"No. Just regular conversation. It was all in the most beautiful couplets of iambic pentameter."

"What'd you do there?"

"That's the oddest thing. I didn't do much of anything. All I recall is sitting in front of a large white vanity with a tabletop mirror, brushing my hair."

"You've got pretty hair." She paused, then asked, "Why'd you come back?"

"I didn't want to. I woke up in the hospital with a sore throat and a really bad stomachache. My father was standing over me, but he walked away as soon as I opened my eyes. He must have found me when he came home from work, and he called an ambulance."

"That's too bad," Hogg said.

"Yeah, I know."

With her worries somewhat eased, Hogg considered Shelly's version of heaven, coupled with her new friend's earlier expressed doubt regarding God's existence, and said, "Can I ask you something?"

"Sure."

"Why do you go to a Catholic school?"

"That's easy. Jesus loves me."

"That makes a lot of sense," Hogg said.

"I get that a lot."

*   *   *

After their chance meeting in the restroom, Hogg and Shelly became fast friends. Hogg even joined us on the *Beacon* staff; she wasn't much of a writer, but she was one hell of a salesperson. Our advertising income and circulation skyrocketed with Hogg on the staff. Remarkably, she had, thus far, emerged from the crucible of schoolhouse cruelty armed with a gentle, good humor; it was an evolutionary leap of survival that Shelly was never able to make. If the demigods of Trinity could have just gotten past their fat prejudice, which most of them couldn't, they would have discovered a likeable, even attractive, young woman in Hogg—a reality, remarkably enough, not lost on Gordon.

"I wish you wouldn't," I heard Shelly tell Gordon as we sat in the *Beacon*'s office.

It was a Friday afternoon that had the expectancy in the air that only Friday afternoons possess: a feeling of the suspension of time between the accomplishments or failures of the weekdays just behind and the possibilities of the weekend just ahead. Adding to the sense of potential was that it was also the night of the Halloween dance, sponsored by the *Yearbook*'s staff. It was the best-attended dance of the school year because, unlike couples' dances like prom or homecoming, dateless losers, like me, could mill about the periphery of the dance floor without being so conspicuous.

Gordon was supposed to be peer editing Shelly's story

as she did the same with his, but his attention was clearly elsewhere. Since Hogg had joined the staff, the frequency of Gordon's attendance in the *Beacon*'s office had risen sharply, and now he couldn't seem to take his eyes off of Hogg. Shelly must have heard the calculations whirring in his brain and anticipated their ultimate sum.

Pulled from his musings at the sound of Shelly's voice, Gordon said, "Wish I wouldn't what?"

"You know I know what you're thinking, Gordon. And I wish you wouldn't. That's all."

"Why shouldn't I?" he asked.

"Hogg's my friend."

"So am I," Gordon said.

"If you are, you'll stay away from Hogg."

Hogg stood across the room looking out the windows and talking on her cell with potential advertisers for next semester's edition, while I sat, brooding over one of my own pieces. I never allowed anyone to see my work before final submission; I've never exactly taken well to criticism, constructive or otherwise. It's a common, if inexpedient, trait shared by many artists. Hey, at least I'm honest.

After my father's funeral, I thought that Shelly and I might become more than friends, but with the addition of Hogg to the staff, Shelly seemed disinterested in tethering her flimsy sense of reality to me, instead choosing Hogg, whose weighty obtuseness served as a more reliable anchor than I. Hogg also served to help Shelly stave off the flights of fancy that she was prone to taking, which inevitably led to her crazy stunts and getting into trouble.

My existence still seemed to inspire little notice from

Gordon. By then, he had firmly established his place on top of the jockocracy of Trinity, no small feat for a swimmer, participating in what—despite the team's success—was considered a relatively minor sport at Trinity. But even the football and hockey players—by far the most macho of all—couldn't help but admire his Hummer, his family name, his authorial celebrity, his growing wealth, his popularity with girls, and even his ripped body.

With fewer than five hundred students, news travels fast and freely through Trinity's corridors, classrooms, locker rooms, and cafeteria. I regularly overheard Monday-morning reports of weekend debaucheries spent by Trinity's warrior class with Gordon. I'd see him with those Neanderthals at school and wonder "Why?" He was so much their better in every way imaginable. They were clearly hangers-on, members of an ever-changing entourage, using him for his ride, his family's lakeside mansion with all its toys, and for the variety of fish (as he'd sometimes refer to girls) that he would find unsatisfactory and leave for them to devour.

But one day, when I watched him lead a pack of these knuckle draggers through the main hallway of the classroom building, I realized that I had it backward. They weren't taking advantage of *him* as much as he was using *them* as background. It was the contrast between him and these unsophisticated, dull, and ordinary guys that made Gordon's attractiveness pop. He needed their banality to frame him, to focus the admirer's eye. An angel among angels is invisible, but an angel among men is a god.

That's why, I believe, he enjoyed his "sympathy fucks" (his words, not mine) better than the encounters with gorgeous girls and women whom he "banged" (again, not my word). He was incapable of overwhelming the beautiful ones with his own beauty; they all somehow felt that they deserved him by virtue of their own attractiveness and felt that, in their coupling, the sense of gratitude was equal. He must have hated that.

That was what led to Shelly's pleading "I wish you wouldn't." But she knew there was next to nothing she could do to stop it.

The Halloween dance began at eight o'clock; I arrived at five minutes till. I wore a pair of green scrubs, complete with a surgical cap and mask, that I'd borrowed from the hospital where I volunteered. I paid Mrs. Hildebrand, the yearbook advisor, for my ticket. Admission was five bucks if you wore a costume but ten if you didn't.

A heavy thumping of bass poured from the gymnasium doors; the song was old, like something from the nineties. The only words I could discern were "Jump! Jump! Jump around!" Multicolored lights flashed from around the DJ's table on the portable stage beneath the basketball hoop. Two spotlights, borrowed from the drama department, were trained on a mirrored disco ball, gift of the class of 1980, which had been lowered from the ceiling; its reflected lights rotated throughout the gym space.

There were fewer than two dozen kids inside—all freshmen except me. Clearly, none of us had received the memo from Cool Central regarding fashionably late arrivals. Thinking me still too socially immature, my parents hadn't allowed me to attend the school dances the year before. I recognized a few kids as former middle-school classmates, but that was from two years ago—an entire epoch in teen aging. I considered leaving. But, instead, I climbed to the top of the bleachers and watched the gym floor fill as if I were peering through the lens of a time-lapse camera. From my perch, I could see that many of the arriving upperclassmen, including the girls, wore a red glow on their faces that I hadn't noticed during school days. Many were sporting what my father would have called "shit-eating grins," and they all were chewing gum. (I don't mean they were costumed as chewing gum, but they were actually *chewing* gum.) Later, I learned that the reason for their late arrivals and strange appearances was that they had been drinking, filling up on the "liquid courage" that would enable the boys to talk to and dance with girls who they otherwise lacked the temerity to approach, and enable the girls to give the boys the kind of flirtation and access that they were other times too prudish, or caught up in appearing to be so, to allow.

Most of the guys had been less than imaginative in their costuming. Many simply wore their athletic uniforms; others came as nerds, punk rockers, and cowboys. The least creative simply wore rubber masks of presidents and monsters they'd purchased at Spencer's Gifts in the mall.

The girls were another story; they were completely unrecognizable from those who walked the halls and sat in the classrooms of Trinity. Just about the only male sexual fantasy they failed to cater to was the Catholic schoolgirl one, which they lived every day. There were countless nurses, librarians, and French maids in impossibly short skirts and cleavage-baring tops. And, apparently, every ingénue of Disney and fairytale fame had been an aspiring Victoria's Secret model; costumed Cinderellas, Sleeping Beauties, Snow Whites, Ariels, Tianas, and Jasmines exposed more breasts and thighs than Trinity had seen since last spring's sophomore-class-sponsored chicken dinner fund-raiser.

By eight-thirty, the gym floor was filled with bumping, grinding—basically dry-humping—teenagers. The out-numbered teacher chaperones had early on capitulated in their attempts to police the dancing and had retreated in defeat to the fringes of the orgiastic ritual. I began to enjoy my out-of-student-body experience. I felt Olympian, high above the mortals performing for my titillation and entertainment below.

I'm not sure how long they'd been there, intermingled with the masquerading multitude, but eventually I spotted Hogg and Shelly. Hogg wore an all-white man's suit, in-cluding a white cowboy hat and a black string tie. A huge unlit cigar dangled from her lips. She was dressed as Boss Hogg from *The Dukes of Hazzard*. Shelly was the Jessica Simpson version of Daisy Duke in a blond wig, brown cow-boy boots, cutoff jean shorts, and a short-sleeved red-checked button-down shirt tied off to show her midriff. Her hair was in pigtails, and she'd dotted her cheeks with brown freckles. I had to cross my legs and fold my hands over my lap to hide my "interest."

Boy after boy, many of whom had made fun of her throughout their years at Trinity, and none of whom had pre-viously shown the tiniest amorous interest in her, tried to pry her away from Hogg to the dance floor, but she successfully rebuffed each attempt. Even Brandon Sullivan, a senior football captain, was initially turned away. I think that she was waiting for Gordon to arrive and be wowed.

And arrive he did.

Shortly after ten o'clock, with less than an hour left in the dance, a commotion arose near the gym entrance. A harem of barefooted silk-veiled belly dancers (all members of the girls' swim team) ushered in Gordon, who was dressed as a Turkish sultan. He wore a satin three-quarter length aqua-blue robe with a black lapel and very short sleeves. A gold fringe ran the length of the bottom cuff; the robe was left entirely open, exposing his still tanned bare torso. The pants were a blousy black silk with an elastic bottom. On his feet were a pair of curly gold pointy-toed slippers that no one but Gordon could have worn without ridicule. The ensemble was topped off with a turban to match the robe, with a fake ruby centered over the forehead.

Gordon made his way through the parting sea of on-lookers directly to where Shelly was standing. A collective gasp sounded when he extended his hand to . . . Hogg, who, suddenly oblivious to Shelly's presence, followed him to the floor, accompanied by a slow song. Soon the mismatched pair were melded into the sea of dancers, rocking back and forth, left and right, from foot to foot, and then I completely lost sight of them for the remainder of the evening.

I did, however, spot Shelly—although I wish I hadn't. After her snubbing, she marched directly up to Brandon Sullivan and cut in on his partner. Before the dance ended, her tongue was tonsil-deep in Brandon's mouth.

Maybe that was the beginning of the end, a sign of her tendency to respond irrationally and dangerously to Gordon's rejection. In any case, in that moment, if she couldn't have Gordon, she'd *be* Gordon.

Both Hogg and Shelly went too far that night—Shelly spitefully, in the back of Brandon's father's Dodge Ram, and Hogg because what choice did she have, on the floor of Trinity's chapel, after being plied with a bottle of Communion wine that Gordon had pilfered from the tabernacle?

The outcomes of the evening were not revealed to me by Shelly or Gordon. Regarding Shelly, gentlemen may never kiss and tell, but Brandon Sullivan sure as hell was no gentleman. As for Hogg, on Monday, when the missing wine was discovered, so too were the black string tie from Hogg's costume and an empty condom wrapper. The tie was easily traced to Hogg through a large number of schadenfreude-inspired witnesses. Hogg was summarily expelled when, for the sake of what she was convinced was love, she refused to narc on Gordon, which could have reduced her punishment to a six-day suspension. Hearsay evidence led Principal Smith to Gordon, who, after a terse denial, escaped unpunished. He was, however, informally assigned to Father Fulop for counseling.

I'm convinced that Gordon unconsciously left the evidence behind on purpose. I think he perceived Hogg as a threat. You see, there's no doubt that Gordon loved Shelly, but not in some easily classifiable way.

"Romantically?" you ask.

No.

"Like a sister?"

Not really.

"A best friend?"

That's not it either.

It was some twisted form of love that required her to be forever inferior to, and emotionally dependent on, him. With Hogg, he couldn't stand the idea of Shelly's attention being diverted from him, so he found a way to remove her. It's just a theory, but one that grew stronger. And, if the theory is correct, Gordon's possessiveness played just as big a role in Shelly's death as her own obsessions.

In the weeks that followed, Shelly grew distant and sullen. While Gordon dove into the start of swim season and made only infrequent visits to the *Beacon*'s office, Shelly stayed long hours, worked weekends, and threw herself headlong into making the final edits and preparing the magazine for December's publication date. She had also assumed Hogg's responsibilities and was already lining up advertisers for next semester's edition. I figured that her mood was the result of Gordon's and Hogg's absences, and that she was working so hard as a way of dealing with her sadness by not dealing with it at all. Concerned for her well-being and selfishly missing her attention, I followed her into the media center darkroom one day when we, the Gordonettes, and Mr. Robbins were all working after school. She had gone to retrieve a ream of paper for the printer.

"Hey," I said, as, with her back to me, she reached for the papers stacked high on an overhead shelf.

Startled, she gasped, half-turned toward me with widened eyes, and formed a shield across her breasts with her arms.

When she recognized me in the strawberry syrup light, she let her guard down. "Oh, it's just you."

"Gee, thanks," I said, playing hurt.

"You know what I mean. You scared me."

"Following you in here was the only way to corner you long enough to talk to you."

"What do you want?" she asked tersely with her lashes fluttering incessantly over eyes that refused to alight for more than a second on anything, including me.

"I want to know what's wrong. You haven't been so . . . so . . . so Shelly lately. Did I do something?" I asked, in the egocentric way all guys believe the world and everything in it is somehow connected to ourselves.

"Maybe, John, you don't know me as well as you think you do," she snipped in a tone I'd never heard her use before. "Nothing's wrong. It's my period," she said, expecting the topic of menstruation to send me reeling like Dracula from a cross, as is typical of most males. Ironic simile, I know.

What Shelly didn't know was that since I'd been a little boy, my mother had sent me on "tampon runs." Literally, I'd run—because my father was at work or, in the last years of his life, unable to drive, and she was too drowning in self-pity to do much of anything. She'd tell me that if I didn't hurry, she'd bleed to death. I know now that she was exaggerating, but I didn't know that then. Because of the dearth of drugstores in our neighborhood, my runs weren't short ones. I like to think that if I had had the inclination, I could have been a fair cross-country runner.

The first time, I was maybe nine years old. I tore into the drugstore and ran right into a white-coated man, who was trying to exit. "Mister, I need help!" I said with tears welling. "My mother is bleeding to death!"

I handed him a slip of scrap paper wrapped in a ten-dollar

bill on which my mother had scribbled, "One box of store-brand tampons."

The pharmacist smiled, then calmly walked me to the feminine products section. On one knee, he explained that my mother was not going to bleed to death ("desanguination" is the term for the type of massive blood loss that may lead to death), and he proceeded to provide a clinical explanation of the female reproductive system. I certainly didn't understand much of the anatomy lecture, but I was relieved to know that my mother was going to live. When I think of that pharmacist today, I imagine him as the type of father who, in what he believes is a loving and rational manner, teaches his children that there is no Tooth Fairy, Easter Bunny, or even Santa Claus.

Anyway, Shelly's attempt at avoidance didn't work. I stood my ground, blocking the narrow darkroom passage.

In the next instant, she was pressed against me, head resting on my left shoulder, arms still draped at her sides and tears drenching my neck and polo.

Unsure of my role, I slowly raised my arms so that I held her loosely and was running my hand down the back of her head and shoulders over her long, silky black hair from where it spilled out from beneath her toboggan. She sobbed convulsively and confessed strings of mostly unintelligible sorrows—some of which I have already shared with you—until, eventually, she regained her composure. She wiped her eyes, her nose, and my shoulder, with tissues removed from the pockets of the black cardigan that she wore over her uniform blouse. The disintegrated tissue left white dandruff-like flakes on my shirtfront.

"I'm sorry," she said in a half-laugh, half-cry.

"It's okay."

"Thank you so much, John," she added.

"For what?" I asked, sincerely unsure of what good I'd done and certainly no wiser for having listened to the causes of her sadness.

"For asking," Shelly said. Then she deftly slid between the sink baths and me and was gone.

A week later, on a Friday afternoon early in December, a day when the first Alberta clipper of the winter had come barreling down from Canada, surfing the current of the fast-flowing jet stream and dumping the season's first measurable snowfall on northern Ohio, I asked Shelly to join me at Gordon's swim meet after school.

She whispered that she couldn't because she was working that afternoon at Planned Parenthood.

So I went to the meet by myself, knowing full well that it was a total violation of the code of teenage cool to go anywhere alone. It's penultimate only to being seen riding a school bus to or from school, which is the irrefutable sign of being completely friendless and lame.

The humidity inside the natatorium was stifling, like a tropical rain forest. I was seated in the first row of the aluminum bleachers, and I half-expected Gordon to swing in on a vine. His entrance was, however, less conspicuous but not much less impressive.

The girls' and then the boys' teams filed out of their respective locker rooms, and Gordon was the last swimmer in line, and the only topless one. The others were all wrapped in red calf-length swim parkas with hoods over their heads; they looked like a line of monks marching to evening prayers. Gordon wore only a pair of black wind pants that rested well below his waistline, to expose the top of the red bikini Speedo beneath. The pants effectively concealed his misshapen foot and calf, as his bared torso drew the crowd's collective stare of appreciation for his Adonis-like build and beauty.

When Gordon's events were called, he'd wait until after introductions, and at the very last second drop his pants, assume his position on the platform or in the pool, and train his eyes on the water in order to avoid catching a glimpse of any untoward stares at his deformity.

As on the deck, in the water he was without peer regardless of the stroke: butterfly, breaststroke, backstroke, or freestyle. What had been pure, brutish athleticism during his sophomore year, Coach Mancini had transformed into a graceful liquidity of motion by his junior season. Gordon's form cut with surgical precision through the water, more dolphinlike than human.

"He's an Aquarius, you know," a woman's voice said from behind me as Gordon dominated his final race of the afternoon.

When I turned in acknowledgment, however, her eyes were glued on the pool as if she had been speaking to no one, or anyone, or, perhaps, everyone.

Then she said, "Aquarians are stubborn, contrary, perverse, unpredictable, unemotional, and detached. Look it up. It's not my fault. It's in his stars."

After Gordon touched the timing pad, having easily won his race, the strange woman rose and exited the natatorium without another word.

As the swim parents seated on the bleacher behind me repositioned themselves into the vacuum created by the strange woman's departure, I heard a father say, "That Byron woman is one queer duck."

When I left the swim meet, the weather couldn't have been more opposite to the sauna-like natatorium, but it being a Friday and there being no one waiting enthusiastically for my return at home, I decided to lean into the wind, brave the face-stinging snowflakes, and visit Shelly at Planned Parenthood. I thought it might make her happy to hear of the Olympian feats Gordon had performed, and I wanted to share with her that I'd met, sort of, Gordon's mother. Okay, yeah, I *really* didn't want to go home.

Planned Parenthood is located on the fringe of what used to be a downtown Ogontz replete with department stores and specialty shops and restaurants but is now nearly full of empty buildings. As I approached, I was relieved to see that there were no picketers outside the clinic. An ecumenical group of pro-life advocates, sponsored by a coalition of Ogontz's Christian churches (the only kind in town), occasionally set up human barricades to frighten away and harass would-be patients, and to express their scorn for a sexually informed citizenry. These advocates were usually armed with poster-sized photographs of aborted fetuses and with cameras, which they sometimes used to take pictures of clients as they exited the building beneath the Planned Parenthood sign. Then they would post the photographs on their website. Apparently, the rain, sleet, snow, and gloom of night did stay these people's puritanical resolve, unlike that of the intrepid U.S. mail carriers.

A tone sounded in the back of the building when I pulled open the single glass door. I felt my testicles shrivel the second I entered the waiting room and a multitude of shades of pinks attacked my senses. I had hoped to find Shelly behind the receptionist's counter, but it was unattended. A vertical rack, full of pamphlets related to sexual health, hung to the right of the counter. I was reading, without actually touching, one on genital warts when a large African American woman asked, "Can I help you?" in one of those tones that conveys the exact opposite meaning of one's actual words.

If not for the counterbalancing pull of her double-wide hips, the woman's boulder-sized breasts, spilling from the front of her scoop-necked red chiffon dress, would have successfully teamed with gravity to topple her to the ground. I immediately understood her agitation with having to rise from wherever she had been parked in the rear to wait on a skinny white boy, who, she presumed, had been unable to keep his puny peashooter holstered and was now suffering the consequences. She made note of my reading selection and, despite her best attempt at professionalism, was unable to mask her disgust.

Her badge read "Sha'niqua."

"Oh. No. I don't need help," I said, responding to her revulsion.

"It's okay, honey; you'd be surprised at the folks who come here. It's nothing to be ashamed of," she said, although it sounded more like "Sure you don't, asshole."

"No. You don't understand. I'm here for Shelly."

Her brow furrowed and her frown deepened; her contempt for me actually increased at my mention of Shelly's name.

"I see," she said. "Did she know you was coming?"

I paused to consider whether the pun was a Planned Parenthood joke and whether I should acknowledge the attempt at humor with a smile or chuckle. An additional nonthreatening glance into Sha'niqua's eyes, however, made it clear that levity was not standard procedure at Planned Parenthood. "Yes."

She hesitated, sized me up, clearly found me lacking in whatever it was she was measuring, and said, "Come with me."

Sha'niqua waddled, accompanied by the *squish-squish* of the fabric from her sleeves rubbing a bossa nova beat against the material on her sides, making the metallic rattlesnake sound of a cabasa. I followed her, conga style, past the receptionist's work area, the director's office, a pair of conference rooms, and a kitchenette, until she stopped and opened the door to an examining room in which Shelly sat with her bare legs hanging over the side of one of those cold vinyl-covered, height-adjustable examining tables with the ass-wide paper strip down the middle. Her face was turned to the wall; she wore a thin hospital robe. A Trinity girl's uniform made a pile on a chair in the corner. My guide shut the door and left without a word, but not before shooting me a look of utter loathing.

"Hey" was my feeble-voiced conversation starter. I had tried but somehow still had failed to put two and two together.

A rapid turn of Shelly's head met my greeting. Mine was *not* the voice she—not so much expected, but had hoped, to hear.

"What are you doing here?"

"I came to see you; I thought you were working."

"I'm not. How'd you get back here?"

"I asked for you and the woman led me back."

"She must think you're the father," Shelly mused, more to herself than to me. A half-smile flickered for a moment, then evaporated from her face.

"The father? Whose father? What are you talking about?" I paused in contemplation. Wait for it. Wait for it. Four. And . . . there we go. . . . My jaw dropped to my chest. "You're, you're . . ."

"Pregnant," Shelly finished.

"You mean . . . Then you . . ."

"Are having an abortion. Am waiting for the doctor."

"Here?"

"Not in this room, no. There's a sort of operating room for the procedure farther down the hall."

"Wow" was my stupid response. Then something even more inane like, "Are you sure?" Then, before I could stop it, "Can I help?"

She smiled at what she knew was my sincere concern.

The smile reassured me that it, she, even I, would be okay. So Shelly.

"Wait. What about your father? Does he know?"

Suddenly stone-faced, she said, "No. He doesn't even know I'm pregnant, and he can never know." Her tone was not ironic. "John, this baby. It's . . . it's my . . ." She stopped herself, then began again. "My responsibility. This is my choice. Okay?"

"Sure," I said. "But don't you have to be . . ."

"Today is my birthday," she interrupted. "I'm seventeen."

"Happy birthday," I said. "But that's still not old enough. You need your parent's permission."

"I got something called judicial consent. Planned Parenthood helped me get a lawyer and petition a judge. It's perfectly legal. They've been wonderful. I couldn't tell my father. I just . . . couldn't."

Just then, a petite short-haired blond doctor with a stethoscope draped snakelike around her neck entered the room, carrying Shelly's chart. "Oh," she said when she saw me, obviously unaccustomed to finding her patients accompanied. "You must be the father."

Shelly tried to correct the doctor, but I dwarfed the volume of her voice with my own. "Yes. I am."

Shelly smiled and raised her left hand to draw me nearer. I took her hand; she pulled me to her and whispered, "Thanks."

"It's time," the doctor said to Shelly. Then, to me, she said, "You can sit in the waiting room. The procedure doesn't take long, less than a half hour."

"No," Shelly said, turning her head to me. "You go home. You've done enough."

The message was clear; she didn't want my company, or anyone else's. She was going to see this through on her own.

As I exited the room, Shelly called me back to her side. "John, promise you won't tell Gordon."

"I won't."

After a carefully monitored in-clinic recovery period, Shelly took a taxi home from the clinic. Since it was Friday, she didn't need to be in school for two days, and since this was her father's honeymoon weekend with his new bride, there was no one at home to ask questions (as if her father would have shown that much interest). Shelly's father and Mary Jane had gotten married at the courthouse that same Friday morning and had driven to Detroit for a weekend of casino gambling. Shelly stayed in bed all weekend. She watched her favorite movie, *Harold and Maude*, repeatedly on her portable DVD player; listened to the entire R.E.M. catalog, and edited a short story she'd been working on for the upcoming edition of the *Beacon*; but mostly she cried.

On Monday morning, she woke early, took a long shower, shook her Etch A Sketch of short-term memory, and returned to Trinity one soul lighter.

9

After about forty-five minutes, I finally spotted the outline of the three south-to-north-aligned Bass islands. It was a good thing, because the pretzels and the can of Sprite were no longer warding off my seasickness. I needed to put my feet on stable ground soon—or else.

Clearly, I was no expert mariner, but I could tell that Gordon had already tacked away from what I thought was our intended destination: North Bass Island. Sure as shit, the blip on the GPS representing the Corsair was veering left from the charted path.

"I thought we . . ."

"Detour."

We were headed for the southernmost of the Bass Islands, the infamous—in these parts anyway—South Bass Island, and the harbor town of Put-in-Bay, originally Pudden Bay but morphed into its current form through phonetic sloppiness. In sixth-grade Ohio history, we had been taught the "significant" role South Bass had played during the War of 1812. It was off the northwest coast of South Bass that Colonel Oliver Hazard Perry fought and defeated a British fleet for no apparent reason, except, after a major naval upset, to provide a stage on which to pronounce heroically, "We have met the enemy and they are ours. . . ."

I had never visited the island, but the stories of the bacchanalian revelry that takes place there during the boating season are legendary throughout the lower Great Lakes area. (There are only two seasons on the islands: boating season and preparing for boating season.) South Bass is New Orleans at Mardi Gras; spring break on South Padre; Las Vegas; Sodom and Gomorrah; Caligula's Rome; the sultry Greek Islands; and Dodge City in amalgam, microcosmically offered in two stacked E-shaped docks and the three-block strip of bars in downtown Put-in-Bay.

For Gordon, the happiest place on earth . . . or so I supposed.

Me? I was scared shitless.

As I stood on the dock waiting for Gordon to stow away the Corsair, he reached into the captain's bin again; this time, he pulled out his notorious human skull drinking cup, which I'd heard about but had never seen, and a handful of purple, gold, and green strands of cheap plastic beads, which he threw to me.

"What are these for?" I asked.

"They don't flash 'em for free, junior" was his cryptic answer.

I soon discovered the beads' function as we walked the docks, pushing our way through the filled-to-capacity public marina. Powerboats ranging from fourteen to fifty-plus feet (many of which bore the Byron Boatyard logo) were jammed inside the steel docks. They rafted off one another three and four deep as we neared land. Each boat was a floating frat house/strip club. The men outnumbered the ladies by at least three to one, but the women seemed to be enjoying the ratio and encouraging the attention. During our trek from where we tied off to the dockmaster's small wooden booth/office on shore, I saw my first real topless woman—that is, the woman was real, not the boobs. I'd learned to discern the difference by the time I'd reached shore and depleted my supply of beads.

Gordon never slowed down or turned his head to look, even when a "girl gone wild" craving his attention called out to him, "Hey, Cutie. I'll show *you* for free," or "Take a look, sugar," or invited him to "party." He couldn't have been less interested.

"What's the matter?" I asked, confused.

"They disgust me. I hate this place."

But we were in his element. Weren't we?

"These people have no class, Keats. No style. They're barbarians. The women are sluts. They pay ten grand on a credit card for a boob job; then, to get their money's worth, they flash them in the face of any pecker head who'll trade them a set of fucking fifty-cent beads. It's pathetic." Gordon looked over my shoulder at the flotilla behind me.

"And these guys, what assholes." He paused to absorb the beer-bellied baseball-capped board-shorted scene. "These losers' idea of seduction is slipping one of these already half-drunk whores a roofie, waiting for her to start feeling woozy, then offering, all gentlemanlike, to walk her back to her boat or her hotel or wherever, where she passes out and the ball-less piece of shit generates enough self-confidence to pull out his pencil dick and fuck the corpse. It's sick. There's no talent here."

I think that was what really bothered Gordon. It wasn't the lack of morality but the lack of artistry. But by the time Gordon had finished his diatribe, I wanted to rush back to the docks and collect all the beads I had given away and throw a towel around each one of the bikini-topped women.

He must have read the guilt on my face, for he said, "Not you, Keats. I don't mean you. You *need* your cherry popped."

I wasn't completely sure what that meant, but I figured it had something to do with my obvious lack of experience with women. I couldn't even begin to imagine what he had in store for me.

After paying the dockage fee, Gordon led me through a downtown park that by day served as a picnic and children's play area but by night became a sort of demilitarized zone/piss stop/make-out area/detox center between the bars and the docks.

"Gordon," I called, incapable of matching his pace. "Where we going?" He ignored my question. "What are we doing here?" No answer. "What does this have to do with Shelly?" He stopped. His patience with my ignorance had reached its limit.

"Have you ever been to *North* Bass, Keats?"

"No."

"I have. Lots of times. The majority of it is a state park. The only marina is state run. What do you suppose the ranger at that marina is going to think when two kids carrying an urn and still dressed in their funeral clothes come cruising in around midnight looking for a dock? Don't you think it might raise a few suspicions? Don't you think he might make a few phone calls? By now they've got to be looking for us. Shelly's old man has to be searching for our asses. If there's one place that we can lose ourselves for a couple hours, this is it. People here are anonymous; the things they do here . . . they don't want to attach their names to. So they don't ask or answer many questions, but for the right price, they *will* tell any lie you pay them to tell. I slipped that dockmaster a hundred bucks to register us under a false name and boat and to play dumb should anybody come asking."

My hangdog expression showed that I'd had my nose sufficiently rubbed in my stupidity.

Gordon's tone mellowed. "We'll do what we came to do," he said. "We'll keep our promise to Shelly and spread her ashes on North Bass, but we've got to be smart. We'll disappear here for a while, sleep a little. Just before dawn, we'll cruise over to North Bass, slip into the marina, and finish this. All right?"

I nodded in agreement.

It was just approaching six hours since we'd ash-napped Shelly, but it seemed like a lifetime ago.

"Wait here," Gordon said.

We had just entered a railroad-tie-enclosed pit that contained a pair of high swing sets; the ground was layered with bits of recycled rubber still warm from the day's heat. (One

151

ten-year study reported nearly 150 deaths in the United States due to unsafe playground equipment, strangulation and swing impact being the most common causes.)

"Where you going?" I asked, more nervous about being abandoned than sincerely curious about Gordon's destination.

"Just wait here. I won't be long." He handed me his skull cup.

The swing had one of those rubber strap seats that fold up around your ass and hips. The oaks and maples in the park blocked much of the moonlight, so as far as I could tell the chains holding that seat climbed past them and attached to stars. Waiting, I didn't swing so much as I swayed, looping in small ovals in the air. Occasionally, a group of revelers stumbled past me in either direction.

The park itself seemed beastlike and sentient, alive with all sorts of cathartic grunts and groans. I tried not to imagine the spewing forth of bodily fluids that were taking place all around me, or their sources of origin, but I instinctively lifted my feet onto the swing and tried to think of something else.

The skull cup.

I had always assumed that Gordon's infamous skull cup was a novelty item that he had purchased cheaply at some souvenir shop, but feeling the cool hardness of its uneven surface and observing its more-yellow-than-white coloring, I knew it was authentic, a real dead man's skull. I almost dropped it at the thought, but my curiosity won out. I began to study it as best as I could in the limited light. Though smaller than I would have thought, it clearly was an adult's.

In order to drink from the cup, the skull had to be turned up-side down and the eye and nose sockets used for gripping, like the holes in a bowling ball. Gordon had hollowed out as much of the bone as had been needed to mold a plastic con-tainer inside the cavity, so that the top of the skull served as the bottom of the cup. As I pantomimed the act of lifting and tilting the skull to drink, it was eerie to watch the flesh-less face come noseless to nose with me.

"Is that him?" A female's voice from the surrounding blackness startled me, ending my stare-down with the near future. But the pronunciation wasn't right, more like "Es dat heem?"

"That's him." The second bodiless voice was Gordon's; he was speaking in a condescending tone, almost as if he were talking to a child.

"He's cute," she said.

"I told you this would be easy," Gordon said as he emerged from the darkness and the trees. His arm was around the shoulders of a tall dirty-blonde. She wore black high heels that sank an inch deep into the soft turf with each step, a denim miniskirt, and a pink sleeveless tank top whose spaghetti straps had fallen to mid-bicep level, leaving her black bra straps exposed. It may have been the moonglow, but her skin seemed pale, almost pasty, as if it were midwinter rather than the start of summer. If not for Gordon's assis-tance, she would have fallen flat on her face.

It was pure Gordon; he couldn't have been gone fifteen minutes, and he had already picked up a girl.

"Keats, meet Nadia."

"Hi, Keats," Nadia said with a windshield wiper wave of her hand, which sent her listing heavily to starboard, only to be righted by Gordon's quick grasp.

"Nadia here is looking to party," Gordon explained. "She has a place above one of the bars and would like it if you would spend some time with her."

"What about you?" I asked. "Aren't you coming too?"

"No. I need to . . . um . . . check on the boat. You two go."

That said, Gordon threw her in my direction. She stumbled toward me. I caught her beneath her armpits, but she still fell so that her nose was literally buried in my crotch. Not strong enough to lift her myself—she was at least a foot taller and probably twenty pounds heavier than I—I laid her down as gently as possible on the rubber-chip mattress. She didn't move.

I marched over to Gordon. "What the fuck, Gordon? Do you really expect me to just hang out with her while you go down to the boat?"

A smirk spread over Gordon's moonlit face. "I don't expect you to 'hang out with her' at all. It's time you become a man, Keats. Like I said, you need to pop that cherry of yours."

"Are you insane? I'm not sleeping with some random girl!"

"I don't want you to 'sleep' with her either."

"You know what I mean," I said. "I don't even know her!"

"Sure you do. Her name is Nadia and she's willing to fuck you. What more do you need to know?"

"Didn't you just say, not a half hour ago, that you hate 'loose women'?"

"She's not a loose woman, Keats. She's a hooker. There's

a difference. Look, this island is full of foreign workers who come here on six-month visas. They get paid minimum wage, which is probably ten times what they'd be paid for similar work at home, if they could find it. Most of them hold down at least two jobs and work sixteen hours a day, seven days a week. Some of the girls, like Nadia here, supplement their income even further with some selective hooking on the side. Hell, you'd be doing her a favor; you'd probably be feeding her family back home or helping her to finance a college education. Just consider it a co-sympathy fuck."

"Why the hell do you care anyway?"

"Relax, dude. I don't. I just thought you could use a good lay. You know, loosen up a bit. But whatever."

Together, we studied Nadia, lying on the rubber with her skirt hiked up, exposing a tiny pink thong and a round Eastern Bloc ass. "Are you sure?" Gordon asked after a moment.

"I'm sure."

"At least help me get her up," he said.

We propped her between us and more-dragged-than-walked her to a nearby park bench, where Gordon gently placed her lying down, faceup. He removed a fifty-dollar bill from his wallet and placed it inside her bra.

"Let's go," he said.

"We can't just leave her," I argued.

"Sure we can," he said, and headed toward the docks.

A cacophonic admixture of music from the bars and the stereos on the boats surrounding us made it impossible to sleep, so Gordon and I talked to pass the time until the island

and its visitors had spent themselves and we could grab a few hours of rest. Gordon lay next to Shelly on the deck of the Corsair, which rocked gently with the passing waves and the occasional wake made by late-exiting boaters. I sat cross-kneed on the steady dock.

"What's up with the skull?" I asked at last.

"My sister, Shelly, and I dug that up on Johnson's Island when we were kids."

"From the prisoner-of-war cemetery?" I asked.

"No. But not far from it. We were digging a trench to recreate the Battle of Antietam, and there it was. A complete skeleton. Shelly insisted it was an Ottawa Indian warrior, but I didn't think so. Anyway, I wrapped the skull in my T-shirt and took it home with me. Actually, I forgot I had it after a while. Found it in a box when I was packing for prep school. That's when I read *Hamlet* in freshman English class. You know, Yorick? The grave digger scene? It reminded me of this skull." He held it up for me to see.

"Why a cup?"

"When I came home to Ogontz after that year with the Brothers, I dug it out. For a while, it just sat on a shelf in my room. But then I thought it could be put to a better and more practical use as a memento mori, a reminder of death like the ones medieval monks kept around. You know, carpe diem, *hakuna matata*, the old gladiator's code: 'Eat, drink, and be merry, for tomorrow we die.' That sort of thing."

I tried absorbing his philosophical musings, but my fingertips were busy impulsively tracing my cheekbones and jawline as an image of my own fleshless face flashed in my mind. "Gordon?"

"Yeah, Keats."

"I should have done it with Nadia, huh?"

"Yes, Keats, you should have."

After a few moments of contemplating what could have been, I heard Gordon's light snore rising from the Corsair.

There was no way I would have been able to sleep on that dock, and I wasn't ready to be left alone with my thoughts. So I said, "Gordon?"

"What? I was almost asleep."

"Let's play the disc."

"What disc?"

"Shelly's. The R.E.M. mix. I can't sleep."

"I can." He was testy but propped himself up on his elbows and went along with it. "The boom box is up front, but don't play it for too long; I want to save the batteries for later."

I lowered myself into the boat, stepped over Gordon and Shelly, removed the disc from my suit coat pocket, retrieved the boom box, and then climbed back onto the dock and repositioned myself with the player on my lap.

"Gordon?" I said again.

"What now?" He was on the verge of losing his temper.

"Which song did Shelly have for you?"

"'Nightswimming.' It's number six. I ought to know; she played it enough," he said, lying flat on his back with his eyes closed to the heavens. "But it's not just mine. It's Augusta's and Shelly's too. She called it 'our song.'"

I put in the disc and forwarded to number six, but I immediately recognized the opening notes to "Losing My Religion." Rather than bothering Gordon again, I pressed the forward button, and the very first word from Michael Stipe's mouth was "Nightswimming." When he reached the second verse in a voice of raspy nostalgia over a piano-driven arrangement, the appropriateness of Shelly's song choice for their less-than-holy trinity came clear: "Nightswimming deserves a quiet night. / I'm not sure all these people understand." It was perfect. Twelve words captured both the beauty and the frustration of the threesome they'd formed.

I pressed pause, closed my eyes, and tried to imagine Shelly's face, but it's weird how soon you forget a dead person's face. I think it's because people wear so many of them that when you try to recall just one, you get a blurred blending that renders that one version, which you're trying so desperately to see, unrecognizable. It's like that with my parents.

"I hate that song," Gordon said before rolling onto his side and turning his back to me.

I ejected the disc and made sure the power was off on the boom box. When I placed the disc back in its case, I realized that another, unmarked disc was already in the other's place. I hadn't noticed it when I'd removed the R.E.M. disc.

"Gordon?"

"Jesus fucking Christ, Keats! If you don't leave me alone and let me get some sleep, I swear I'm going to throw you in."

"What's this?" I asked, ignoring Gordon's rage and holding up the case with the mystery disc inside.

"How the fuck should I know? You had the disc. She must have put two discs in one case by mistake. What's the big deal?"

I realized that not only had I not bothered to listen to

the disc since she'd given it to me, I'd never even opened the case. "It's no big deal; it's just not like Shelly. I mean, she could be careless about a lot of things, but not about her favorite CDs."

I tried to make out any markings on it in the moonlight but couldn't. "Do you have a flashlight?" I asked Gordon.

"In the bin," he said, before sitting and finally giving up on trying to get any sleep before morning.

I jumped down into the boat and found the flashlight. Gordon met me at the captain's console, where I shined the beam onto the disc.

"That's not a CD," Gordon said. "It's a DVD. There's a movie or something on there that she must've wanted us to see."

"What *exactly* did Shelly tell you? Have you told me *everything*?" I asked.

Gordon hesitated, stupidly (or so I thought) still weighing whether it was time to include me in Shelly's full confidence. "All she said was that if anything happened to her, you'd have the disc. 'Bring the boom box and Keats. He'll have the disc.' That was all."

I allowed a few moments for it all to soak in. "If anything happened to her?" I said. "What does that mean? Why would she have thought that something was going to happen to her? Why would she have made all these plans for us? Unless . . ."

"Unless what, Keats?"

"Unless she . . ."

"She what?"

"She . . ."

"Go on. Say it. Unless she knew that she was going to die."

"You mean . . . Shelly killed herself?"

Once more I got the look of utter indignation regarding my apparent thickheadedness. "Don't be an idiot, Keats."

That said, Gordon closed his eyes and the door on any further discussion.

Alone with my thoughts, I turned my attention to the stars and searched for clues.

10

I remember that I blamed Shelly's sadness during that November and December on Hogg's expulsion; on Gordon's aloofness; on the coming of winter, which also marked the end of sailing season; on her difficulty adjusting to her new extended family (remember, her father had hastily remarried in early December); and, obviously, on her abortion. It wouldn't be until the near fulfillment of our pledge to Shelly that I would learn from Gordon the true motivation for her melancholy.

Shelly's piece for the *Beacon* that semester, which she began in earnest shortly after the night of the Halloween dance, reflected her atypical darkness of that period. It was a short tale titled "Since He . . ." It tells the story of a wealthy family unanimously considered exemplary as a model of Christian piety. That is, until the father is discovered with his throat slit ear to ear, on the floor of his study beneath the emptied wall safe, the apparent victim of an interrupted home invasion. The police quickly determine that there had been no break-in at all and that the killer had to have been a family member. Lacking in duplicity, the daughter, under interrogatory duress, admits to the killing, committed with the aid of her mother. Their plea that the murder had been precipitated by the daughter's victimization at her father's incestuous hands falls upon the disbelieving ears of the townspeople, and the jury summarily sentences both mother and daughter to death.

"Since He . . ." was a huge success both for the *Beacon*, which sold more copies of that particular issue than of any other in its fifty-year publishing history, and for Shelly. Her emergence as a talented writer helped to transform her weirdness into quirkiness and lubricated for her the hallways of Trinity for the remainder of her time there. Her schoolmates, if not exactly inviting her to join in their reindeer games, at least turned their attention to finding fresher meat to skewer. Mr. Robbins encouraged Shelly to enter the story in various contests or to offer it to publications catering to young writers, but, to my disbelief, she refused.

It was that same fall semester of their junior year, and for the same issue, when Gordon, at the last minute, finally submitted something to be printed in the *Beacon*. He'd been reading Shelly's story and knew it was good. He could have let her have the day, but he went ahead and stole it, for, in all honesty, it was most likely *his* story that caused the spike in sales, but as perhaps only Mr. Robbins and myself knew, Shelly's was the work of greater literary depth and quality. Gordon's was a masturbatory piece of self-aggrandizement, but the irregularly reading public of Trinity was incapable of discerning the difference between artistry and sensationalism.

"Asmodeus" is the title of Gordon's story. The title refers to the Judeo-Christian demon of lust. The narrative was a condensed version of what would become his second Manfred novel under the same title. The original, published in the *Beacon,* is a simple morality tale set in the near future at St. Jude's, a coed Catholic high school similar to Trinity. The protagonist is a Goody Two-shoes senior named Toby who vies for the affection of the homecoming queen and class salutatorian, the virginal Rachel. His archrival for Rachel's affection is a recent transfer student named Con, short for Conrad.

Con is nothing like Toby and Rachel, who are both academically gifted rich kids from traditional homes; both very likely to succeed. Con is the only child of an immigrant Scottish widow; she sleeps all day and works nights as a cashier at Wal-Mart in between getting high and sleeping with any number of low-life losers that she escorts to their tiny thin-walled two-bedroom apartment. (In case you haven't figured it out, Con is Manfred's son, his mother a vampire turned by Manfred. The losers she picks up? Dinner. Consider the stake through Manfred's heart at the end of the first novel solved and a series born.)

Initially, Rachel finds Con repulsive. In fact, she finds all of the boys who have attempted to woo her repulsive. Including her senior homecoming dance, she has attended seven different formal dances with seven different boys, each of whom went home with bluer balls than the blue of Con's piercing eyes. Toby has waited patiently, but he is goaded to act when he recognizes a look in Rachel's eyes as she watches Con ride out of the student parking lot on his Indian brand motorcycle, a look identical to the way Toby looks at *her*.

Over time, and in juxtaposition to all of the other boys she has ever known, Con's moody bad-boy demeanor and hard-luck life begin to appeal to Rachel. Through his feigned lack of interest, Con ignites a longing that she didn't think she'd ever feel. Ashamed, during confession she reveals her lust to Father Raphael and emerges armed with an arsenal of Hail Marys, Our Fathers, and Glory Bes to combat her sexual urgings, but her prayers prove inadequate to quell her primal lust for Con.

With Father Raphael's urging, Toby finally reveals his love to Rachel and reclaims her through a nostalgic recounting of their twelve years of parallel paths to the present and by imaginatively portraying her likely future of ruin and ultimate damnation.

In an act of altruistic self-sacrifice, unwilling to burden her with his own torturous curse, Con surrenders his impossible love for Rachel, leaves St. Jude's in a bilious puff of motorcycle exhaust, and rides off into a Midwest midnight. (Motorcycle fatalities have risen by nearly 7 percent in the past five years.)

The sarcasm-proof morons at Trinity loved it. Even the faculty swallowed it hook, line, and sinker, but Gordon knew that, even though his dull-witted, God-fearing readers would never have admitted it, if they could have traded lives with or fucked any one of the characters, they would have unanimously chosen Con.

11

"Keats."

I vaguely heard my name, but it failed to stimulate any kind of synaptic reaction or verbal response from inside the syrupy morass of my muted consciousness.

"Keats."

There it was again. This time a little more forceful and accompanied by something poking at my rib cage, a poking that chased what had been my temporarily unfettered thoughts and reconnected them to the weighty and disappointing reality of a body that was scrunched, fetal position, on a cold, hard, and momentarily unidentifiable surface.

"Keats! Wake up. We've got to go."

Gordon. It was Gordon. Somehow, at some point in the night, I'd managed to fall asleep on the dock with a moldy-smelling life preserver under my head for a pillow.

"What time is it?" I asked for no relevant reason other

than to delay my ascent to the surface of awareness and to prevent a crippling case of the psychic bends.

"Time to get the fuck out of here. Let's go. Undo that spring line and hop in," Gordon directed.

I had no clue what a spring line was (I was picturing a Paris fashion show), but since there was only one rope still tied to the cleat on the dock, I figured that was it. I undid the simple knot and slid on board.

"Here," he said, and handed me the urn. "Hold Shelly."

The surface of the urn was warm. Gordon must have slept with Shelly snug to his body. I smiled at him.

"What?" Gordon asked defensively.

"Nothing," I said, but he knew that I knew.

A quiet pall had descended on the early morning that would have seemed impossible during the raucous hours just prior. It evoked a stillness unlike any I had ever experienced growing up on my busy, well-lit Ogontz street, where cars whizzed past at all hours no more than fifty feet from my bedroom window, and sirens seemed to blare constantly. In my neighborhood, one learned early to discern the sympathetic wail of an ambulance from the angry command of a police car from the abject terror of a fire engine. Here, there was only the primordial quiet of an inland sea. The sole sounds were the occasional lapping of current against the dock pilings and the groaning of a too taut line being stretched to its excruciatingly painful extreme like an accused heretic on the rack.

Gordon gently turned the ignition switch as if his delicate handling would somehow convince the engines to understand our need for stealth. Unlike my rousing, theirs was immediate and enthusiastic, like two puppies at play, but even their boisterous barking wasn't shrill enough to penetrate the depths of drunkenness into which most of our neighbors had descended. Gordon's goal was to limit as severely as possible any record or awareness of our coming or going, so we idled out of our slip and out of the docks, into the harbor, leaving a barely discernible and untraceable wake writ on the water's surface.

As we inched out into the narrow latitudinal channel separating South from Middle Bass Island, Gordon turned on the running lights and eased the throttles forward. "It'll be a short run," he said.

Since the sun was still a good hour from peeking its nose over the eastern horizon, Gordon reconfigured the GPS settings and navigated according to the phosphorescent images splashed on the radar screen, rather than trusting his eyesight alone.

Our course sent us skirting around the west coast of Middle Bass. Between it and farther to the west lies what the screen identified as Rattlesnake Island. It was a diminutive privately owned island that Gordon tried to convince me was owned by members of a Cleveland Mafia family and was used alternatively as a hideout, as a sort of sit-down center for the bosses of Midwest mob families, and as a summertime getaway.

"During Prohibition, it was used as a way station for whiskey runners smuggling booze from Canada," Gordon explained. "You know, a bunch of the boats they used were the original wooden-hulled *Byron* speedboats that my family made. Rattlesnake has a private airstrip, a helipad, a par three golf course, and a fully staffed clubhouse with a whole herd of chefs flown in from the home country as demanded."

It may have been Gordon's bullshit imagination, but in the spirit of our own romantic quest, I bought every bit of it.

On course, we made a dogleg right around the even smaller, uninhabited freckle of earth known as Sugar Island off the northwest coast of Middle Bass. The Corsair was headed directly for the state park marina on the southeast corner of North Bass. The sky had begun to turn the gray of fired charcoal, and the lake had begun to show its morning green complexion, occasionally washed over by the white-caps that had begun to transform our heretofore smooth run into a speed-bump-lined strip of nautical highway.

"What's yours?" Gordon half-yelled, apropos of nothing, over the roar of the outboards and the splash of the fiberglass hull. With one hand, he breakfasted on what remained of the pretzels, as he steered with the other.

But I knew what he was asking; he wanted to know which R.E.M. song Shelly had assigned to me. "'Try Not to Breathe,'" I said. "It's pretty depressing."

"I've never heard of it."

"It isn't one of their most popular songs. It's an old one and wasn't on the radio much, even when it was released. She'd play it for me sometimes while we worked on the *Beacon*."

"How's it go?"

"I'm not singing it," I said, fully aware of my tone deafness.

"What about the lyrics? I mean, why did she pick it?"

I said, "There's a line in the song that I think spoke to her somehow. I think it made her think of me."

"So, how's it go?" Gordon demanded.

I recited, "'I have lived a full life / And these are the eyes that I want you to remember.'"

There was a moment of dead air between us.

"That's fucked up," Gordon finally said.

"You don't know the half of it."

"That was Shelly's problem," Gordon continued in his half-shout. "She started to take everything way too seriously. She became a drama queen. She wasn't like that when we were kids, but somewhere along the way she became super-fragile. Almost to the point where I didn't want to hang around her, you know?"

I didn't have the nerve to tell him that it was him, as much as anything else, that had created her brittle self-image.

"There it is," Gordon pronounced, as he pointed toward a strobe flashing intermittently in the distance to our right. "Off the starboard bow. That's a channel marker. A red buoy. 'Red, right, return.'" He recited what he informed me was the mariner's mantra for orienting one's craft upon return to port, and he situated the Corsair so that we passed the buoy on the starboard side. With the throttles pulled back, we slunk into the unoccupied marina, which provided fewer than twenty slips.

"Why are we stopping here?" I asked. "I thought we were going to the north side."

"We are. But there's no dock there anymore. The state dismantled it to keep trespassers away."

North Bass offered none of the advantages that the majority of the high-spending boating crowd desired, namely alcohol and breast-flashing women. Fewer than a dozen residents lived year-round on the state-owned nature preserve (that's the island's official designation), and if near-total neglect was the means by which to establish and maintain such a preserve, then the Ohio Department of Natural Resources was doing an enviable job.

It was no secret, however, that many at the statehouse viewed the island's offshore location as ideal for the construction of a mini Vegas, so they did as little as possible to encourage the productive usage of North Bass. In the lawmakers' wildest and wettest dreams, ferry services (transportation tax), hotels (bed tax), souvenir stores and stands (sales tax), and fully staffed bars and gambling houses (income tax, sin tax, and property tax) would one day transform a budget deficit in the millions of dollars into a budget surplus.

Not knowing when the ranger's shift and patrol would start, we hurried to begin our approximately one-mile hike to the north shore, with Shelly, her discs, and the boom box in hand.

12

As I've already made clear, Gordon flat-out hated Shelly's stepsister Claire. He thought her pathetic, but in late March of his junior year, after having returned to Ogontz giddy with his second individual and another team state swimming championship, Gordon relented. That night, when he arrived home from the team party at Coach Mancini's and parked the H3 half on the circular driveway, half on the front lawn, Claire was waiting on his porch with a homemade banner of "Congratulations!" draped diagonally across her chest and splitting her impressive boobs. She was holding an already quarter-empty bottle of top-shelf vodka, which she had pilfered from her stepdad's liquor cabinet.

Well inebriated himself from the gin-laced water bottle he'd been sipping at the party, and as horny as hell, he was able to overcome his antipathy for his psycho-stalker. Gordon flashed his high beams to signal her into the Hummer, which she entered with her jaws already flapping. "Blah,

blah, blah, blah, blah" was all he made of Claire's prattle as he took several swigs from the long smoked-glass bottle of France's finest vodka.

A little bit of making out preceded a thirty-second screw in the back of the Hummer. Gordon's uniform khakis never passed his ankles, nor did his school-issue blazer or tie come off, while Claire's skinny-legged jeans and black with white polka dots boy shorts clung to her right foot like a bear trap. (In a typical year, there are only three deaths by bear attack in North America.) Her royal-blue flyaway cashmere cardigan was opened wide to reveal a white cami and a lace bra pushed up and over her breasts.

When he awoke in his bed the next morning, hungover and confused, he prayed that the tryst inside his Hummer had been a dream. But when Claire's onslaught began only moments later, he knew there to be no such luck. He ignored phone message after phone message; he deleted unread text after text. The very second Gordon stepped onto his front porch or activated the garage door, Claire came running. If he snuck out back to hop on a Jet Ski or into one of the water crafts, she was waiting onshore when he returned. At school those last two months of his junior year, she haunted him to the point that he frequently just stayed home. Worst of all and despite his protestations, many were beginning to think them a couple.

It wouldn't be until August, however, that she'd begin to show.

* * *

On a Friday afternoon in early May, five months after her abortion, Shelly finally brushed the remaining surface layer of dirt from her shallow grave of depression, climbed out, and reclaimed her space among us living.

It had been a harsh winter.

Shelly had played host briefly during her leechlike step-sister's introduction to Trinity. Soon, however, Claire had found Gordon and ditched Shelly. Prior to the Key Club's Christmas toy drive, Shelly quit as president, and she stopped volunteering at Planned Parenthood. Not once did she perform an act of civil disobedience, and she carried out her duties at the *Beacon* with halfhearted indifference and didn't provide a single submission. By spring's arrival, Shelly had been reduced to a faded shade of her former self.

Lost in the self-pity caused by my own increasingly shitty reality, I wasn't much of a friend to her. The paltry funeral we'd provided my father had drained dry the shallow pool of our family finances. His disability checks stopped coming; and the government aid we did receive was quickly eaten up by utilities and grocery bills. Sometimes—and I know being poor is no excuse, but having money gives you no right to judge either—my irregularly washed and re-worn school clothes were less than fresh, so I avoided contact with everybody at school and rarely showed up to help Shelly with the *Beacon*. Like her, I offered nothing for inclusion, and also like her, if for different reasons, I was disappearing.

Tom, still healthy, dropped out of college for the spring semester and took on additional hours busing tables at a local restaurant in order to make at least minimal payments on my tuition at Trinity. I volunteered to transfer to Ogontz Public, but he insisted that our Catholic school education had been a source of pride for our father, and transferring wasn't an option. I could have applied for tuition assistance, but my father would have been mortified. He was prideful that way. I'm sure that if I'd been a head taller and seventy-five pounds heavier and I could have rifled a football or dunked a basketball, Trinity would have found a scholarship for me. But I wasn't, and I couldn't. And brainy little shits like myself do not much inspire alumni to crack open their wallets.

Meanwhile, sitting in a permanent haze at the kitchen table, my mother seemed intent on joining our father by starving or by smoking herself to death at a world record pace.

It was Gordon who conjured Shelly's resurrection.

That Friday, Shelly and I sat, sharing a computer and completing a final edit of the spring edition of the *Beacon*. For his part, it was the first time that Gordon had set foot inside the room all semester, having had, until recently, turned his attention away from the *Beacon*'s needs in response to his editor at Pandroth's insistence that he get moving on the sequel to *Manfred*.

As Gordon entered the room, he dropped a folded copy of that day's *Ogontz Reporter* across the keyboard. "Do Not Remove from Library" was stamped in lipstick red across a banner headline reading "Indian Uprising!"

"What's this?" Shelly asked.

"Got it during study hall. It reminded me of you and Johnson's Island when we were kids. Remember?"

The article reported that two nights previous, a band of Ottawa had stormed a small beach on North Bass, planted the flag of the Ottawa Nation, and set up a headquarters in an abandoned farmhouse. A spokesman for the tribe, identified only by the name Neolin, placed calls to reporters at the Ogontz newspaper, Cleveland's *Plain Dealer*, the Toledo *Blade*, and the *Columbus Dispatch*. He announced the Ottawa plan to resettle peacefully in their ancient fishing village on North Bass and to return to what he called the Way. Neolin referred to the reverse exodus as "a rejection of modernity and of America's depraved culture of excess and greed" and as an attempt "to reunite the scattered sovereign nation of the Ottawa." Finally, Neolin expressed the naïve hope that the Ottawa efforts would be met in a spirit of respect and reparation by the state of Ohio, but, if necessary, the settlers were willing "to pursue any measure in their demand for justice, cultural independence, and repossession of the Ottawa Nation's homeland."

When Shelly lifted her eyes from the newsprint, it was as though she had been born again, and I actually thought that she was speaking in tongues. It was, rather, an unrelated string of words in the Ottawa language—which she had learned during her childhood fascination with the tribe— that was pouring out of her, rhapsodically, and in euphoric recognition of what she was convinced was to be her new life's purpose.

Shelly rose to her feet and announced in a trancelike tone, "I'm going."

"Going where?" Gordon asked incredulously. "To North Bass? Don't get mixed up in that shit, Shell. Sounds to me like those Ottawa are digging trenches for a battle they can't win. You have better ways to waste your time."

"That's just it, Gordon. I don't. And I'm tired of wasting my time. This might be my chance to do something that actually matters. I don't care if it takes all summer. I'm going."

"Christ, I didn't show you the damn article actually believing you'd want to join the revolution. I just thought you'd get a kick out of it."

"Come with me, Gordon. It will be like when we were kids but for real."

"Me? Don't think so. As soon as school is out, I'm heading to Europe with my agent and my mother. *Manfred* is now available in over fifteen foreign languages. My agent wants me to do a few meet-and-greets and sign a few autographs, and I plan to check out some of those foreign tongues for myself." He actually winked at me. "Besides, my editor is really on my ass about the next novel. Nope. I pick my battles more carefully than that. This one isn't mine. I'll see you around." With a brief wave of his hand, Gordon was gone.

One more Gordonian boot to the belly.

Shelly turned to me. "What about you, John? You want to come?"

I had thought that I would do anything for her, would follow her anywhere. But, let's face it, I was a chickenshit. "No. I'm, you know, not much for causes."

I'm not sure why I wasn't instantly and forever dead to her after that.

I hadn't told Shelly, but I had recently gone digital. Over

the winter, during my poverty-imposed house arrest, I had opened free accounts on several social networking websites popular with teenagers and college kids, and I'd begun posting some old poems and short stories. Positive feedback from online "friends" had motivated me to construct my own Web page. The number of hits I was receiving was steady, so I needed time to write and update my site. I was hoping to begin advertising soon and turn the page into something profitable. I knew it wouldn't be much, if anything, but I hoped to contribute something to the family income.

"No problem," she said stiffly before leaving me to finish the edit.

13

To reach the one paved road on North Bass, promised by the GPS app on Gordon's phone, we first had to make our way across a wet weed-strewn mufflehead-infested field. Mufflehead is the locally applied nickname for a nonstinging, mosquitolike insect that plagues the lake region every June. We were still in our clothes and dress shoes from the wake. I carried Shelly in both hands, while Gordon walked with the boom box on his shoulder like an eighties "beat boy," searching for a flat slab of concrete and a clean piece of cardboard. After only a few steps, our socks were dew drenched, our feet were soaking wet, and our ears, eyes, and noses were filled with insects. The faux-leather uppers of my Shoe Warehouse loafers were becoming unglued and beginning to separate from their soles. And although it was still too dark to identify species, every few footsteps sent an unhappily roused critter scurrying or slithering out of our path.

The route to the Ottawa campsite would take us past the

airstrip (all the inhabited islands had a similar runway for small planes; it was the only way to get to or from some of the islands during the winter months once the lake froze and the private boats and commercial ferries were dry-docked) before dead-ending on the north coast of the island near what had been the short-lived self-proclaimed sovereign outpost of the Ottawa Nation. The so-called paved road, however, was more of a dirt path covered in loose stones, stones that must have been suffering from some form of island claustrophobia, since so many were making a mad attempt to join our journey and to escape their exile by stowing away in our shoes.

Even at such an early hour, with the sun still low on the horizon, I began to sweat profusely, adding to my increasingly "aromatic" condition. It was the dawning of one of those oppressively humid nearly tropical summer days around the lake. Incredibly, Gordon didn't appear to be the least bit daunted by the swampy climate. However, due to the heat and exhaustion, we walked at a sluggish pace, and Gordon's limp grew slightly more pronounced. His face showed the beginnings of a beard, one of those rugged shadow-beards that some lucky guys are able to grow. I, on the other hand, have "summer" facial hair. You know, "summer here, summer there." I could have plucked my boyish beard rather than shave it.

Since the beginning of our odyssey, I'd had the feeling that Gordon was keeping something from me. I knew we were going to spread Shelly's ashes, but I sensed that there was something more that he wasn't telling me. So as we walked, I pried. "Shelly only gave me the CD. I didn't know why until you told me. What *exactly* are we supposed to do? We just play her song and scatter her ashes?"

Gordon sighed, dispirited by the necessity of expending energy in speech, then said, "She wants us to spread half her ashes on the water and half on some beach near the Ottawa camp, all while playing that stupid song she likes—*liked*." He paused. "I'm just glad nobody has to hear—or, better yet, *see*—us playing it. I mean, Christ, 'Shiny Happy People'?"

In unrehearsed synchronization, we said, "So Shelly," and laughed.

"What about the DVD?" I asked.

"Don't know. Like I told you last night, she never mentioned it to me."

We continued in silence, taking our left turn toward the airstrip, lost in contemplation of Shelly, and growing weary of our task.

"Gordon?"

"Yeah, Keats."

"Shelly had an abortion."

I don't know what inspired me to share it or if it counted as a violation of my promise to Shelly never to tell him, but it just came out. Maybe, unsatisfied that Gordon had yet to come fully clean, I was hoping for a little tit for tat. You know, quid pro quo.

Gordon stopped dead in his progress, set the boom box on the ground, and turned his head toward me. "She what?"

"She was pregnant and had an abortion," I said.

"No shit. I didn't know she had it in her," he said. The comment was so full of double entendre that I chose to ignore it, but the tone of his voice lacked something. The sarcasm was hollow, and the usual appreciation of his own wit was missing.

I'm not sure how to characterize his facial expression while he grappled with the hurtful fact that Shelly had shared such an intimate secret with me but not him: Was it surprise? Disbelief? Anger? Jealousy?

"When was this?" Gordon finally asked.

"About a year and a half ago. December of your junior year."

Gordon winced. "Why didn't she . . . Why didn't you tell me?"

"She asked me not to. I thought that, maybe, you . . ."

"Got her pregnant?" Gordon gave voice to my unfinished thought.

"Did you?"

"No, Keats. I didn't. Why would you even think that?"

"I don't know. It's just that . . . when she first saw me in her room at the clinic, I'm pretty sure that she was hoping I was you."

"Clinic? What clinic?"

"At Planned Parenthood. She volunteered there."

His expression betrayed that he had had no clue that Shelly had worked there.

"So? What does that even mean, 'she was hoping I was you'? Are you jealous that Shelly and I were so close? Is that it?"

"No. That's not it," I said, hoping to slow the momentum of his fast-rising anger.

"Shelly and I go back a lot further than you and her and that stupid *Beacon*, Keats."

He was venting; I'm pretty sure that he knew he was being stupid, but it was like he couldn't help himself. I thought that, perhaps for the first time, he was wrapping his brain around the fact of Shelly's death, and the anger over the senselessness of the whole thing was finally blowing the top off the volcano of his typically cool surface. Violently he grabbed two handfuls of my shirt and lifted me to the very tips of my toes. I quickly positioned Shelly between us as a buffer, and for an instant, I thought he was going to reveal something, but he abruptly let go of me with a halfhearted push.

"You know what? Fuck you, Keats." He didn't look my way; instead, with his hands on his hips, he studied the bluing sky over the runway, searching. "Just . . . fuck you," he repeated, but less angrily this time.

Gordon picked up the boom box, and we resumed the march. Geisha-girl-like, I trailed at a safe distance.

When he reached the road running parallel to the runway, he stopped and waited for me to catch up to him. I wasn't sure what he was going to do. I admit, I was nervous.

He turned his head to face me, smiled big, and said, "I knew all along. Shelly told me."

But he was slipping. I could tell he was lying.

He acted as if he'd been screwing with me the entire time, but I knew he hadn't been. He was simply attempting to remain my superior regarding all things Shelly.

"Had you going, though, didn't I?" he said through a put-on smile. "But it wasn't mine, Keats. The baby. It wasn't mine." The smile was gone and his tone was earnest. "We weren't like that, Shelly and me. I suppose there were times when she wanted to be, but I couldn't think of her in that way. She damn well may be the only girl I never did see in that way, but I didn't."

With that he turned north and resumed walking.

After a few steps, I asked, "No one will be there, right?"

"Be where?"

"The place. The beach where . . ." I couldn't say it.

"Yeah. It's been, what? Over a week? There might be police tape or something roping it off, but there shouldn't be any people there."

"What about press?"

"Hell," Gordon said, "they're long gone. Shelly and the Ottawa rebellion are yesterday's news."

"I guess you're right. I hope you're right; otherwise, we'll have a tough time finishing this thing."

"Oh, we're going to finish it," Gordon said. "You can count on that."

14

Just more than a year before her drowning, on the day after Gordon shared with her the news of the Ottawa occupation, and the Saturday before Mother's Day, Shelly's least favorite day of the year, Shelly set sail in *Ariel* for the Ottawa camp on North Bass. With a steady headwind blowing from the west, she was forced to tack aggressively throughout the nearly four-hour sail. Wearing a life jacket, a cardinal-red flotation jacket, foul-weather bibs, and with her sockless feet snug inside a pair of old leather Top-Siders, Shelly arrived off the coast dripping wet, fatigued, sore to the bone, and, for the first time in months, relatively optimistic.

Shelly shared this and the story that follows on the last night I saw her. She damn near glowed in the telling, simultaneously enraptured by the memory of having experienced it and devastated by the knowledge of the impossibility of living it again.

* * *

In the late eighteen hundreds, the Ottawa were one of the most powerful tribes on the islands and along the southern shore of Lake Erie, but they were forcibly resettled by the United States government to the Oklahoma Territory. Shelly's obsession with the tribe began with a third-grade History Day project and continued until she died, as one of the two casualties in what I like to call the Ottawa Massacre. Backed by the expert testimony of a cartographer, who maintained that North Bass actually lay in Canadian waters, the chief of the present-day Ottawa tribe had recently claimed ancestral property rights and fishing rights to the island. Everyone involved, however, suspected that his actual motivation was to construct an island casino to match the one already flourishing in the northeastern corner of their current home state.

From a good one hundred yards offshore, Shelly spotted several men moving about the property that the Ottawa had reclaimed, thus far unopposed. The men were all shirtless and wore blue jeans and work boots. Shelly was unsure of their purpose, but intermittent clangs of metal led her to believe that they were engaged in fortifying their position or in improving their living quarters.

As she drew closer, blended voices began to reach her. She couldn't yet differentiate one from another, but she could discern a surprising lack of worry in their combined tone.

Fewer than fifty feet from shore, she remained undetected.

To her surprise, Shelly saw that the metallic clanging was not caused by labor but by horseshoes finding their mark. Laughter and playful banter rang from the improvised horse-shoe pits, and the smell of barbecuing meat wafted on the breeze and nauseated her vegan sensibilities. Except for a few scattered rifles leaning against trees, the scene looked more like a picnic than a territorial takeover.

Only when she let down her single sail and began to scull her way toward a dilapidated wooden dock did anyone notice her approach. It was a young man, dressed like the others, who came running in her direction. Only his disruption of their game by crossing between the stakes—completely oblivious to the potential of taking a horseshoe to the side of the head—alerted any of the beer-swilling invaders that Shelly was there. Even so, only the young man showed any concern for or interest in her arrival.

He was tan (melanoma is the most deadly form of skin cancer; cancer in general is the second leading cause of death in the United States), almost too tan—even for a Native American—for so early in a Great Lakes summer, and, unlike the potbellied others, his body was taut and angular, not mus-cular so much as lean. As he slowed and strode toward Shelly, his hair fell, longish and lustrous, from his scalp and blew back slightly, like a sheer black curtain. He looked like the instrument-less lead singer of a hard rock band.

"Go away," he warned her as he arrived and stood at the end of the bowed and partially submerged dock. "You are not welcome."

Shelly was taken more by the earnestness of his expres-sion than by the beauty of his perfectly symmetrical face,

187

which housed the darkest eyes into which she had ever peered. His eyes lorded over the high promontories formed by his cheekbones, and over the thin nose and lips that were etched into a straight-line scowl, which appeared more put-on than natural. An adorable dimple cleaved his chin.

"*Wow-kwing on-je-baw,*" she said to herself in her half-remembered, stilted Ottawa. It means "He comes from heaven." Then, out loud, ignoring his command, she said, "You're him. Aren't you? You're the one in the paper. Neolin."

Unsettled by Shelly's correct identification, the young man studied her face in search of recognition, defying the obvious impossibility of being already acquainted. Finally, he said, "I'm Neolin. How'd you know? There were no photographs."

"I can just tell," Shelly answered, presumptuously throwing him a line to tie off her boat.

Holding the rope limply, Neolin said, "I told you; you aren't welcome."

"Don't be stupid. I'm here to help. *Boozhoo,*" Shelly said as she rose and extended her hand for assistance onto the dock.

"Booze what?" he answered.

"*Boozhoo.* It's Ojibwa for 'hello.' I'm surprised you don't know that."

"No one, except maybe for a few elders, speaks the old language. But, how do you? Are you Odawa?"

Shelly noticed his clear pronunciation of the "d." Never more disappointed in her white-bread origins, she answered, "No. But I did a history project once and used to pretend to be Odawa." She corrected her pronunciation.

Suspicious, Neolin grasped Shelly's still-extended hand and helped her up and onto the dock, but he misjudged the required effort, and his backward momentum would have sent him plummeting into the clear green algae-tinted water, if not for Shelly's grabbing on to the massive silver belt buckle he wore on a thick leather belt through the loops of his faded boot-cut jeans. The back of her hand pressed against the thin trail of hair climbing to his belly button as she helped him to regain his balance. After allowing Neolin to find his footing, she unconsciously let her fingertips linger a little too long just inside the waistline of his blue jeans, until Neolin directed his eyes in that direction. She snapped them away suddenly, as if she'd touched something red hot.

Composure regained, he asked, "Can you teach me?"

"What? How to stand up?" she joked.

"No," he answered, oblivious to her attempt at humor, "to speak Odawa?"

"I'm really not that fluent, and I don't think I even speak it correctly. What about those guys?" she asked, pointing toward the picnickers. "Can't any of them teach you?"

"They know nothing and couldn't care less about our heritage or the Way."

Shelly remembered the reference to "the Way" from the newspaper article. "Then why are they here?"

Neolin's face fell like the side of a glacier. Without explanation, he turned away and walked toward the shore.

Confused, Shelly called, "Wait. What did I say?"

"Go home," he yelled back, not stopping or turning.

"I'll teach you," she said, with just a trace of desperation betraying her budding girlish infatuation.

Neolin halted. He paused. "Okay," he said, finally turning his head. "Come with me."

Shelly unzipped her jacket, slid out of her pants, and threw them carelessly into the sailboat. Wearing a pair of soccer shorts, navy blue with white striping, and a white T-shirt with a head shot of a smiling Bob Marley airbrushed onto it, she dropped to her knees and reached into the boat to extract the backpack of supplies she'd brought with her. Rising to her feet, she snuck a look back at Neolin and realized that he had been watching her with something more than curiosity. Shelly blushed.

"Where to?" she asked.

Neolin squinted in the sunlight and pointed past a tiny tent village, which had been constructed beneath a copse of large elms, to the run-down farmhouse. "There. That's our White House."

Shelly smiled. "Isn't that ironic?"

After Shelly entered the musty headquarters, the old wooden spring-loaded screen door slammed shut, startling her. A damp coolness greeted her inside, as if the house were air-conditioned. The windows, at least those that weren't painted shut, had been thrown open in a futile attempt to air out the place and to let in light.

To the immediate left of the door, a set of stairs in disrepair ascended to the second story. A makeshift table, consisting of a sheet of warped plywood spread across two rickety sawhorses, sat surrounded by stacked milk crates, which served as chairs, in the middle of what had once been a living room, or what Shelly generously described to me later as a "parlor."

Doing her best to situate her skinny ass on top of the rigid milk crates, Shelly asked, "So, why are you here?"

"I thought you read the article."

"I don't mean here, as in on the island; I mean *in* here, while everyone else is out there?" She threw her thumb over her shoulder toward the front lawn.

Neolin made a lemon face, but the wistful tone of his voice betrayed his hurt when he said, "What? With those guys? I don't need them. They're just muscle. They won't be here for long."

"Why you?" Shelly asked. "Why did they put you in charge? You're so . . ."

"Young?" He finished her sentence.

"Cute."

She actually had intended to say "young" but had bailed after his defensive reaction. Her response temporarily staggered Neolin. When he regained his mental footing, he said, "I'm the only one who went to college. Well, for one year anyway. Ottawa University."

Shelly laughed, thinking it was like when her father said that he'd graduated from the school of hard knocks, but the hurt in Neolin's eyes betrayed his seriousness. "You weren't kidding," Shelly said apologetically. "It's a real school?"

"Yes. It's a *real* school."

"I'm so sorry. I didn't mean to offend you, but I've never heard of it."

"It's in Kansas on what was once Odawa reservation land, before Baptist missionaries promised to build a school in exchange for the property, and promised to let Odawa go for free. But I'm not going back."

"Not going back?" Shelly echoed. "Why not?"

"It's not really Odawa. The students and professors are almost all Anglo and Christian. I'm the minority at a college named for my people and on our land. I've decided it's time to come home. To my real home. Here in the land of my ancestors. I attended a meeting of the tribal council and reminded them of 'the Way' that we were meant to live. I told them about my plan to reclaim some place in our people's journey. I did my research. This island seemed the most promising. Almost no one lives here. To be honest, I was surprised when the chief encouraged the council to not only give its approval but also give financing and some men to help get started."

"But do you really believe—" Shelly began.

He cut her off. "I have to. I can't go back. My only option is living here according to the Way, or . . ." Neolin didn't finish; instead he rose, walked to the front bay window, and looked out over the frontage of the property to the lake waters beyond. Two hundred and fifty years rewound in fast motion. He seemed to be returning in his imagination to the day when all in his current line of vision had been Ottawa. He cursed his ill-timed life.

Shelly watched his silhouette inside the dust-mote-crowded sunlight streaming through the window. "What exactly is 'the Way'?" she asked.

Neolin turned and faced her so that he was backlit,

washed in an ethereal aura. Then he floated (I know that he walked, but Shelly described it as if he floated "like Jesus on *South Park*") toward her and sat at her feet (this is going to be cringe-worthy), "Indian-style," on the dust-covered hardwood floor.

He raised his eyes to meet hers and said, "Do you know the Odawa word '*pimadazin*'?"

She shook her head.

"It means 'a good, healthy, and moral life living in a community with others.' It's obtained by following the seven *ways* of the Odawa: purity in mind, purity in heart, purity in body, humility, honesty, love, and respect." He ticked off each one on a finger as if he'd memorized them for a test. "Taken all together, they are *pimadazin,* or the Way."

"But why couldn't you find that in Oklahoma? Why'd you have to come here?"

"Have you been to northeast Oklahoma?"

"No."

"It's wide open, flat country. For over two hundred years, the Odawa have tried to farm. Either the land is no good or we're no good at farming, or maybe both are true. Besides, our nature is to hunt and fish and trade."

"That's what *Odawa* means," Shelly interjected proudly. "'Trader.'"

"Yes. Even I know that. But now we have joined the native tribes who have opened casinos to screw the whites. Only, in the end, and like all the others, we will mostly screw ourselves. A few will get rich, but most will squander their share of the payouts inside the very casinos that were meant to liberate them from the poverty, alcoholism, and boredom."

His outrage was palpable and rising. Neolin paused to collect himself, then said, "I am sorry for my anger. It was not true to *pimadazin*.

"Besides, look at this place." He rose to his feet and returned to the window. "The green of the grass and trees, the blue of the water. It's beautiful. It's filled with life and possibility. Where I come from, it's brown and dry and full of death."

"And death is so bad?"

"Well, of course."

"What makes you think that they will let you stay?" Shelly changed the subject. "This island, most of it's owned by the state now."

"Why wouldn't they? They're not using it." He let loose a smile that was indicative of either naïveté or cunning, Shelly wasn't sure which.

"Even if they let you stay, what will you do? How will you survive?"

"I don't know. Fish. There are fisheries in port cities all along the coast. I've done some research. We'll buy a boat and nets, and we'll sell our catch to the fisheries here or maybe in Canada."

Shelly could tell that he was rambling and hadn't really thought through the whole relocation thing. "What do you know about boating and commercial fishing?" she asked.

"I've fished before. Many times."

"What? With a cane pole in a creek or from the shore of some lake that even I could throw a stone across? Haven't you noticed the size of this lake? Get a few miles from shore, and it may as well be the ocean. And wait until you see the storms it kicks up with almost no warning."

Her words deflated Neolin.

"It *is* much bigger than it looks on a map," he admitted.

Not wanting to let him off her tenuously implanted hook, Shelly let out some slack in her line and allowed him to enjoy the illusion of swimming freely once again.

"I know it won't be easy, and it won't happen quickly, but I believe I can do it—if the government will leave us alone. The time is now. I can feel it." He was regaining his confidence. "The Odawa need to know that I've returned to reclaim this island for them, to give them dignity when they leave their pathetic farms and the casinos and return to the old ways. *Pimadazin.*"

"How about the guns?" Violence was the deal breaker, the one nonnegotiable factor in all of her schemes. (The accidental discharge of firearms accounts for approximately 1 percent of teenage deaths annually.)

"A temporary necessity. The men insisted," he said. "I'd prefer not to be armed, but the government's history with secessionists leaves us little choice. If it makes you feel better, I'm a terrible shot."

Shelly weighed this compromise against her supposedly engraved-in-stone insistence on peaceable protest, then said, "I want to help."

"You? What can you do?"

"First of all," she stalled, having no ready answer, "I can handle any kind of boat. I—well, my father—has others that I can use to get supplies or whatever."

"We have boats and we can get supplies for ourselves," he said.

"Well." She was thinking fast, trying to offer some way of making herself necessary. "I've got a laptop, and I can write. You'll need to get the word out. I can start a Web page."

"But the Way demands that one turn away as much as possible from modern conveniences and technology."

"I'm not Odawa. So technically, *you* won't be in violation."

Neolin laughed and said, "You've got a point there."

"So I can help?"

"Let me think about it. C'mon. Let's get out of this stinking house. It's a beautiful day in Odawa country. I'll show you around and you can teach me my language."

Shelly was tempted to reach for his hand but resisted the urge. Instead, she followed him out, taking a long look at his broad shoulders, tapered torso, and rounded ass.

When they emerged, the sun temporarily blinded them, but they could hear clearly the off-color comments about Shelly from the men, who had finished their game of horseshoes. Most were sitting on fold-up cloth lawn chairs and eating burgers and dogs from the grill. They'd obviously begun to feel their beers. Shelly liked nothing about the way the biggest one, standing with a rifle resting over and through his folded arms, leered at her. She'd seen that look before.

Ashamed of the men's disrespect toward his guest, and sensing a challenge to his command, Neolin feebly attempted to assert himself. "The floors and the steps in the house need fixing, and we need to turn over the ground out back for a garden." It was meant to be an imperative statement, but it came out declarative, like he was stating a fact rather than giving an order. No one moved. An awkward silence hung in the air. "Daniel? Benjamin? Aaron?" Still, not one of the men responded. "After lunch, then." He tried to save face.

Without turning, he reached back, grabbed Shelly by the wrist, and pulled her past the men, whose laughter deeply wounded his pride. Shelly ran a few strides to draw even with him. He led her toward a heavily forested patch of land abutting the western edge of the property.

"Where are we going?" Shelly asked.

He didn't respond but stormed ahead of her again and resumed dragging her after him. The path they followed was mostly overgrown. Thick undergrowth and low-hanging branches slowed their progress. More than once a deer suddenly burst from out of its resting place in the cool of the shade. Eventually, the sound of lapping surf meandered its way through the thick forestation. When they emerged, they stood on a patch of secluded beach with gray-brown sand. It was no bigger than a large outdoor patio and was surrounded on three sides by trees.

Unsure of Neolin's intentions, Shelly stopped, dug her feet into the sand, and asked, "Why did you bring me here?"

But Neolin was pacing so frantically along the surf line and was in such a bad temper that he didn't sense her nervousness or hear the question clearly.

"What?"

"Why are we here?"

He stopped and looked around as if to take stock himself, of where they were, and of why they'd come there. He pointed back in the direction of the camp and said, "Those . . .

those assholes make me so angry. I mean, I get so frustrated . . . so pissed off that sometimes I come here to get away, to refocus."

"It's okay," Shelly assured him.

"No! It's not okay!" He said it a little too aggressively.

"What's up with their names?" Shelly asked, trying to get his mind off of their insolence. "I mean, Daniel? Aaron and Benjamin?"

"What did you expect? Crazy Horse? Three Bears? Geronimo?"

Shelly's shoulders shrunk at his sarcasm.

"I'm sorry," he said.

"But your name is so unlike theirs."

"It's not my real name. Neolin was a Delaware prophet who taught the Way and inspired the Odawa to resist the whites back when this was our home. My real name is Gabriel Smith." He raised his arms and rolled his wrists outward, like Christ displaying the nail holes in his palms to the doubting Thomas. "Look at me. Do I look anything like a Smith?" After a dramatic pause, he said, "That's what this is about. I've got to find myself, and I won't—I can't—do that inside some lousy casino in Oklahoma."

"Then let me help you," Shelly said.

He placed his hands on his narrow, almost girlish hips, laughed, smiled, and said, "You are one persistent pale-faced girl."

"Buddy, you have no idea."

15

Gordon and I made our way beyond the North Bass airstrip.

"I'd kill for a little bit of breeze," I said.

"All I know is that when we get there, I'm dropping this damn boom box."

"What's with that thing anyway?" I asked. "Couldn't we have used something smaller?"

"No way," Gordon answered. "She insisted that we use this one. It's the one that we'd use when we were kids, playing in her pool or sitting on the dock. I'm pretty sure it once belonged to her mother. I guess you could call it an heirloom."

"Not much of an inheritance," I said.

Changing the suddenly nostalgic mood, Gordon said, "The first chance I get, I'm jumping in the damn lake. I'm sweating my nuts off."

"I don't really like the water," I said.

Maybe it was exhaustion, but at that point during my first

prolonged exposure to Gordon, I found myself in a confessional state of mind. Gordon looked at me as if I'd told him that I was some kind of alien.

"Keats," he said through his strained incredulity, "you live two blocks from a Great Lake."

"I know, but you've been to my neighborhood. Do we look like the yachting type?"

"You've got a point. The brothers aren't exactly much for water sports."

"When I was a little kid, my dad used to say to my brother and me, 'Tom. Johnny. Let's go check on the water. See if it's still there.' This is when he could still walk—"

"Whoa," Gordon interrupted. "Still walk? What's that mean? Is your dad handicapped or something?"

"Maybe he's yanking my chain," I thought. I mean, it had been nearly two years since the funeral. Didn't *everyone* know my father had died? I couldn't imagine that he'd make light of such a thing, but I'd already learned not to assume anything with Gordon. Yet the softening of his expression and what I know was sincere compassion in his eyes betrayed that we were—and I realize this sounds as corny as hell—sharing a moment. Go ahead. Snicker. Maybe it was our shared fatherless condition. I don't know. He didn't say and I didn't ask. However, from that moment on, for at least the remainder of our mission, we were more than friends of Shelly's. We were friends.

"Go on," Gordon said.

"We'd go down to the bay," I continued. "Tom and I would skip stones while Dad sat on one of the big slabs of concrete that had been dumped there as a breakwall. He'd just sit and stare at the water like it was talking to him or something, whispering secrets. But we never went in, just played along the edges."

"That's sad," Gordon said. "More than sad. Unnatural."

Again, Gordon's ambiguity made it difficult to pin down his meaning. I wasn't sure if his "unnatural" referred to my father's death or my landlubber status.

"What did you do for fun?"

I stared at him blankly. I'd never really thought of fun as being some kind of requirement for living. I'd always figured that fun was not for a child "intellectually advanced for his age," as I had often heard myself described by teachers. Fun was not for a white boy forbidden to play outside in an otherwise all-black neighborhood. Fun was not for a kid with walking-dead parents haunting his house. Fun was not for a wannabe writer who was certain to have been granted too short a time in which to make an indelible mark. There had always been too much to read, too much to be afraid of, too much sadness, and too much yet to be put into words to be able just to go out and have fun.

By the end of that day, however, I would realize that all of the pursuits that I thought I didn't have time to experience were the very things I needed to do if I had any hope of having anything meaningful to say, anything to contribute.

"I flew a kite once," I offered pathetically.

"A kite? Was that after you'd finished a quick game of marbles? For Christ's sake, Keats, it's the twenty-first century."

I ignored Gordon's sarcasm and continued my recollection. "I was only seven or eight years old. It was April. Easter

Sunday. My dad was only just confined to the wheelchair. I had jelly beans and some marshmallow Peeps in my Easter basket, and this cheap paper Spider-Man kite." I paused, then went on. "Most of the kids in the neighborhood had been dragged to church services and the corners were empty. My dad stayed on the porch, shouting instructions. I took off down the sidewalk with my kite trailing at shoulder height. Then the wind took it. It flew as high as it could go, and I walked back to my front yard, careful not to snag the string in a tree branch or something. We watched the kite. I felt the wind tugging at it. In my little kid brain, I thought the kite was trying to lift me up—out of that place. I remember thinking that I wouldn't resist if it did."

"Then what?" Gordon asked, pulling me out of my flashback.

"They shot it."

"What!"

"Three guys, still wearing their church suits. Four or five quick shots. Obliterated the thing. It was probably a dare or something. Haven't flown a kite since, but sometimes I still imagine that a big wind will come and blow me out of there."

"Yeah. You and your dog Toto too," Gordon said.

"Something like that."

We were drawing near to the north shore. It meant that the culmination of our quest and our final farewells to Shelly were approaching. Bowed by the emotional weight of the past few days and the literal weight of lugging around her ashes since the night before, I simultaneously dreaded and looked forward to letting go of her.

"Do you think we'll see her again?" I asked.

"See who?"

"Shelly."

"You mean like in heaven or some shit like that?" Gordon said with his typical irreverence for all things sacred.

"Yeah."

"Nope. Don't believe so. This is it, Keats. One shot," said Gordon.

"Me neither," I said, before I hedged. "At least, I don't think so."

"No shit? I always thought you were one of the good guys. I'll be damned."

"Very funny."

"Did you have some kind of revelation when I stopped to piss back there, or what?"

"No," I answered. "I've been thinking about it a lot since Shelly died, and it just doesn't add up."

"Slow down, Keats. I don't want any part of an ontological meltdown."

"I have no idea what you're talking about," I said.

"Sure you do. You're a smart guy. You just don't know you know."

I was surprised, and pleased, to know that Gordon thought of me as smart.

"You're talking about the existence of things—what we know exists and what we don't know exists. How we know it, and what we're even capable of knowing in the first place. You'll hear it all in Fulop's senior Introduction to Philosophy class."

"Oh," I said, pretending his explanation had cleared it up.

"It's like you've burst some kind of existential cherry, and I don't need to be blamed for it. I've already got enough blood on my hands, and I'm tired of being blamed for shit I didn't do."

Again, I had no idea what he was talking about. What was with Gordon's obsession with cherries? "Anyway," I said, returning to my thought, "I don't believe any of it either: the soul, heaven, hell, God, the devil."

"Whoa. Slow down there. Don't get all Nietzsche on me. I didn't say I didn't believe in *anything*."

"What do you believe in?" I asked. "Sex, drugs, and rock and roll?"

"Those are pretty good places to start, but even I'm not so shallow as that. There might be something more, some kind of power. I just don't think it's the dude they teach at school or in churches. As far as I'm concerned, 'God' is just a word, a metaphor for whatever the fuck makes you hard, and heaven's a metaphor for the wishful thinking that's actually the nothing that comes next. Like I said, there may be something out there, some kind of creative force or energizing spirit, but I don't believe there's some judgmental prick with a shitty sense of humor waiting for the last laugh. At least, I sure hope not."

"That's what Shelly said too."

"Well, Shelly was weird, not dumb."

"What if you're wrong?" I asked, ignoring his sloppy characterization of Shelly.

"Then I'm fucked, but what if *they're* wrong and by listening to them, I waste my life saying no to damn near everything that makes me feel good and alive? I need more than men in black saying 'Because I told you so,' or some bullshit holy book full of more nonsense, contradictions, and God-sponsored cruelty than Homer could have imagined in a thousand epics. Nope. That shit's not for me. I'm betting on the bird in this hand"—he actually grabbed his crotch—"and fucking every burning bush worth fucking. If you want to see Shelly again, take off that stopper and take a long hard look, because that's all that's left and all the reunion you're ever going to get."

I took the absence of an immediate and directed lightning strike as a point in Gordon's favor, but I backed away a few paces just in case. (On the average, there are ninety fatalities each year in America due to lightning strikes.)

"What's that?" Gordon said, surveying the hazy blue sky with both eyes and ears.

I mimicked his tilted head posture and sensory activation. "It sounds like . . ."

"A plane." (You have a one-in-eleven-million chance of dying in a plane crash.) After he finished my sentence, he pointed over my shoulder toward the south and the mainland. "Let's go."

"We did just pass the airport," I reasoned with him.

"I know, but it's flying awfully low and circling without being in any hurry to land, at least not until it finds what it's looking for, and I think that may be us. I don't know; it just doesn't feel right. We need to hurry. I can feel it."

"Shelly's dad?" I asked.

"I don't know. Maybe."

I felt Shelly swishing around inside of the urn as we ran.

part three

I.

DEATH IS HERE AND DEATH IS THERE,
DEATH IS BUSY EVERYWHERE,
ALL AROUND, WITHIN, BENEATH,
ABOVE IS DEATH—AND WE ARE DEATH.

II.

DEATH HAS SET HIS MARK AND SEAL
ON ALL WE ARE AND ALL WE FEEL,
ON ALL WE KNOW AND ALL WE FEAR,

III.

FIRST OUR PLEASURES DIE—AND THEN
OUR HOPES, AND THEN OUR FEARS—AND WHEN
THESE ARE DEAD, THE DEBT IS DUE,
DUST CLAIMS DUST—AND WE DIE TOO.

IV.

ALL THINGS THAT WE LOVE AND CHERISH,
LIKE OURSELVES MUST FADE AND PERISH;
SUCH IS OUR RUDE MORTAL LOT—
LOVE ITSELF WOULD, DID THEY NOT.
—PERCY BYSSHE SHELLEY, "DEATH"

16

The summer between my sophomore and junior years—
between Shelly's and Gordon's junior and senior years—as I
worked on my writing and website, Shelly was on North
Bass, and Gordon was overseas. The three of us were largely
incommunicado (nothing atypical as far as I went, since the
Beacon had been my only consistent link to either one of
them and, obviously, there was no summer edition). That
June, my mother passed away, and not long after, Tom dis-
played signs of the onset of his tuberculosis.

At only twenty years old, he felt the burden of being the
man of the house, and he didn't always deal with it in what
you might call "appropriate" ways, especially after Mom died.
He'd made some pretty shady friends at work who'd introduced him first to pot and cocaine and eventually to heroin.
I know I should have done something, but put yourself in the
situation we were in, and you tell me what you would have
done. To make matters worse, Tom had been lazy in treating

his diabetes (number six killer of Americans), and neither of us had healthy eating habits. I assumed that his lingering cough, constant lethargy, and weight loss were due to the drugs and poor diet.

His health deteriorated. He was fired from his job, for his constant coughing was giving everyone the fantods as they wondered what he might be spreading. Besides, he looked like a zombie; his appearance was enough to drive potential customers screaming from the restaurant.

When I finally convinced him to go to the clinic at the county health department, the doctor diagnosed his tuberculosis (not to mention his drug usage, which led the doctor to also have Tom tested for AIDS—negative thus far). The precautionary test for TB ordered for me came back negative. Tom was prescribed a combination of antibiotics that required vigilant regimentation, which I knew he would struggle to maintain, in order to be effective. But at least he was being treated.

My mother had died in her sleep. One noontime in late June, I realized that I hadn't heard her stir all morning. I found her lying in bed, already bluing. I knew she was dead, but I called 911 anyway. Then I called Tom. One of the EMTs notified the same cut-rate funeral home that had handled my father. By midafternoon, my mother was on a gurney being wheeled from house to hearse. She was buried next to my father with even less ceremony than his "blue light special" interment. It sounds awful, I know, but her death was sort of anticlimactic. She'd all but died that day years earlier when my father had received his ALS death sentence.

With my mother's passing, we felt freer to seek any and

all of the governmental assistance for which we were eligible but that our father had abhorred and our mother, as head of the household, had been too cataleptic to pursue. Pride and honor are nice and all, but you can't eat them, and they don't pay the utilities.

Thinking Shelly might go with me to the cemetery, I called her house. But the woman who answered the phone (I assumed it was her stepmother) curtly communicated that she hadn't seen Shelly in days. She offered me Shelly's cell number, but by that point I'd already determined it had been a bad idea to call, so I didn't take the number. I figured that Shelly was preoccupied with the goings-on at North Bass that summer anyway.

Although I completely lost touch with Shelly from when school let out in June until it began again in early September, in between composing and posting new poems to my website, I was able to follow Gordon's book tour through blogs on his professionally administered page. So much happened to all of us during those months he was away. It was the summer that changed everything.

After bleeding dry the overwhelmingly female market of young adult readers in America, that spring Pandroth had unleashed a number of foreign language editions of *Manfred* into the European market. Its author, accompanied by his agent, Ms. Martin, and his mother, followed soon after— fangs bared. When the four-week tour of book signings and appearances concluded, Gordon successfully bullied his mother into allowing him extended vacation time, with a brief visit to western Turkey and a prolonged stay in Greece, both of which had held a special place in his imagination since his early readings of Homer. In an effort to ease Catherine's worry, Ms. Martin arranged for Johnny Hobhouse, a recent Columbia grad and an intern at her agency, to fly over and serve as Gordon's chaperone for the remainder of his pilgrimage.

Upon his liberation from his matronly cotravelers, Gordon's blogs grew infrequent. I mostly learned of his Aegean adventures and Shelly's own quixotic summer the following fall from Shelly. Apparently, Gordon emailed her with occasional updates, attaching photographs of himself in various locations. In one that Shelly shared, he was dripping wet inside a peeled-to-beneath-his-waist wet suit as he emerged in the half-light of dusk from a large body of water. According to Gordon's email, he had just recreated Leander's swimming of the Dardanelles, a strait separating the Aegean Sea from the Sea of Marmara, not far from the ancient city of Troy.

The idea for the swim had originated years ago at the Rood, where Willie had shared the story of Leander and Hero, and had even posed Gordon as Leander for one of his sketches. In the myth, Leander of Abydos and Hero of Sestos fall in love during a chance encounter at a festival honoring Aphrodite. However, Hero's parents refuse to allow their daughter to enter into a relationship with a boy from the rival city-state directly across the Dardanelles—or the Hellespont, as the strait was then named. In defiance of her parents, Hero agrees to Leander's plan for her to light a lamp in her bedroom tower window as a landmark by which he can navigate as he braves the turbulent waters and secretly swims to her. The ritual continues nightly. One evening at the onset of winter, however, a strong wind extinguishes Hero's lamp in the midst of Leander's crossing and leaves him floundering, directionless, until he drowns in watery confusion. Spotting his lifeless body washed up on the rocks beneath her tower on the following morning, Hero throws herself from the window to die next to Leander.

When Gordon finally emerged from his swim, he was met by Hobhouse, who snapped the photograph sent to Shelly. As it turned out, Hobhouse had more than a few wild hairs of his own, and Ms. Martin couldn't have picked a less suitable chaperone for her boy genius.

From northeastern Greece, they relocated to the Athenaeum InterContinental luxury hotel, located twenty minutes from the nightlife of downtown Athens but near to the Acropolis, the Parthenon, and the Temple of Apollo. The hotel's close proximity to the metro made it an ideal launching pad for their planned adventures. Initially, their itinerary consisted of the stuff of standard Greek vacations, but it was soon discarded in favor of a more epicurean, less touristy stay. The pair began sleeping until noon, and then commencing their daily ritual of afternoons spent at the beaches of Glyfada, light dinners and coffee in any of the numerous cafés in Athens, and clubbing until dawn.

One morning, however, Gordon broke from their established cycle of sloth and debauchery, cut short their morning slumber, dragged the hungover Hobhouse from bed, and rode the municipal bus from Omonia Square to Cape Sounion, the southernmost tip of the Attica peninsula.

There they visited the ruins of the Temple of Poseidon. As if to touch the past and to link himself inextricably with his self-acknowledged patron god forever, Gordon snuck past the barriers and carved his name into the base of one of the remaining pillars, while Hobhouse distracted the security guard with a perfectly timed bout of vomiting.

"That is as close to immortality as either one of us will ever come," Gordon told Hobhouse upon extricating himself from the cordoned-off temple.

"Whatever," Hobhouse moaned, badly in need of some serious hydration and a nap before the night's revelries.

Hobhouse quickly grew accustomed to being blown off by Gordon whenever his ward made the company of a local beauty. In fact, on their first full day in Athens, while the two of them were shopping in the boutiques of Kolonaki, Gordon met three sisters who, in Hobhouse's estimation, were all in their early to middle teens. Made uncomfortable in their company by his own relatively advanced years, Hobhouse excused himself.

Gordon, meanwhile, accompanied Teresa, Mariana, and Kattinka to their suburban home northeast of downtown Athens. Among the three of them they didn't appear to share ten words of English. The Macri sisters' home was a four-story Grammatikos stone maisonette with a view of the Evoikos Gulf, and was worth more than a million euros. Compared to downtown Athens, it was rural, uncongested, and, if nothing else, free from the incessant smog that lingered over the ancient city.

No sooner had Gordon set foot on the dark German hardwood of the first-floor living room, than the squealing sisters scattered to their respective bedrooms. Gordon stood stock-still among a collection of abstract sculptures and paintings until the girls returned; each was wrapped in a bath towel and nothing else. Gordon had a sneaking suspicion that he wasn't the first boy they'd collected and brought home.

Teresa, the one Gordon thought to be the youngest (perhaps thirteen), took him by the hand and led him, followed by her two sisters, through a sliding glass door into a first-level pool and Jacuzzi area. Without ceremony or hesitation, the sisters dropped their towels, joined hands at the pool's edge, and jumped in as Gordon watched.

Treading water, the three formed a line of synchronized swimmers and turned to their guest. "Well?" Kattinka, the oldest, asked.

Cross-armed, he pulled his T-shirt up over his head and tossed it onto the concrete deck. Giddy, I'm sure, with the possibilities before him, he slipped out of his sandals and dropped his pants so that they covered his feet. He then dove into the water, swam beneath the surface, and stalked the girls' bottoms like a great white. (A person's chance of being killed by a shark is 1 in 264.1 million.) The girls scattered. Their squeals reached Gordon through the warbled distortion of the water, and he was once again comfortable and in his element.

They played—literally played—for nearly an hour: shark tank, volleyball, keep-away, and chicken fights, and he taught them to call "Polo" to his "Marco." Gordon felt as if *he* were thirteen years old again, splashing in the back bay with Shelly and Augusta. He couldn't remember a happier time in the intervening years.

The time machine was soon broken, however, and the games ended, when they heard the glass door to the living area sliding heavily on its track. Through the smell of chlorinated water, Gordon caught a whiff of an exotic perfume wafting in the air as he surfaced. He made out the shapely figure of a woman standing poolside with arms crossed as the girls called what Gordon took for helloes to the woman without the slightest hint of shame or concern for having been caught skinny-dipping with a boy.

Tarsia Macri was the water nymphs' mother. In her late thirties, she could have easily passed for twenty-five.

Calmly, as if making the most mundane of requests, Mrs. Macri said something in Greek, and the girls, moaning their reluctance, swam to the concrete deck. They reached up, pulled and then pushed their glistening nubile bodies in perfect synchronicity from the pool, wrapped their towels around themselves, and scurried back, dripping wet, into the house.

Alone with Mrs. Macri, Gordon waited for his scolding.

"Well?" she said in a stilted English that perfectly matched Kattinka's earlier invitation to jump into the water. Indicating that he too was expected to remove himself from the pool, Mrs. Macri revealed no obvious intention of chastising him for his behavior with her daughters, or any intention of averting her gaze.

Unabashedly, Gordon mimicked the girls' exit and stood, dripping, two feet in front of her, awaiting further instructions.

Mrs. Macri slid her sunglasses to the tip of her nose and gave Gordon's body a once-over from bottom to top and back down again. "What happened to your leg?" she asked.

He actually appreciated her bluntness, especially compared to the idiotic manner most people employed in order to pretend not to notice, but before he could answer, she turned and walked away, announcing that dinner would be served in half an hour.

As he showered in the guest bathroom, Gordon imagined several scenarios, in anticipation of what the Macri females had in store for the evening. The fantasy he settled on was that Mrs. Macri was a cougar who fed on the flesh and fluids of young men, in an ever-increasingly difficult quest to maintain her own youth and to forestall her inevitable march into the living-death of middle age. She used her daughters as bait to trap her victims and lure them to her lair, where she ravished and drained her boy toys in exquisite tortures that even Gordon couldn't imagine but was dying to discover.

His erotic musings were abruptly interrupted when a panicked Mrs. Macri burst in and threw his clothes over the top of the glazed glass shower door.

"What's going on?" Gordon asked, sensing that his burgeoning fantasies were going to remain just that—fantasies.

"You must go," she insisted as Gordon attempted to pull on his sopping wet clothes.

"But—"

"No talk. Just go."

From the pool deck, Gordon heard the bass voice of a man

who, to inspire this kind of terror, could only be Mrs. Macri's husband. The girls' birdlike voices were intermingled with the man's.

With his pants barely covering his ass and his shirt worn inside out, Gordon, still soaking wet, carried his shoes and followed Mrs. Macri down to the first level, where she shoved him through the kitchen and out the back door.

Dismayed and pouting, Gordon sat down impudently on the steps, which led to a rear alley. He finished dressing, gathered his dignity, made his way around to the street in front, and walked toward Athens in search of a taxi.

It would seem that, at least for the first part of his stay in Greece, Gordon was still Gordon.

But on a mid-July afternoon two weeks later, Gordon met a girl. I don't mean the typical "Gordon girl" but one who sincerely interested him and with whom he developed an actual platonic relationship bordering on friendship. Although, it began inauspiciously.

The beach was unusually crowded. Gordon and Hobhouse had begun to fold up their beach chairs early and head back to their rooms, when Hobhouse elbowed Gordon in the side and said, "Hey, look." With a backward nod of his head, he directed Gordon's attention to a petite young lady with her long black hair gathered into a muffin-sized bun. She lounged on her back in a relatively modest—for a Mediterranean beach—black bikini with silvery spangles reflecting the sunshine like so many constellations. On first glance, Gordon guessed her to be his age or maybe a little older. Her eyes and nearly half of her face were covered by a massive pair of sunglasses. Most interesting, however, was that she held a Greek language version of *Manfred* in one hand, and, while fully engrossed, she turned the pages with the other.

"I can't pass this up," Gordon said, carelessly dropping his beach accoutrements to the sand. "This is fucking kismet."

He weaved around and stepped his way over a minefield of bronzed and baked bodies of all shapes and sizes until he stood at the foot of her chair like a human eclipse blocking the sun. "That's mine," Gordon said, hoping she could understand his English.

Assuming he referred to the in-much-demand beach chair on which she lay, the girl said, with only a slightly stilted accent, "Fuck off. You Americans still think you run the world. The chair was empty. I took it. Now, go get a Big Mac." (Heart disease is the number one killer of Americans in general but only the number five killer of teens.)

Her attitude seemed more affected than authentic, as if part of a general attitude regarding American tourists.

Gordon laughed, which really angered her.

"What's so funny?" she asked, lifting her torso and positioning herself on her elbows, now appearing genuinely annoyed. "You think it's all some kind of joke, and then you're shocked when jet planes fly into your skyscrapers. Only then, you stop with the laughing."

I know, *not* cool. But it made Gordon stop laughing all right. "I'm sorry, but I meant *that*. That's mine." He pointed at the iconic cover of her copy of *Manfred,* which she held against the side of her thigh.

Confused, she sat up completely and looked around her

219

and under a pile of newspapers for something she must have missed.

"The book," Gordon said. "I wrote it. Look in the back. There's a picture. It's a couple of years old, but I think you'll recognize it."

She did as he suggested, then lowered her sunglasses and looked knowingly into Gordon's eyes. "Now I'm sorry," she said sincerely, but without any apparent regret for her anti-American rant.

Rather than receiving the instant adulation to which he'd grown accustomed from his cultish readers, Gordon was surprised by her almost total lack of amazement or sense of privilege. "It's my little sister's. She left it in my bag. I had nothing else to read."

Noticing the bookmark hastily stuck nearly three quarters of the way through the novel, he said, "Well, at least your little sister must be enjoying it."

"My sister's an idiot," she said.

The dark young lady swung her shapely thighs and winnowing calves to the side and off of the chair; her realignment revealed a tiny tattoo, between her ankle bone and Achilles tendon, of a pale yellow star outlined in red, with a matching "17N" in its middle. She stuffed Gordon's novel and her newspapers into an enormous beach bag, which matched her suit, in a show of disgust.

Gordon quickly sat down beside her. "Wait," he said. "Can't we talk?"

"Talk? Of what? And why? So you can ask me to show you around Athens while you pretend to be interested, until the famous boy author from America can convince the starstruck native girl to allow him inside her pants?"

"I was thinking coffee, but I'm open to your plan."

She literally harrumphed and stood, before releasing and shaking her luxuriant hair so that it fell in shiny raven-black tresses over her shoulders and down her slender back. She bent forward at the waist, shook out some sand from her top, and then suddenly snapped to a vertical position while corralling her hair with both hands along the sides of her head. With a magician's sleight of hand, she ran her locks through an elastic hair band and gathered it into a ponytail. Back arched, elbows akimbo, and breasts thrust forward and up, she momentarily struck a pose worthy of sculptor's marble. Finally, after picking up her bag, she made a show of stomping away through the torrid sand without a word of farewell.

Something about it was too over the top, too meet-cute, Gordon thought. Without much concern, he put the failed attempt behind him. He'd struck out before, and he certainly would again. Based upon the lecture he'd given me two years earlier at the *Beacon* regarding his courage in approaching girls, I'm sure he thought, "What's going to happen will happen. There's no sense worrying about it."

He hurried to where Hobhouse stood, watching and enjoying Gordon being blown off for a change. "Looks like the Mighty Casey struck out," Hobhouse said.

"That's only the first swing," Gordon replied.

They returned to the hotel for a regenerative nap before diving headlong once more into the Athens nightlife.

* * *

"It's her," Gordon said, breaking the silence that had usurped the rightful place of dinner conversation. "She's here."

He reached across the small circular table that he shared with Hobhouse at the O Glykis café, and pulled down the menu that Hobhouse had been studying with rapt focus. Hobhouse, like Gordon, enjoyed his food, and in large quantities. Whereas Gordon might compare their three-part days to a sort of triathlon, for Hobhouse, their daily routine was best described as a well-wrought three-act play: the beach served as rising action, and the clubbing as denouement, both sandwiched around each night's climactic dinner, which he could patiently prolong for hours. Knowing that he wasn't spending a dime of his own money only added to his culinary pleasure.

The O Glykis was somewhat removed from the congested cafés on Eterias Square, so Gordon was surprised when he spotted the brusque brunette from the beach seated near the café entrance, out of which the waiters appeared and disappeared in their white aprons. He was certain that she hadn't been there when they'd arrived. One of the waiters, Gordon noticed, paid particular attention to the girl, especially considering that she had ordered nothing but a coffee in the time that Gordon had been aware of her presence.

"Who's here?" Hobhouse asked, more than a little perturbed by the interruption of his dinner planning.

"The girl from the beach," Gordon said.

"Well, that narrows it down to several thousand."

"The black bikini," Gordon said, "reading my book."

"That's an unlikely coincidence."

"You think so?" The sarcasm dripped. "I'm going over there."

"If at first . . . ," Hobhouse began, but Gordon was already gone.

"I saw you," she preempted him. "I saw you but did not care. I sat anyway, believing I made myself clear and you'd be a gentleman. But, no. Here you stand. Typical."

With his hands braced against the black iron chair in front of him, Gordon asked, "Why do you dislike me? I get the whole 'stupid American' thing, but don't you think you're being just a little unfairly prejudiced? I mean, you don't even know me."

"Oh, I know you. I've seen you in the magazines and on the Internet. You are the all-American boy, no? You are everything I hate about your country, and now you are poisoning mine."

"Christ, comrade, relax," Gordon said.

As was the case earlier, she made a show of leaving, but as she rose, the overly attentive dark-haired dark-eyed (it seemed everyone in Athens was dark-haired and dark-eyed) waiter—with full sideburns flanking a gaunt face and protuberant nose beneath the longest eyelashes Gordon had ever seen on a man—made an almost imperceptible pause as he passed her table, while simultaneously locking eyes with the girl, and she slunk back into her chair as if on orders.

Gordon sat down.

"What if I told you that the guy you've seen in those magazines isn't real? That I'm not that guy?"

She shrugged her shoulders, while she stared over his, out into the street; she was either truly disgusted by Gordon or afraid of his charms. "I'd say you are a liar."

Gordon continued, "What if I told you that, even if I am in some small ways 'that guy,' I want to change? Would you believe me . . ." He had wanted to use her name in direct address, but realized he didn't know it, so he paused, hoping she'd respond to his cue. And she did.

"Zoe."

"Zoe?" Gordon repeated. "Is that short for something? Is there a last name to go with it?"

"Just Zoe. That is all you need to know."

The waiter returned and asked, "Do you stay?"

Zoe's lips separated to respond, but before she could give voice to whatever her answer was going to be, Gordon gave a presumptuous, "Yes."

Gordon turned and signaled his intention to stay to Hobhouse.

Exasperated but not surprised, Hobhouse smiled insincerely and flipped off Gordon.

"What's with the tattoo?" Gordon asked Zoe. Beneath the table, he felt her cross her legs in her dark denim jeans, as if covering the mark. "What's the 17N stand for?"

Because his description of the tattoo was accurate, and a simple Google search would identify the symbol anyway, there was no reason for Zoe to dissemble. "It represents the seventeenth of November." She pronounced it as if it would generate a surprised response.

"What's that? Your birthday?"

"No," she said, thinking he must be the most ignorant boy on earth. "It is a"—she hesitated, choosing her words carefully—"a political organization."

"And you're a member?"

"Sort of."

"And you have to get a tattoo when you're a member?"

"No. Only I have such a tattoo."

"Why not a butterfly or a flower or your boyfriend's, the waiter's, name?"

Gordon saw that Zoe was thrown by his characterization of her relationship with Rony, the eyeballing waiter; her face betrayed her surprise.

"So, I'm right. He is your boyfriend."

"He is *not* my boyfriend, and it is irrelevant. For your information, the 17N were Greek patriots and freedom fighters."

"You said 'were.' But you also said you are a member of this . . . What did you call it? A political organization? So, which one is it?"

"You are not like most Americans. You listen. But do you learn? That is yet to be determined," she said.

"I do," Gordon said, "and I'm still waiting to learn the answer. Are you a member or not?"

Rony stopped and refilled Zoe's coffee cup, then lifted the glass pot toward Gordon. "Yes?" he asked, but Gordon sensed a greater implication in the gesture than the mere offer of a cup of coffee.

Gordon waved his hand and said, "No. Thank you."

Rony turned again to Zoe, who shook her head, then answered Gordon's question as Rony waited on the patrons in his section, giving regular furtive glances back at the two of them. "My father was a member. A founder, actually, but now he's in jail."

"I take it that has something to do with this 17N?"

"Yes."

"What did he do?"

"He *did* many things—all for Greece."

"If he's such a hero, why is he in jail?"

"My father fought for the people against the puppets and appeasers in parliament who continue to whore out our country to foreigners and then persecute their own sons and daughters. My father is a great man," Zoe insisted. "There are evils that must be done, sacrifices that must be made, even innocents who must suffer, for the greater goal of Greek sovereignty."

"Those sound like the justifications of a terrori—" Gordon began.

Before he could finish the word, Gordon felt the cold sting of a slap across his face, which set off a ringing in his ears. With temporarily blurred vision, he watched Zoe rise. He listened as she declaimed, "Don't you ever use that word about my father or my friends. We are no more terrorists than your own American revolutionaries. Like them, we demand self-rule in our own country. We would rather die than live under the boots of America, our so-called allies, with their military bases and economic blackmail, or live with the

Turks despoiling Cyprus, or with any ties to the EU or the panderers from NATO."

With her point abundantly made and with his interest sincerely piqued, Gordon begged Zoe to sit down. The lesson in geopolitics was coming too fast for him to process through the ringing-turned-buzzing inside his head, but he appreciated her passion. With a show of reluctance, she sat down with her arms folded. With a puckered mouth, Zoe turned toward the street.

"Tell me more," Gordon said. "Please."

She turned her narrowed eyes toward him. "Why? So you can insult?"

"No. I'm sorry. I want to know more about this 17N and whatever it is they do and why they do it." The sudden burst of social concern was unfamiliar to him, but it was all so Shelly. Reflecting on the irony of it made him laugh.

"And now you laugh," she said.

"I'm not laughing at you. I'm thinking of a friend back home who should probably be having this conversation instead of me."

"Is he too a famous writer?" she asked in a subtly mocking tone.

"She," Gordon corrected her. "She is a writer, but she is not famous."

"She is your girlfriend?" Zoe dropped her hands onto her lap and sat tall with her shoulders drawn back. Intently, she studied his face and looked for any tics or eye movements that might indicate deceit in his forthcoming answer.

Pleased with the implications of the question—her

interest in his relationship status—Gordon purposefully hesitated, hoping that she might unconsciously reveal a budding romantic curiosity, but her expression was granite. Finally, he said, "No—just a good friend."

Without segue, Zoe began. Speaking in a tone reminiscent of a junior high History Day presentation (probably the result of the English as a second language thing), she said, "As I said, '17N' stands for the seventeenth of November. On that date in 1973, a group of law students at the Athens Polytechnic, protesting the tyrannical policies of the American-backed military junta and demanding the rights of democratic citizens, were set upon by tanks and soldiers. My father was one of those students. Twenty-four protesters were murdered."

"What happened then?"

"After a brief period of full martial law, the Regime of Colonels collapsed under the combined weight of the blood it had spilled at Polytechnic, its own infighting, the resistance of patriotic military officers, and the contrary will of the people."

"If the dictatorship was ended and, I assume, democratic reforms enacted, why 17N?"

"That night changed my father forever. He rose the next day a Marxist. Together with his brothers—both of whom had been arrested and tortured by the military police for just having Communist acquaintances—and a small group of others, they formed and operated as 17N until they were arrested."

"So, what do you and Rony call yourselves?"

Zoe leaned across the table, a move that exposed the tops

of her breasts and more than ample cleavage over the top of the white peasant blouse, which she wore off her bare shoulders. "We are 'the Struggle,'" she whispered.

"Sounds more like an alternative rock band than a terr—" He corrected himself. "Freedom fighting organization."

To Gordon's surprise, not only did she not take offense at his near slip of the tongue and haul off and slap him again, but she actually smiled, exposing perfectly straight and perfectly white teeth.

Abruptly, she straightened, rose to her feet, and said, "We'll talk again."

Before he could inquire why, where, or when, she was gone, having disappeared into the Athens night, leaving him to pay for her coffees.

I despised the way Gordon had of one-upping Shelly and of denying her even the smallest amount of happiness that didn't flow from his own doing or his mere presence.

When they were kids, his Civil War games pulverized Shelly's Ottawa peace councils. When Shelly began a friendship with Hogg, Gordon destroyed it. When Shelly's Gothic tale of murder should have been her moment, Gordon contributed his little vampire story and stole the spotlight. When Shelly joined the Ottawa on North Bass, Gordon suddenly discovered his sociopolitical conscience and joined a revolutionary cell of Greek Communists. I hate it that so much of what should be Shelly's story is about Gordon. But then, so much of her life was too.

Now, you know Gordon. How genuine a conversion could his have been? And could it all have been purely co-incidental? I'll let you draw your own conclusions.

As Shelly told it, Gordon awoke the next morning to a knock on his hotel room door. Spying only an empty hallway through the peephole, he opened his door to the full length of the chain lock, and still saw no one. At his feet, however, was a shoe box wrapped in plain brown paper and tied with string. After unlocking the chain, he held the box to his ear and listened for ticking. His conversation the previous evening had stoked his imagination.

Back inside the room, he sat on the floor at the foot of his bed and undid the string and paper. When he removed the lid of the shoe box, he discovered a book with one red and yellow word across the bottom: "Che." This was the title of John Lee Anderson's biography of Che Guevara, the hand-some son of Argentinean aristocracy turned guerilla fighter, Marxist rebel, and trusted intimate of Fidel Castro, the leader of the guerilla revolutionary forces during the overthrow of Batista's Cuba. Guevara's portrait filled the remainder of the cover. Gordon stared, mesmerized by Che's handsome, swarthy bearded face and longish tousled black hair beneath a single-gold-starred-in-the-center black beret. For the next three days and nights, Gordon left Hobhouse to his own de-vices. He didn't leave the room, didn't shower or shave. Occa-sionally, he ordered room service and, when exhausted, slept, but for most of that time, he read from the eight-hundred-plus-page tome. Whenever his eyes grew weary or his brain teemed with new ideas and impressions, he paused in his reading and studied the black-and-white photographs of Guevara at the varying stages of his life.

On the fourth morning, he received a phone call from Zoe. "We'll pick you up at the main entrance at noon" was all she said before hanging up without waiting for a confirmation or to answer any of his million questions.

Gordon dragged himself into the bathroom and, this time, actually flipped on the light. Bracing himself with a one-handed stiff arm against the wall, he took a nearly orgasmic piss. When he turned his head and, for the first time in more than three days, studied himself in the mirror, he nearly had a stroke. For a brief sleep-deprived moment, with his brain besotted by revolutionary zeal, he could have sworn it was Che himself staring back at him in the mirror. He showered but kept the beard.

At exactly noon, Rony and Zoe arrived in a beat-up, most likely stolen, silver Toyota Corolla with rental plates. Rony, behind the wheel, reached across and threw open the front passenger-side door. Zoe sat in back in a hooded white terry-cloth beach cover-up.

"What's up?" Gordon said.

Eyeing the beard, Rony and Zoe exchanged glances over the front seat and laughed. Remembering Gordon's sarcasm on the day at the beach, she said, "What? No beret, comrade?"

Embarrassed by his overzealousness, Gordon blushed but felt relieved by his decision to leave in his room the beret that he had bought that morning.

Rony pulled onto the busy Syngrou Avenue and turned up the radio that pumped what Gordon would soon learn was rebetiko, a bluesy form of folk music, heavy on stringed and simple percussion instruments, that gives expression to the complaints of the poor and the oppressed and to the universal bullshit of living.

Gordon tried to initiate conversation over the too loud music. "We going to the beach? If we are, I didn't bring a suit."

Nothing.

"It's hotter than balls," he said.

Nothing.

"I read the book."

Nothing.

"I hear Socrates fucked little boys."

Nothing but a roll of Zoe's eyes. He quit trying.

Eventually, the Corolla rolled up to the outskirts of the Plaka, Athens's oldest neighborhood. It rests directly beneath the Acropolis. The Plaka has pretty much been abdicated by the indigenous people of Athens to those in the business of fleecing tourists. Quaint in the way nothing authentic really can be, it is filled with museums, cafés, shops, restaurants, street vendors, and street performers. The tourists flock to the Plaka, naïvely unsuspecting of the sharp-toothed smiling, scamming, and pocket-picking wolves among whom they mingle.

The preponderance of pedestrian tourists had caused the closing of most streets in the village, so Rony parked near Syntagma Square in the center of Athens. They walked up Nikis Street to where it ran into Kydathaneon, which they followed into the Plaka. Upon reaching the central square,

Rony and Zoe consulted their watches and, as far as Gordon could tell, made plans to rendezvous; then Rony took off and disappeared into the crowded streets.

"Hold this," Zoe told Gordon as she handed him the same overstuffed black beach bag she'd carried on the day they'd first met.

He held her bag while she undid her cover-up to reveal the spangled black bikini top and a pair of tiny khaki-colored shorts that failed to contain the whale-tail of her black thong panties. After stuffing the cover-up into the bag, she removed from it and put on the oversized sunglasses and a pair of high-heeled sandals, which she exchanged for the tennis shoes she had worn for the walk from the car.

"Come," Zoe said, and led him toward a small grocery advertising Greek wines and foods, and containing a variety of items resembling those of any convenience store in America. She checked her watch as they walked, before coming to a stop outside the store. "He's late," she said.

"Who's late? Where are we?" Gordon asked.

No sooner had the words passed his lips than a clerk emerged from the entrance of the store, untying a full apron from around his neck. He walked toward them and handed Zoe the apron and a tiny slip of paper. She quickly scanned the paper scrap, handed it and the apron to Gordon, and said, "Let's go."

"Go? Where?"

Zoe was already entering the cavelike darkness of the store when he grabbed her by the elbow. "What's this?" Gordon held the slip of paper before her eyes.

She pulled his arm down, like the lever of a slot machine,

while nudging him backward until his back was against the doorjamb. She pressed herself hard against him, rose onto her tiptoes, looked up into his confused eyes through her sunglasses, and put on a smile, as if they were a pair of lovers engaged in a moment of playful intimacy, and in a sweet voice incongruous to the words' meaning, said, "Are you stupid?"

Sliding seamlessly into her improvisational routine, Gordon slipped his arms around her waist, placed his hands against the smooth skin of the small of her back, leaned forward, and turned his ear toward her.

"It's the code for the cash register," she said, before taking her leave with a dismissive two-handed shove against his chest, accompanied by canned laughter.

Still processing the purpose of his holding the entry code for the store's cash register, Gordon watched as Zoe worked the aisles of the shop like they were a Parisian catwalk, before finally approaching the pated middle-aged man behind the counter, who had been ogling her since they'd entered the store. Because the clerk—who, it suddenly became clear to Gordon, was obviously Zoe's compatriot—had gone on break, the owner was manning the store single-handedly. Zoe strutted her way to the counter, where she placed her elbows on the surface of the glass top, shoved her breasts within several inches of the owner's nose, then stood upright with her shoulders thrown back, all the while engaging him in some kind of coquettish conversation. She twisted her torso and her head (giving the older gentleman total freedom to gape unchecked at her breasts in profile) and pointed questioningly toward the glass-doored stand-up cooler containing a variety of beverages in the back of the store.

Eventually, the storekeeper came around the counter and accompanied Zoe to the cold drinks. In a single glance, she communicated to Gordon, "Now's the time. Do something that matters. Join the revolution. Be one of us." He didn't hesitate. It was a dare he couldn't pass up. It was like sex in public: the accelerated heart rate, the hyperawareness of surroundings, the slightly metallic taste of fear, the sheer joy of perversion. He slung the borrowed apron over his head, walked behind the counter as if he owned the place, punched in the code from the scrap of paper he palmed, and pressed enter. The drawer slid silently open. Eschewing the coins, he calmly removed the multicolored stacks of euro bills: yellow two hundreds, green one hundreds, orange fifties, blue twenties, reddish tens, and gray fives. The currency, which he folded over and stuffed into the front pocket of his cargo shorts, impressed him as no more than Monopoly money. After gently closing the drawer, he strode from behind the counter directly toward the door.

Returning to the early afternoon light and heat, he removed the apron from around his neck, balled it up inside his fist as much as possible, and waited for Zoe across the street from the grocery.

When she exited, Zoe spotted him standing conspicuously still among the to-and-fro of the pedestrian traffic. Instead of crossing, she turned and reversed their route of ascent. Gordon mirrored her movement. With one eye on the onrushing pilgrims to the Plaka and Acropolis and one eye on her, he watched as, with her bag swinging from her shoulder, she deftly converted her hair into a ponytail and took a floral print summer dress from the bag. Then, with quick-change artistry worthy of a Vegas show, she pulled it over herself to cover the bikini top and short shorts.

She walked past the abandoned Corolla and reunited with Rony in Syntagma Square. The clerk from the grocery stood next to him, smoking a cigarette. Gordon joined them and returned the apron to the clerk, who, clearly suspicious of Gordon's motives, dropped the half-extinguished cigarette to the ground and smeared it against the concrete with the heel of his motorcycle boot.

Zoe pressed herself against Gordon as she had done in the store. Rising to her tiptoes, she whispered, "The money," as he turned his head to listen.

Zoe's warm breath, brushing zephyrlike past his ear, caused every one of Gordon's nerve endings to quiver. He felt Zoe's upturned palm pressing against his stomach. As discreetly as he could, he reached into his front pocket and passed the bills to her.

For an added touch of realism, Zoe planted a fleeting kiss on Gordon's lips, leaving them whetted and wanting more, while Rony studied the ground at his feet.

The vignette completed, she turned to the others. "It's not much," she said, referencing the cash, "but it'll help. And it won't get the attention of the *batsos*," which is the Greek equivalent of Americans calling the police pigs.

Wordlessly, Rony removed his backpack, partially unzipped the top, and set it at Zoe's feet. Inside was a collection of men's and women's wallets pilfered from the pockets and purses of the Plaka's visitors. His abundant haul earned for him a genuine look of appreciation and affection from Zoe, which left Gordon stung with jealousy.

"What now?" the clerk, who had had enough of the "feel good," asked. "I can't go back. The old man is a lecher, not an idiot."

"Obviously, George," Zoe answered. "There's plenty more to be done."

"Good." He walked to a nearby trash can and deposited the apron. "I hated that job."

The three Athenians began to converse in their native language. Frustrated by his lingual exclusion, Gordon interrupted their conversation. "Hold on. No more Greek. Either speak English or I'm out."

"We're sorry, but Rony's English is not so good," Zoe explained. "Let's get out of here and we'll talk."

They hopped a city bus in Syntagma Square; the scrolling green digitized sign in the front window momentarily flashed "Pireas," an area Gordon had already mentally bookmarked as a must-see destination during his time in Greece. He didn't know much about Pireas other than its status as the largest port in all of Europe and its serving as the jumping-off point to the Greek islands. These two attributes—although on a much larger scale—made Pireas somewhat reminiscent of Ogontz, and even while sitting inside the inadequately air-conditioned and crowded city bus as it made its way southwest from central Athens, Gordon could feel the atmosphere outside becoming familiar as they neared the coast.

Something simultaneously the product of man's collective primordial unconscious and of Gordon's own peculiar lakeside upbringing activated in his soul and reoriented the gyroscope that had been spun off-kilter in the headiness of the last five days' romantic reverie. The wave, which had begun its run that afternoon at the beach and had swept him headlong into the middle of a radical insurrection in a nation of no relation to his own, had finally broke. Gordon sat on the bus, dripping wet in the excitement of radicalism, and realized he had to make a choice: clamber out at the next stop, dry off, and return to his insulated American skin, or stay on board with his new comrades and ride the next wave of this nascent revolution.

A tone sounded through the speakers in the ceiling of the bus. The driver announced the stop. A cluster of exiting riders gathered at the middle double doors.

Gordon didn't move.

Zoe made eye contact with him and flashed a knowing smile.

The bus reentered the bedlam that is Athens's traffic anti-pattern.

With the reassuring understanding, which he didn't share with his new friends, that the extent of his involvement would be limited by the length of his summer vacation, he determined that the cause was exciting enough and worthy of his participation, even to the preclusion of his intention to visit the exotic Greek isles and inevitably make the conquest of their women.

For the four weeks he had remaining in his stay, he would commit himself to the Struggle and hopefully bed its dark-eyed Athena of the black spangled bikini.

*   *   *

It was easy for Gordon to bribe Hobhouse to provide the necessary corroborating cover for Ms. Martin and Catherine, and to post an occasional blog entry, and Gordon himself phoned home sporadically to describe the places he had supposedly visited—usually with a Fodor's travel guide spread open on his lap to provide the text and imagery with which he filled his descriptions. Catherine's suspicions were once aroused when her credit card statements revealed several large cash advances. In typical fashion, he berated her for the violation of his privacy and threatened to cut her off financially and filially should she continue to interfere in his personal life, and, as usual, she cowered, shriveled, and looked the other way.

By August, Gordon had abandoned Hobhouse and the hotel for a tiny unfurnished two-bedroom apartment above a fish market, an apartment he shared with the ever coming and going members of the Struggle, whose standard mode of serial occupancy was to change residences frequently, take only short-term leases, and always pay ahead in cash. If such arrangements couldn't be found, in the summer, they slept on beaches or in parks; in winter, they slept in student hostels or metro stations or, occasionally, one of their own family homes.

Gordon learned that Zoe and Rony were legitimate second-generation revolutionaries. However, except for the occasional genuinely oppressed token foot soldier, who seemed more inspired to revolution by the room, board, and hookah that the Struggle provided than by revolutionary zeal, they all were young and from middle- to upper-class backgrounds. Gordon easily identified those of aristocratic roots by the nurtured, spongy softness beneath their hard manufactured shells. They were tough talkers; he knew the type well. He'd encountered dozens of them at the Rood.

Gordon told Shelly that by then he had figured out that Zoe and Rony had pegged him as one of these disposable idealists who was ripe for manipulation. Their plan (which totally worked, by the way) all along had been to lure him with Zoe's and anarchy's sexiness, to seduce him further with the romantic life of Che Guevara, to test his commitment and pull him in deeper with the addictive thrill of deviance (knocking off the grocery), and, finally, like the others, to drain him of his money in support of the cause. But by then, he told Shelly, he didn't care.

As early as the bus ride to Pireas, Gordon consciously chose to play along. Why not? He had the time. He had the money, spawned from the biannual royalty checks for sales of *Manfred* and *Manfred*-related merchandise. He thought the cause legitimate, and he sincerely relished the role of rebel.

The plan was simple. Once the police wagon cleared the sidewalk and the gate closed behind the wagon, Rony would punch the gas pedal and pull directly into its path. The sudden acceleration would be Gordon's cue to throw open the side door of their van. Zoe and George were to fire directly into the cab at the driver and the officer riding shotgun. After opening the door, Gordon's job was to spray the front of the vehicle with gunfire, with the intention of blowing its tires, disabling its engine, and rendering it useless to pursue its attackers. By the time the police in the rear of the wagon exited, or reinforcements arrived, the Struggle members would have already driven the van to a nearby parking lot, where a stolen Land Rover would be waiting for their ditch and switch. DNA testing and modern forensics made it imperative not to leave any trace of evidence behind; therefore, they would need to change clothes in the Rover and carry their guns with them until they could be safely dismantled and disposed of. They had an email prepared to be sent to various media sources boasting responsibility for the ambush on behalf of the Struggle. It was, obviously, vital to keep their individual identities anonymous.

Gordon later told Shelly that he waited all day for Zoe and Rony to chicken out or simply to change their minds, or for some circumstance to arise and cause an abortion of the mission, but they didn't and none did. He crouched in that van with his hand on the cool metal of the latch. What at first had seemed romantic had turned real and scary.

To steel himself against his rising anxiety as he waited for his cue, Gordon repeated the mantra, "The future is past. The future is past." It helped if he put what had yet to happen in the clear and calm of retrospect. It would allow him to perform his scripted role, free from the hesitations of conscience and choice-making. "The future is past. The future is past. . . ."

As if second-guessing themselves and their role in the ambush, the rear tires of the van spun in the roadside gravel beneath him—like him, searching for the necessary traction.

Gordon says he still doesn't remember opening the van door. When the tires' rubber finally bit into the road, the van lurched suddenly forward and threw him backward with his hand still clutching the latch. The door flew open with or without his conscious intention, and the game was on.

Cliché or not, from that point on, it all happened for Gordon in slow motion.

Almost immediately, the Kalashnikovs in Zoe's and George's hands exploded with deafening reverberation inside the van. There was no hesitation in their actions. They moved with the confidence of true believers, the conviction of the converted, the faith of martyrs. Gordon watched them for what couldn't have been more than a second or two. Each on a knee, waving their weapons in a short oscillating manner. Both of their mouths were wide open. Their lips, left exposed by the holes in their masks, appeared chimpishly pink and fleshy and were stretched wide, baring their teeth and tongues. He watched as they let loose primitive howls unheard among the rat-a-tat-a-tat of their weapons.

Still clinging to the latch with his left hand, Gordon swung his right flank around so that he was firing his gun single-handedly with indiscriminate aim in the direction of the hood and undercarriage of the police wagon.

Just as suddenly as it had started, it stopped.

With the tires squealing exhilarated shouts of triumphant baptism, Rony sped from the massacre.

"Don't!" Zoe screamed at Gordon as, Orpheus-like, he stuck his head out of the still open door to look back at the hell they'd left behind. Slinging her strap-on Kalashnikov over her shoulder, she lunged and reached desperately to stop him, but it was too late.

In the fleeting glimpse Gordon stole as the van made a

hard left turn, Gordon saw the police wagon's front fender biting into the concrete street. He saw water spilling and steam rising from the radiator that his own blasts had ruptured. And having rendered the wagon immobile, he felt the momentary flush of the pride of accomplishment rush through him.

Panning upward, peering through the jagged frame of shards of glass where the windshield of the wagon used to be, Gordon saw the top of the driver's head with blood-matted hair slumped over the steering wheel, and the inside of the cab splattered with pinkish matter. Scanning to the left, the officer who had been riding shotgun was still strapped in by his shoulder belt but was virtually headless, except for the mushy ruins.

Then, it all went black.

There was light again as the stunned Gordon was shepherded from the van into the Land Rover, where Zoe ripped the stocking cap off over his head and began to strip him of his clothing. She was already free from her disguise. Again, she wore the black bikini top, shorts, and sandals.

"I can do it myself," he said, coming to his senses.

"You must hurry. Get down behind the seat," Zoe commanded him.

In the front passenger seat, he saw George crouched on the floor beneath the dashboard. To Gordon's right, Zoe was crouching.

Gordon discarded his outer layers of clothing, which Zoe gathered and stuffed into her beach bag that already bulged from her own and George's clothes. In his white tank top and blue and white floral board shorts, Gordon lay across the

243

backseat, invisible to the outside. From the streets and side-walks, Rony appeared to be the only one inside the vehicle.

The configuration of their bodies placed Gordon's glassy eyes in direct line with the steely gray of Zoe's, but she looked through him, not at him. Gordon's thoughts wallowed in the horrific events of the just past. Hers remained Lady Macbeth–like, focused on present exigencies and future necessities. Her performance in the previous five minutes had "unsexed" her in Gordon's eyes. Her behavior hadn't been so much manly as reptilian, cold-blooded, and cruel. He could no longer re-member what he had found so alluring in her. The thought of making love to her became repulsive.

The plan was to dump the vehicle, then scatter and in-dependently make their ways to the beach at Glyfada (where Gordon had first encountered Zoe). There, they'd reunite, stake out a spot, build a fire like many other beachgoers, and spend the remainder of the night burning their clothing and dismantling and dumping their weapons in the ocean.

Gordon never made it to Glyfada, nor did he ever see the others again.

Hobhouse was sound asleep in his room at the Inter-Continental, butt-naked and napping with arms and legs outstretched like a prone Leonardo da Vinci's *Vitruvian Man*.

"Christ, Hobby. You've put on fifteen pounds."

"Twenty-five," Hobhouse said, wiping the sleep from his eyes, cobwebs from his brain, and vestiges of cream sauce from his lips. "You don't look so hot yourself."

Gordon had lost weight in the nearly four weeks they'd

been apart. His hair had grown unruly, and he hadn't shaved since the night on which he'd met Zoe and Rony in the café.

"We've got to go," Gordon said.

"Go? Go where?"

"Home."

"We are home."

"I mean home, home." Gordon began to gather articles of Hobhouse's clothing from the floor and to form a pile on the foot of the bed.

"What? What about—"

"What about nothing," Gordon said. "We're going home. I've already booked us on a red-eye to Kennedy. Now get your fat ass moving."

"But . . . ," Hobhouse began, but abruptly ended his protest. The dream was over.

It was Shelly who received Gordon's call from New York asking to be picked up at the Detroit Metro Airport, where his connecting flight would be landing that afternoon.

When he emerged from behind the tinted glass of the automatic sliding doors to baggage claim, he was met by Shelly and Claire, who was already five months pregnant but only beginning to show. He shot Shelly a "What the fuck?" look as she came around the rear driver's side of her father's Suburban, but she adroitly dodged the shoot-to-kill stare, ran to him, and hugged him, full of appreciation that he had asked her to meet him. Shelly rose onto her tiptoes and threw her arms around his neck, which he'd shaved during his New York layover.

Shelly whispered, "She wanted to come," as if that explanation would suffice to ease his consternation. Somehow, it did.

"So Shelly," thought Gordon, "to bring along Claire." Unlike most people, Shelly didn't love religiously, in a worshipful and covetous way, demanding exclusivity. She was willing, even eager, to share all whom she loved, believing love not to be a finite pie with only so many slices to go around but infinite and endless manna from the universe. She believed that love generated itself forever anew, and expanded in ever-widening circles unless, as is typically the case, it was impeded by the petty jealousies and the small-mindedness of the majority, who have been brainwashed by parents and churches and governments, competing for their slices of allegiance and affection.

Holding Shelly by the elbows at arm's length, Gordon looked her up and down and drank in the satisfying taste of the familiar. Her skin, golden brown, as if she'd spent every second of summer vacation out of doors, set off the snow-whiteness of her teeth inside the first genuine smile Gordon had seen in a long time. A smile for which he was sure his return was only partly responsible. She had summer secrets to tell that would explain her rejuvenation from the mysterious gloom of the previous winter and spring. He wanted to hear them, but not until he had unburdened himself of his own sinful summer tales.

Speeding south and then east on Midwestern interstates, and with his own special flair for poetic license, Gordon regaled the girls with stories of his European adventures, at least right up to the final day. That he'd save for Shelly alone, to barter it for her secrets.

They wanted to hear it all: the book signings, the famous places he'd seen, the people he'd met. He told them of his reenactment of Leander's swim, the beaches and beauties, the Grecian nightlife, the shrine of Poseidon, the Macri sisters, and he told them of the anarchist friends he had made and with whom he'd stayed for a while in Pireas. Claire was oblivious to the Peloponnesian War, so, much less was she aware or interested in the civil unrest occurring in modern-day Athens. But with Shelly's years of experience reading Gordon's body language and decoding the inflections in his voice, she communicated with knowing eyes her understanding that there was more to the story to be shared later.

At Kennedy, Gordon had picked up a USA Today and found only a paragraph under the headline "Leftist Group Claims Responsibility for Attack." An unidentified Greek authority spoke of the probability of future unrest propagated by anarchist groups of the extreme left, but he also expressed doubt that the group, responsible for the murder of the two officers and identifying itself as the Struggle, had yet to establish a significant membership or to create the infrastructure necessary to pose a "consistent or serious threat beyond relatively minor and cowardly acts of terrorism." Clearly, the "authority" was chumming. The article contained no mention of individual suspects in the ambush, but the investigation was ongoing.

* * *

That night, having ditched Claire, Gordon and Shelly sat, side touching side, at the end of his dock. Gordon's feet dangled ankle-deep in the still water; Shelly, legs crossed at the ankles, swung hers a few inches above it. For a long time, they sat silently. Their internal antennae tuned to the universe, they'd lost all sense of self and of the bullshit of the world beyond the dock. Shelly broke the spell with a laugh of remembrance, and for a while they recounted the summers of their childhood, but they grew pensive when the conversation advanced to their impending senior year and the choices it would demand they make in the fashioning of some future beyond Ogontz and, most likely, each other.

Wanting to savor every delectable second of the Gordon-filled present before he'd spin out of her orbit once again, she said, "So tell me the rest of the story."

"What story?" Gordon played coy.

"These friends you made in Athens. The girl in the black bikini and the others."

Gordon told her everything with no sense of shame or fear of being betrayed or consideration for Shelly's feelings for him. He began with the "chance" encounters with Zoe at the beach and at the sidewalk café and his immediate infatuation with her. With a passionate zeal, if not with total conviction, he told her of his reading of *Che* and of his newfound "sympathy for the plight of the masses, who, worldwide, continue to be systematically victimized by the very institutions in which they place their hopes for justice and a decent standard of living." He told her of knocking off the grocery store.

He told her of the other members of the Struggle, of the stinking apartment above the fish market, of the weapons they'd collected and the bombs they intended to build and to detonate. Then, he stopped short.

Although she was conflicted by the pride she felt over the social consciousness seemingly awakened in her previously pathologically egocentric best friend, contrasted with the revulsion to the Struggle's preference for violence, Shelly knew there was still more to tell, and she urged on his confession. "And?" she prodded.

Gordon hesitated in his response.

"And," he began, then stopped again, then began once more. "Shelly, you can't tell anyone. I mean it. This is some serious shit."

(Of course, Shelly told me. But you know how that goes. *"I promised I wouldn't tell anyone, so you can't tell anybody else."* Eventually, everyone and their brother tells only one other person until the entire school or town knows the secret. Luckily for Gordon, I really didn't have anyone else to tell.)

It was the only time in her life, she said, that she saw Gordon completely vulnerable; the only time she was 100 percent sure that he was telling an absolute truth untainted by ulterior motives.

To reassure him of her complete trustworthiness and to lighten the tension of the moment, Shelly reminded him of the blood oath they'd sworn when they were kids, and she declared the covenant still binding.

"We killed two cops." He vomited the words as if they'd

been rising repeatedly from his gorge for the past forty-eight hours, swishing around his mouth and gagging him with their acidic truth, demanding to be spit out, only to be forcefully swallowed and temporarily restored inside his poisoned bowels.

Shelly's face washed pale; she'd just been made an accomplice. Stupidly, she responded, "Oh."

Gordon rushed to plug the holes sprung in Shelly's reservoir of faith in him. "I said 'we,' but I didn't actually kill anybody. They did. Zoe and George, or whatever their names really are." Even in his own ears his plea of innocence sounded inane. "I know. It was stupid."

"Stupid? Defacing a national treasure is stupid. Being conned by firm boobs and a round ass is stupid. Robbing a store is stupid. Murder is criminal; it's evil. What am I supposed to do with this?"

"Shell, I don't know what I was thinking."

"I do. You were thinking about getting off that black bikini." She attempted to hide her disgust. "For such a smart guy, Gordon, sometimes you are so predictable." For Shelly, "predictable" was about as pathetic a label as a person could have.

"You're right. I'm not going to lie. I did want her, but I'm telling you, it was more than that."

Shelly wanted to believe him more than you can possibly know. "Go on."

"It happened fast. One minute I was crouched inside the van; the next I was looking at what was left of two dead cops' heads splattered inside the truck."

"What then?"

"I left," Gordon said. "We were supposed to rendezvous, but I bolted. Seeing those two cops changed everything."

"What? Guilt? Shame? Utter self-loathing?"

Gordon looked at her like she was the crazy one.

"No. I *liked* it too much. The adrenaline high was incredible. I couldn't believe I'd been a part of something so . . . so . . . cool. That's not the word. Radical, extreme. I don't know, but I realized that I've got too much shit to do before I go and play martyr for someone else's cause—noble or not. When I saw those cops wasted, I knew that if I rejoined the Struggle, I'd go all in. Instead, I got on the first plane I could and called you as soon as I arrived in New York."

"They got away with it, then?"

"As far as I know."

"You're a fugitive, Gordon." She couldn't believe that she was the one giving voice to reason. "When they're caught—and they will be, you know—one of them will identify you, if for no other reason than the attention it will draw to their cause."

"I know. I thought about that. What am I going to do, Shell?"

"Get a lawyer. That agent lady must know someone."

"I thought about that too. I can't. They'll want me to narc out my friends and to cut some kind of deal. I can't do that. I'm not a snitch."

"Then you better hope the black bikini and her gang don't get caught, and don't be surprised when your 'friends' contact you and blackmail you for more money. They've got you, Gordo. Looks like you got your wish after all. That Zoe chick fucked you big-time."

"It's not funny, Shelly."

With typical Gordonian disregard for segue, he asked, "What about you? What's with the sunny disposition? When I left, you'd gone all Sylvia Plath and shit."

"Ha-ha," she said, but Shelly had been waiting for this opportunity for a long time. For her own emotional well-being, she needed to share with somebody the events that had culminated in her still-to-remain-a-secret-to-Gordon abortion that I had crashed the previous December. And Gordon was the only person who might understand, and with whom she could trust her secret shame—well, most of it, anyway.

A thick cloud cover blocked the moonlight. Shelly was grateful for the tar black of the August night; it rendered them nearly invisible to one another, reducing each to a puny voice struggling to penetrate the darkness. Emboldened by the near opacity, Shelly shared a story that, had Gordon been visible, would have caused her to see the typically impervious Gordon Byron turn red with embarrassment, rage, and disgust.

"You know my father," Shelly began rhetorically.

"Asshole," Gordon said curtly and matter-of-factly.

"Not always," she reacted. "He wasn't always."

"To me he was . . . is."

It wasn't argument that Shelly sought.

"He never liked me," Gordon continued. "Since we were kids, he always hated me. As if everything was my fault. Like I—"

"He raped me," Shelly blurted, stopping Gordon mid-rant.

Nature's evening choir filled the interval of his shocked disbelief with the intermittent croaking of frogs singing bass harmony to the melodious tenor chirping of the crickets.

"He what?"

"Please, Gordon. Don't make me say it again."

Gordon scrambled to his feet. "He can't get away with it."

Rising to her knees, Shelly groped above herself in the darkness until she found a balled fist and pulled him back to the surface of the dock with both of her hands. "Sit down, Gordon. He has, and he will." She sobbed. Tears fell in torrents. "I didn't tell you so that you would go all knight-in-shining-armor and defend my honor or make some kind of ridiculous scene."

"Then why did you tell me? What do you want me to do?"

"I don't want you to *do* anything! It's not about you doing something or some*one*." Sniffles punctuated each sentence. "I just needed to tell somebody. I needed to tell *you*. Because sometimes I think it never happened. I start to think I made it all up, or it was a nightmare, or my fault. And I need to know that I'm not crazy, and to remember that it *was* real. And, for his own good, every time he looks at me, my father needs to know that I remember and that he's responsible. But I need someone else to know and to help *me* to remember."

"But, Shell, it's sick. He's sick. He needs help."

"No. It's not like that. It only happened once, and something good has come from it."

"Oh, Christ! You've got to be kidding me. Do you even hear what you're saying?"

"It was the drinking, and since that night, he hasn't been drinking anymore. Besides, I don't think he even meant it."

"Didn't mean it? You can't be serious! You can't accidentally . . . do that."

"I *am* serious. My mother's been dead for nearly my whole life. Since then my father has never"—she hesitated, searching for the appropriate euphemism—"*been with* another woman."

"How do you even know that?"

"I just do. He misses my mother so much. I get that. It's the only thing we've ever had in common. You've seen pictures of my mother, Gordon. You know how much I look like her. That night, I think he stumbled into my room by mistake."

Gordon looked confused. "When was this?"

"Last October, the night of the Halloween dance. Remember? That was the night I was with Brandon Sullivan after the dance. I'm sure you heard the rumors."

Gordon winced. "Aw, Shelly."

"Anyway, when I sat up in bed, he called me by my mother's name. I tried talking to him, telling him it was me, Shelly. I tried screaming. He didn't listen or stop. He just kept calling me Mary, and . . . when he finished, he passed out on top of me." She paused, remembering. "That was the worst part." Shelly stared off into the darkness at the red lights of the marker buoys bobbing on the surface of the deep channel, traveled by the massive freighters that took on thousands of tons of coal at the Ogontz docks. "I couldn't move him or get myself out from underneath him," Shelly continued. "His weight pressed down on me. Alcohol oozed from his pores and breath. The scruff of his beard scratched my face and neck. His . . . his . . . thing pressed sticky and wet between my thighs. I just lay there, staring at the ceiling and crying."

"I don't know what to say, Shell," Gordon said.

"When he woke up, he must have been sober. He raised himself up and turned his face to look at me. For less than a second, I think he still thought I was his wife. Then— Gordon, if you could have seen his face—he recognized me and realized what he had done. He tried to say something; his lips quivered, but no words came out. He rolled off me and pulled up his pants with his back toward me. When he got to my bedroom door, he looked back as if to speak, but didn't. We haven't spoken a word to each other since. He won't talk to me; he won't come anywhere near me. Within weeks, he married Mary Jane, although he hardly knew her. I think it was his way of guarding against it ever happening again."

There was a pause as Gordon tried to absorb what he'd heard, and Shelly dried her face with her shirt. A light, moist breeze began to blow across the bay, turning their arms and legs to gooseflesh. Above, the once dense cloud cover thinned, allowing the moon to emit a luminous glow.

"Wow," he finally said. "I guess that explains the whole Plath phase."

"But I'm better now," Shelly said. "Way better."

"Yeah. What's up with the 'shiny happy people' routine?"

"Shut up, Gordon. Don't make fun. You know I love that song."

"I know it, but I'll never accept it."

"Do you remember that night—we were sitting right

here—when you told me about Annesley and how much you loved her?"

"Yeah, I remember," Gordon said sheepishly, as if embarrassed by his short-lived romantic period.

"Well, now *I'm* in love, and I'm happy. I didn't believe I *could* be this happy."

Gordon's gut didn't wrench. His eyes didn't turn green, nor his face red. Shelly said he seemed more disappointed than anything. She said it was simply as if Gordon could already see how it would end, and it wasn't going to be good.

"I guess that explains it," he said.

While Gordon had been gallivanting around Europe and Greece that summer, Shelly had been experiencing her own quixotic adventure. Her father's guilt-inspired avoidance of her provided Shelly with carte blanche freedom of movement. What few limitations had ever existed on her comings and goings were completely lifted. No itineraries needed to be filed; no "check-in" phone calls placed; no curfews enforced. Generous amounts of spending money regularly appeared on her nightstand.

For her part, Mary Jane had abdicated any claim to parental authority long ago, when, shortly after she'd moved in with Claire and Frances, she'd asked Shelly to "do something about your appearance." The black outfits, self-shorn hair, and black eyeliner were "bringing me down," she'd said.

"Why don't you and Claire go on a little shopping date? It'll be fun," You-can-call-me Mary Jane had said. "She can help you with a makeover! You just watch how the boys come calling."

Shelly had flipped her the finger. They hadn't spoken since.

That summer, Shelly spent many more nights on a sleeping bag on the floor of the old farmhouse near to Neolin than she spent in her own bed. After opting to replace her sailboat, her primary means of transportation to and from the island, with the sixteen-foot Boston Whaler powerboat, a belated seventeenth-birthday present from her father that appeared one day at their dock with the key in the ignition, she came home only when she needed a good shower, or to collect odds and ends: additional clothes, eating utensils, books, and the provisions uniquely required by a female squatter.

The Ottawa settlers had quickly established a congenial relationship with the merchants of Put-in-Bay. Since no one really gave a damn about the sham nature preserve on North Bass, the locals considered the Ottawa harmless—at least for the time being. All branches of law enforcement, from local to federal, regarded any heavy-handed crackdown as a potential public relations nightmare. The unofficial policy was to play nice and wait out the Ottawa, at least until they'd proven that they could withstand the claustrophobia of an ice-locked winter, or until Ohio's voters passed legislation to allow casino gambling and recognized the Bass Islands as the perfect location for such gaming houses. Said legislation was set to be included on November's ballot.

On the first of June, a relief company of Ottawa tribes-men arrived. Their sensibilities were more sympathetic to Neolin's aims, and their personalities were more amenable to accepting leadership. The constant complaining of the initial settlers over the lack of modern conveniences disap-peared. Life on the island improved significantly. The tent city in the front yard was exchanged for dormitory-style liv-ing inside the farmhouse, and civilization arrived in the reestablished capital of the Ottawa Nation when the cistern and septic tank were made operational. Shelly's own seem-ingly indomitable spirit of revolution had almost been bro-ken during her first extended stay on the island, almost broken by the sharing of an outhouse with ten men. Happi-ness is running water.

In addition to cell phones (service was shoddy on the island anyway), Neolin conceded to the use of Shelly's lap-top for monitoring events on the mainland and for commu-nication purposes, and he pretended ignorance of the portable DVD/CD player that Shelly smuggled back with her on one of her runs home.

By the end of June, the garden was beginning to show promise for a bountiful harvest. Although the farmhouse was in dire need of a paint job, the major repairs had all been made, the grounds spruced up, and the bowed boards on the dock replaced. Though less frequent in their patronage of the Put-in-Bay nightlife, the second wave of settlers maintained positive relations with their suppliers in the village. Shelly and Neolin established a division of labor that required each community member, including themselves, to rotate through the more menial jobs—such as housework and yard work, cooking and cleaning—and the more enjoyable task of taking the Kodiak rafts to South Bass for supply runs.

All were expected to attend the communal evening meals, which served as social, planning, and bitch sessions. The most common topic was when to expand the compound and to allow for the reverse migration of a larger cross-section of the Ottawa population, namely women and children. Some of the men had grown mildly envious that Neolin, as de facto leader, had the benefit of Shelly's companionship. To all observers, if not vocalized or physically acted upon by the two of them, the relationship appeared romantic—a perception the men shared with good-natured teasing of the couple.

Happy with the fast progress of the nation, Neolin was reluctant to initiate the reverse migration and inject such a radical change into the dynamic that had been effectively established. But the men's concern had inspired two realizations: one, it was necessary for him to surrender the mantle of leadership in order to meld into and become completely of the people in the true spirit of the Way; and two, he was falling in love. A consensus of opinion determined that a request would be made to the chief and tribal council in Oklahoma that the council discuss the matter of further settlement and deliver its opinion on the repopulation of North Bass in a timely manner.

Neolin didn't expect a quick or favorable response. Throughout the resettlement process, communication with the tribal council had been suspiciously irregular. He optimistically told himself that the elders were confident in his leadership and supportive of his mission, but his other read was that they were completely indifferent to his utopian dream of nation-building. He preferred the former interpretation but suspected the latter to be closer to the truth.

One late mid-August afternoon, when the humidity chased the heat to nearly unlivable heights, Neolin and Shelly each grabbed a towel and hiked through the woods to the small sandy beach that Shelly had followed him to on the day when she'd first crashed his revolution. Sapped by the heat, the lake lay flat, with a curtain of haze rising from its slow-to-boil water. Neolin stripped down to his boxers and Shelly to her mismatched white bra and purple panties, and, facing toward the seemingly boundless Canadian waters, they cooled themselves by lolling in the nearshore shallows, because the Oklahoma boy couldn't swim.

"I can't believe it," he said.

"What's that?" Shelly asked, although she knew exactly what he meant.

"Any of it. This place. My plan actually working. You."

"I know. It's kind of great," she said.

"It can't be real. It can't last. It can't really work. Can it?"

"Why not? Why can't we be happy? Why can't we do anything we want? Why can't we change the world?"

"But what if it only works here? You know what I mean? What if this is some magic place where the regular rules don't apply, and the second we leave here, none of it will continue or have ever happened?"

"Then we'll never leave," Shelly said.

"I don't plan to, but you start your senior year in two weeks."

"I'll be eighteen soon. I can sign my own dropout papers."

"I can't let you do that. Besides, what would your father say?" Neolin probed the exposed family nerve gingerly, for fear of being cross-examined regarding his own dysfunctional childhood spent with an alcoholic mother, and never knowing his "just passing through" Delaware father, who'd made him a half-bred target for ridicule among his mother's Ottawa people. But Neolin was curious as to the mysterious man whose generosity toward his daughter had been redirected toward Neolin's cause.

"He probably wouldn't *say* anything. I told you we don't talk."

"Yeah, but you've never told me why."

Shelly hesitated, weighing the pluses and minuses of that explanation, then concluded, "Another time."

"I really wish you *could* stay here, but you have to go back. You'll regret it if you don't, and, someday, you will blame me."

"But I'm happy here," she said in the pleading voice of a child.

"If only it was as simple as that." Neolin thought for a moment before turning to look at her leaning backward, exposed and vulnerable, with her palms pressed flat in the sand beneath the wrist-deep water. Her hair was wet, pasted back over her ears and against her neck. Her legs were splayed out in front of her with only her toes exposed like a chain of tiny islands. The silky fabric of her saturated bra, with the right strap draped loosely off her shoulder, clung tightly to her breasts. Compelled, he rolled onto his hip and leaned toward her. Shelly remained still, welcoming him in. She met his mouth firmly, and, with the conviction of the newly baptized, they kissed for the first, and only, time.

Despite Shelly's plea to extend their getaway, wisely, Neolin rose, dripping, from the water, dried off, and got dressed.

"Come on." He beckoned her with an outstretched hand. "The men will talk, then tease me to no end if we don't get back."

"Only if you promise that the next time we'll pick up right where we left off."

"I promise," he said.

Holding hands and laughing as they broke through the wood line where it met the front-yard clearing of the compound, they came to a sudden stop. A look of stunned disbelief fell across Neolin's face as Shelly's washed pale.

"They're here," he said.

Shelly immediately recognized all but one of the Ottawa men standing near the dock. It was the original group of settlers, along with a portly middle-aged man wearing blue jeans and cowboy boots despite the August heat.

"Who's the fat one?" Shelly asked.

"The chief."

"What's he doing here?"

"I don't know, but it can't be good," Neolin said in an ominous tone.

"Maybe he wants to see the progress we've made," Shelly offered.

"I hope you're right, but I don't think so."

As Neolin finished his sentence, the chief's eyes found the two of them, and a smile, as phony as a politician's in primary season, spread across his ruddy pockmarked face. Immediately he began a tottering march to where they stood. Behind him, the old and the current settlers intermingled, exchanging greetings and shaking hands before moving purposefully toward the house.

With a big paw extended, the chief reapplied his gap-toothed smile, and from still twenty yards away, he called, "Gabriel—"

"Neolin," Neolin interrupted the chief. "My name is Neolin."

"Huh?" the chief said, perplexed, before remembering. "Oh, that's right. Neolin, how are you?" He offered his meaty palm for shaking.

"I'm good," Neolin answered. "What can we do for you? Why are you here?" His tone bordered on being insolent.

"This is Odawa land. And you seem to have forgotten that I'm the chief."

Sufficiently humbled, Neolin lowered his gaze and apologized.

Shelly interrupted their pissing contest by loudly clearing her throat.

"This is Shelly. She's been helping." Neolin made the introduction.

The chief didn't bother to acknowledge her.

"*Boozhoo,*" Shelly said, undeterred, using her Ottawa greeting.

Neolin's eyes snapped to her. Shelly described that it was as if the word had reset his mind to the day when she'd first arrived at the dock and she'd greeted him in the identical fashion. He started to say something, but as his mouth formed the words, from the corner of his eye he saw the men, past and present, carrying supplies from the house toward the dock.

"Wait!" he called. "What are you doing?" He took a step in their direction, but the chief positioned his bulk between Neolin and the house.

"It's over," the chief said with unquestionable finality.

Shelly said she had never seen such sorrow possess a person's face so immediately as it did Neolin's upon those two words.

Ignoring the chief's claim, Neolin tried to work his way past him. But the big man was surprisingly light on his feet and strong of arm. He easily corralled Neolin and kept him at bay. The evacuation continued as Neolin crumpled to the grass at the chief's feet and wept the tears of the defeated and dying.

The chief turned to Shelly and commanded with no equivocation, "Go home."

They were the words of a father, spoken in an authoritative tone, which she had never heard until that very moment. It began a momentum deep inside her that she was unable to stop. She said that she remembered walking slowly toward the Whaler with her head turned back and her eyes glued on the weeping Neolin, who never, whether out of shame or resignation, lifted his eyes or hand to convey goodbye.

*   *   *

"That was a week ago this morning," Shelly told Gordon then, and told me just a few hours later. The sun was already coming up on a new day behind them and casting their small shadows onto the surface of the bay. The sky was clear and blue; it was going to be a beautiful day. The previous day's humidity had been chased away by the overnight breeze. Shelly and Gordon had been talking all night. "I haven't heard from him since. Gordon, I'm worried."

"I can see that," he said. "I'm sure it will be okay," Gordon said, more dismissively than sympathetically.

In the next instant, suddenly inspired, Shelly sprang to her feet. "Wait here," she ordered Gordon.

"What? Where you going?"

Ignoring his questions, she sprinted toward her family property, across the dew-drenched grass and the fence-enclosed inground pool that lay between the bay and her house. In the murky light of morning, Gordon watched her enter the combined cabana/pool supply shed and emerge with her boom box the size of a large suitcase.

"Oh, shit," he said out loud.

Upon returning, she read the chagrin in his expression. "C'mon, Gordon. Like when we were kids."

She didn't wait for or want his opinion. She placed the boom box at their feet, pressed play, grabbed Gordon by his two limp-wristed hands, and performed a sort of waltzy maneuver and spin beneath his noodly arms as several string-dominant measures of an orchestral tune blew from the speakers at a decibel level that threatened to wake both of their pathetic excuses for parents.

Suddenly, the orchestra was replaced by an infectiously upbeat melody and the voice of R.E.M.'s Michael Stipe singing what sounded much like a children's song in both tune and lyrics: "Shiny happy people laughing . . ." Shelly joined in the singing, released Gordon's hands, and danced around his maypole rigidity, hippie-like, spinning and twirling in her bare feet with her arms over her head, singing through the first verse.

"C'mon, Gordon, sing with me," she pleaded. "'Shiny happy people holding hands,'" she sang along to the refrain.

Over her head, Gordon watched a light switch on in what he knew to be her father's bedroom window. It was followed by the appearance of his stout figure standing and watching between glass and curtain, nearly filling the window's width.

Their eyes locked. Even at that distance, Gordon's expression betrayed his knowledge of Shelly's father's heinous deed.

In spite and with gusto, Gordon joined Shelly in the second verse as she continued her dance, oblivious to her father's ocular presence.

He soon disappeared inside the room, and Gordon stopped singing as Shelly finished the song and dance and collapsed to the dock, pulling Gordon down with her, laughing.

In her giddiness, Shelly failed to hear the gears grinding in the clocklike machinery of Gordon's head as he considered Neolin's threat to what Gordon believed to be his own rightful place at the top of Shelly's hierarchy of affection. He wondered what, if anything, he could or should do about it.

Exhausted from their singing and dancing, recounting their summers passed, and sharing emotional catharses, Gordon and Shelly lay down side by side on their backs on the earth, watching the moon beginning its descent from its teeter-totter top as the sun continued its ascent behind them.

"I'm glad you're back, Gordo."

"Me too. I missed you, Shell."

Minutes of silence passed. They rose and hugged.

"Talk later?" Shelly asked.

"Talk later."

Then they set out on their separate paths to the back entrances of their respective homes. Midway to his door, Gordon called out to her, "And I don't just mean this summer. I mean all these years since we were kids and have kind of gone our own ways. I mean it. I've missed you."

Shelly stopped abruptly. In the slowly advancing light of dawn, she studied his face for any sign of sarcasm, but his emotion seemed, for once, to be unequivocal and genuine. "Thanks, Gordon. That really means a lot."

"No problem," he said.

They turned and walked on.

"Hey, Shell," he called, stopping her one more time.

"What?" Shelly returned through the laughter of mock exasperation.

"I love you."

Gordon disappeared inside his screened-in back porch, leaving Shelly standing frozen, slack-jawed, with her flip-flops dangling from her hand.

Still attempting to rescue her heart from the flash flood of emotions Gordon's declaration had unleashed, Shelly entered the downstairs kitchen, where she found her father, Mary Jane, and Claire all seated at the kitchen table. Claire and Mary Jane had clearly been crying, and her father wore a grave expression.

"What?" Shelly asked, assuming that she was the cause of their chagrin.

Then a second tidal wave struck.

"Claire's pregnant by that Byron boy," Mary Jane said, breaking into a dramatic show of convulsive sobbing, and throwing her arms around her daughter.

No longer able to conceal her "baby bump," Claire had been forced to confess her pregnancy to her mother and stepfather. Surprising to all, except Shelly, who knew that her father's right to moral indignation had been forever relinquished, Mr. Shelley made no bellicose show of anger. Although, clearly, he detested Gordon's self-insertion into the Shelley family sphere.

Shelly looked directly into Claire's eyes. "Does Gordon know?"

"I haven't been able to talk to him alone yet. You had him all night," Claire said before letting go another barrage of tears.

Shelly rolled her eyes.

"When Mommy noticed my belly this morning," Claire continued, "I had to tell her. Oh, Shelly, Gordon will answer *your* call. Could you . . ."

Shelly didn't wait for Claire to finish her request. There was no more to hear or to say. It was all so Gordon.

As she exited the kitchen, Shelly heard Mary Jane comforting Claire by assuring her of the "cute selection of maternity clothes available for expectant mothers these days." And she raved about how "the upstairs guest room will make an adorable nursery."

Despite Claire's claims of loving Gordon, she was forbidden to see him. Although the likelihood was light-years beyond the planet Remote, should Gordon demand them, there was little that the Shelleys could do to deny his rights as a father, but they were under no such obligation to welcome him into their already-dysfunctional-beyond-belief family. Regardless of whether Gordon embraced the role of father or not, the Shelleys would insist that he provide his share of financial support. Through the machinations of his attorneys, however, as of this writing, Gordon has yet to accept his paternity or to take the test that would condemn him to it, financially or otherwise.

Even for Shelly, Claire's pregnancy was so egregious as to severely limit their already-marginal sisterhood.

Initially, Shelly believed that, should Gordon be the father, her choice of Neolin over Gordon would be easy. However, as Gordon vehemently denied his guilt and she, as in all things, believed him, Shelly's lifelong store of love for Gordon weighed heavily in her decision-making.

17

Poised for its demolition duty, a bulldozer sat in the side yard like a dog made to wait with a treat resting on its nose until given permission to eat by its sadistic master. Stapled to trees, to the remains of a wooden fence, and to the pilings of the dismantled dock, cardboard signs with garish orange letters on a black background warned "No Trespassing!" Strips of tattered and limp yellow crime scene tape still hung, knotted to the front screen door handle and around several pillars on the porch. Entering the compound, catching our breath, and eyeing our surroundings, Gordon and I stopped and exchanged dubious looks. He had forgotten his pledge to jump immediately into the lake for a cool, cleansing bath.

The circling plane that had caused our mad dash had flown off without landing at the airstrip. Although it was only midmorning, swampy heat had descended and mercilessly accelerated the pace of our fast-diminishing personal hygiene. We were more than twenty-four hours removed from a shower, and our deodorants had finally punched out after pulling overtime shifts. With our teeth unbrushed, dress shirts pit-stained and wrinkled, pants dust-covered and tattered at the cuffs, and shoes pretty much totaled, the possibility of running water and toiletries left behind inside the farmhouse was far more alluring than the prospect of crossing through the death scene before us was dissuasive.

We climbed the steps, tiptoeing around the indelible once-red-now-brown stain that lay in frozen cascade from the porch down over the first two steps to where the blood must have pooled on the bottom one. A pink flier, issued by the Ottawa County Housing Authority, declared the house condemned. All the windows had been boarded shut with plywood sheets, including the one through which the tear gas canister had been launched. Desperate for refreshment and relief from the direct heat of the sun, Gordon kicked in the front door. After he had set the boom box on the sawhorse table next to a box of odds and ends and I had put Shelly down on an upturned milk crate, our efforts were rewarded by the discovery of cold water, still trickling through reluctant pipes to the kitchen sink, where we took turns rinsing out our mouths.

After washing, we walked solemnly around the completely unfurnished first floor, sharing the stale remains of a tattered plastic sleeve of saltines, which I'd found in an otherwise empty cupboard. Scattered mice droppings inside the cupboard and on the countertop indicated on whose leftovers we were feeding. The air was stifling, but it was still a relief to escape the sun.

"Look," I said, pointing to a single bullet hole in the wall that separated the "parlor" from the dining room. Long since removed, the bullet had frayed the wallpaper before lodging in a two-by-four stud. Tiny remnants of wood shavings and drywall—most likely from when detectives had dug out the bullet—still piled on the floor beneath the hole among scattered shards of window glass. Our heads turned in unison, following the .308-caliber round's reverse journey, from its temporary home in the wall, through the now boarded-up windowpane, the side of Neolin's head as he'd emerged onto the porch, across the front yard, to the verge of the tree line, and back into the womb barrel of the sniper's rifle.

"Just think of the horror story that bullet could tell," Gordon said as we stood in silent contemplation.

"How did this happen?" I asked.

The question was rhetorical, but he answered anyway. "This is what happens when you care too much."

Mindlessly, I began rooting through a box of stuff on the table: a few books, pens and pencils, and an old-fashioned pirate's spyglass. Then I saw Shelly's portable DVD player inside its leather case.

"Check this out!" I said.

Gordon immediately understood the cause of my enthusiasm and pulled the stowaway DVD from his pocket. "Let's play it. Find out whatever the fuck it is she wanted us to see so badly."

I removed the player from the case and slid the power switch to the on position. The amber-lit power indicator immediately blinked a distress signal to warn of its low battery.

"Hurry," I said, opening the maw of the player for Gordon to slip in the disc, whose revolutions whirred complainingly when I pressed play.

On the eight-inch screen, a pair of a young man's legs, shown only from the knees down, in brown dress slacks and shoes, descended a fancy staircase.

Gordon, recognizing the scene immediately, laughed.

Confused, I asked, "What is it?"

"Just watch," he said.

In the bottom left corner, the title *Harold and Maude* appeared, followed almost immediately by the slightly palm-muted strumming of opening guitar chords beneath the tinkling cascade of high register piano keys that begin Cat Stevens's infectious "Don't Be Shy."

Gordon's face could barely contain his smile. "So fucking Shelly," he said. "She loved that movie."

The battery ran out and the disc spun to a stop before the end of the first verse, and before the camera had panned upward to reveal Harold.

The screen went black.

I reached for the eject button but Gordon's hand stopped me. "Don't," he said. "Leave it." He snapped the lid closed. With fingers lingering and tracing slow circles against the player's hard plastic cover, he lost himself for a moment inside thoughts or memories, before finally ejecting the disc himself and returning it to the case.

A slow-dropping awareness of the world outside entered the room in the form of a fast-approaching roar.

"Do you hear that?" I asked.

"Hear what?"

"That noise?"

Tilting his ear toward the still open front door, Gordon said, "A boat. A big boat."

We ran to the door and looked out past the dock toward the north, where we could see a cigarette boat, at least forty feet long, with its bow high out of the water and throwing a massive wake as it sped directly toward us.

"Get that . . ." Gordon hesitated, not sure of the word. "That pirate thing out of the box."

"The spyglass?"

"Yeah. Get it."

"Do you recognize the boat?" I said, handing him the spyglass.

"Not sure." He extended it to its full length. "Shit!"

"What?" I said. "Who is it? Coast guard? The police?"

"No. Just who I thought it would be. It's him. Shelly's father."

"Who? How could he know?" I was panicking, betraying my fear. I had never been in trouble before. "Why wouldn't he just call the police?"

Gordon lowered the spyglass. "The plane must have spotted us after all and radioed to him on his boat. Trust me, he wants nothing to do with the police," he added.

"What are we going to do?" I asked. I was on the verge of a complete meltdown.

"We're going to finish what we came here to do. That's what." He spoke with such matter-of-fact conviction that it immediately calmed my nerves.

"But how? He'll be here in a few minutes."

"That boat's too big for what's left of this little dock out front here. He'll have to go clear around to the marina. By then, we'll have done right by Shelly, but we can't waste any more time." He took a deep breath, turned to me, and smiled that Gordon Byron smile that betrayed just how much he enjoyed being him, betrayed his complete self-assurance that no matter how things turned out, he'd be just fine. "Let's go, Keats. Let's finish this."

With that, he scooped up Shelly and the discs and left me carrying the boom box and chasing him out the front door, down the steps, and toward the wood line.

"Where are we going?" I called.

"You'll see."

18

Gordon's dawn profession of his love sent Shelly reeling—the best and worst thing that had ever happened to her.

I saw her that day at new student orientation. Mr. Robbins had asked us to set up and man a booth for the *Beacon* at the Clubs and Organizations Fair in the just-completed new gymnasium, which had been largely funded by Shelly's father's donations.

In the two years I'd known her, I'd been conditioned to Shelly's flightiness, but I'd never seen her so distracted. She constantly checked her cell phone for phantom texts and missed calls.

During occasional breaks in the steady stream of girls in braces, short shorts (both athletic and khaki), and form-fitting belly-baring spaghetti-strapped tops of varying hues that advertised their brand-new boobs (uniforms were not required for orientation)—all of the girls asking, "Where's Gordon? Is he gonna be here?"—Shelly dropped the bombshells of

Gordon's declaration of his love, Claire's pregnancy, and her feelings for Neolin.

"So, what are you going to do?" I asked.

"I don't know."

Once it was clear that Gordon wasn't coming, few of the attendees paid any attention to us nerdy wannabe writers; instead, the Warriors-to-be queued in long lines at the foreign language club booth (cool trips), the student government booth (looks good on a college application), pep club booth (awesome postgame parties, and they were handing out candy bars), and the Teens for Christ booth. (Rumor had it that Father Fulop, as club advisor, took seniors on small-group retreats to his cabin on some lake in Michigan, where he provided alcohol and some first-rate weed.)

"Does Gordon know about this Neolin?"

Shelly's crestfallen appearance revealed the answer, as she fell under the weight of an irony avalanche caused by Gordon's profession of love just when she thought she'd been able to move past him and into a relationship with a non-soul-sucking boy.

"What am I going to do, John?" She turned the question on me.

"I don't know this Indian guy, but in the time I've known Gordon, I've watched him go through girls like Kleenex. I'd hate for you to be the next tissue out of the box."

Shelly rolled her eyes. "That's a pretty shitty metaphor, John."

"Sorry."

"Besides, I'm not just some *girl*," she said. "It's different with Gordon and me. We've been best friends since we were kids. He wouldn't treat me like one of the Gordonettes."

"Well, maybe that's just it. You've been *friends* a long time. Maybe that's all you can ever be."

"He told me he loved me."

"I know, but." I trod softly. "Love can mean a lot of different things to different people, and I'm not sure there's room in his heart for both of you."

Shelly's defensiveness regarding Gordon's sincerity told me all I needed to know of her intentions. Gordon had finally summoned her into his world. No summer romance, however intense, and no litany of Gordon's past imbroglios (Annesley, Caroline, Mrs. Guiccioli, the Trinity girls at the clinic, Ms. Yancey, and Claire) had the power to dissuade her from answering his beckoning call.

When she arrived home late that afternoon, still stewing over her dilemma and exhausted from lack of sleep, Shelly went immediately out back, sat on her dock, selected her R.E.M. playlist on her MP3 player, inserted her earbuds, and waited for Gordon, just where they'd meet when they were kids. Hours passed. Exhausted, she fell asleep curled up on the warm wooden planks with her arm extended beneath her head and with her cell, set to vibrate and cupped in her hand, next to her ear.

"Shelly . . . Shelly . . . Shelly." Each pronunciation of her name was accompanied by a gentle shake of her arm, each repetition clearer than the last. "Shelly."

"Gordon?" she said through her grogginess as she brushed her hair from her face and removed her earphones.

"No, silly. It's me, Augusta."

"Augusta?" Shelly repeated in sincere bewilderment mixed with obvious disappointment.

Hands on her hips, Augusta pouted her lips and feigned hurt. "Gee, thanks."

"No. I'm sorry," Shelly said, and rose to hug her long-separated fellow musketeer. "It's been so long. I didn't recognize your voice, and"—she hesitated as she looked Augusta up and down—"you're beautiful."

And she was. A feminized version of Gordon, she'd grown quite nicely into her father's genes. Having lived three years removed from her brother's long shadow, she oozed the warmth and confidence that she'd lacked as a child.

"It's been . . ." Shelly paused to do the math.

"Three years," Augusta finished for her.

"You must be in college. Right?"

"William & Mary."

"And you've been living . . ."

"With my aunt and uncle in Virginia. When Cousin Annesley moved out after college, they offered me her room. They were very insistent, really. I'm fairly certain Catherine jumped at the chance to finally be rid of me."

"Oh, I don't think—" Shelly began a halfhearted defense of Catherine.

"It's okay," Augusta interrupted. "I never really belonged here. And other than Gordon . . . and you"—she added this last as an afterthought, and then turned and surveyed the water—"and this, I haven't missed it."

"Gordon didn't tell me."

"He didn't know. That was one of the conditions Catherine insisted on before giving up guardianship. I wasn't allowed any contact with my brother or you—or anyone, for that matter, who might disclose where I was living."

"What about now?"

"I'm an adult now. I can go where I want. Besides, Catherine still receives income from my father's family's boatyards. My aunt applied the pressure that gave Catherine little choice but to allow me to come."

"Well, how long have you been home? How long are you staying? Have you seen Gordon?" Shelly fired the questions.

Augusta answered them in order, "I got in this afternoon. Just a few days. And I just woke him too. Oh, look. Here he comes."

Shirtless, in a pair of frayed khaki cargo shorts that sagged at the hips and sat a hand's width beneath his belly button, Gordon ran his fingers through his mussed hair as he navigated, barefoot, down the sloping back lawn to the bay shore.

Shelly's gasp at the sight turned Augusta's head. "He's beautiful, isn't he? He can't help it. You should have seen him when I woke him. He sleeps in the nude, you know."

Shelly could only nod in response to Augusta's evaluation, and mutter "Yeah," as odd as that might have sounded coming from his half sister. Then Shelly said, "I mean . . . I didn't know that . . . that he . . . you know . . . sleeps . . . I mean, I know he sleeps, but . . . Yes, he is . . . beautiful, I mean."

"Look what I found," Gordon said through a smirk and a cigarette dangling from the corner of his mouth—a habit he'd picked up in Europe. He pulled three rolled joints from his front pocket. "Didn't even know they were in there, but it looks like our lucky night."

With the sun setting purple and orange directly in front of them, Gordon lit and took a long drag from the first joint, clamped between the thumb and index finger of the "okay" sign he pressed to his lips. He passed it left to Augusta, who, unlike Shelly, was no marijuana virgin. Two hours passed. They reminisced. Two more joints were smoked. The mood was mellow, the conversation increasingly uninhibited. Their circle, in the spotlight of a full moon, became continually smaller until their bare knees touched. Augusta told of her onetime experiment with ecstasy, which led to her first, only, and awkward girl-kiss. Shelly shared the story of her short-lived wrestling match with Brandon Sullivan. The truth was, he'd "finished" before he could pull his "thing" from out of his pants. And she told of her romantic kiss on the beach with Neolin. Gordon, not interested in Shelly's Indian summer, interrupted her telling with a dare.

"What do you say we swim like when we were kids?"

"You mean . . . ," Shelly began.

"Naked!" Augusta was already up, untying her bikini top, which she proceeded to swing like a double-barreled slingshot three times around her head before shimmying out of her cutoff jeans and thong. "Now you," she said, turning to Gordon as if Shelly weren't even there.

Gordon took a long, deep drag, flipped the blunt hissing into the water, rose, and dropped his shorts to his ankles. He kicked the shorts into his hand and swung them three times over his head in mock imitation of his half sister.

"Well?" Gordon said, holding Augusta's hand with his left and reaching out for Shelly's with his right.

She had yet to change out of the oversized black concert T-shirt she'd picked up at an alternative band festival in Cleveland a summer back. As she began to lift her shirt, she was mortified, remembering the old maximum-support bra she was wearing beneath, and the granny panties she had on under her athletic shorts. "Turn your backs," she said.

"What?" Augusta laughed.

"You heard me." Shelly held firm.

"C'mon," Gordon said to his sister.

After tossing her unsexy underthings into the dark perimeter, Shelly said, "Okay."

When they turned, Gordon's eyes sparkled with appreciation while Augusta's glared with envious acknowledgment of Shelly's nearly commensurate beauty, but after they had joined hands and jumped in unison into the water and played a few rounds of Marco Polo with hands much less innocently targeted than when they'd been children, it was Augusta who demanded and received the majority of Gordon's attention. She repeatedly climbed onto his broad shoulders and dove into the water, her body glistening in the moonlight. She girlishly splashed water at him to rouse his mock anger and a retaliatory bear hug, followed by a tandem toss of their bodies beneath the surface. All the while, Shelly stood off to the side, smiling awkwardly with her goosefleshed arms crossed over her breasts. Eventually, blue-lipped and shivering in the night air, she climbed out and ran toward her house with her arms holding and pressing her clothes against her nakedness.

"Hey, Shell! Where ya going?" Gordon called when he

realized her absence and spotted her running, bare-assed, toward her house.

For a moment, Gordon remained still, staring into the darkness into which she'd disappeared, but in the next instant, he was once again frolicking in the water with his more-than-sister.

Although she damn near staked out the Byron home 24/7, Shelly didn't see or hear from Augusta or Gordon for the remainder of that final week of summer. Her calls went immediately to his voice mail and her texts were not returned. She rationalized it away as the siblings maximizing the short time that they had to catch up and be together after so many years apart and before Augusta left for college. It would have been petty, she reasoned, to expect anything else. Besides, he had told her that he loved her.

The mere possibility of being Gordon's girlfriend immediately preempted Shelly's nascent relationship with Neolin. Its roots, unlike the layered and intertwined roots of her relationship with Gordon, were still shallow and easily ripped from the soil. Less than two full weeks removed from Neolin's kiss, North Bass may as well have been the north pole, for all the thought Shelly had given it once Gordon had declared his love.

After Shelly's exile from North Bass, events went badly for Neolin—at least, according to an article that appeared in the *Ogontz Reporter*, which was delivered every day at the *Beacon* through a Newspapers in the Classroom program. When I tried to show her the article on that second day of school, Shelly, after a quick glance at the headline, walked out of the room. The article stated that Ohio's prolonged economic recession had caused voter sentiment to poll strongly in favor of passing casino gambling legislation on the upcoming November ballot. Developers were waiting, shovels ready, to break ground on North Bass casinos, restaurants, condominiums, and resorts. All of which had made the pesky presence of the Ottawa intolerable.

Questioned by the reporter, the Ottawa chief revealed that an agreement had been struck with the legislators in Columbus. Legislators had assured him that if his people vacated peaceably (thereby avoiding a public relations disaster that might shift public sentiment away from passage of the gambling bill), the state of Ohio would pay the Ottawa people of Oklahoma a goodwill offering of a percentage of all slot machine profit generated on the island in perpetuity. Not perfect, the chief told the reporter, but better than nothing. He called it "a rare victory for native peoples" and "a long overdue reparation."

In an accompanying photograph, Neolin stood, wearing a disconsolate expression, next to the chief, whose arm appeared, not so much to be affectionately wrapped around him but to be propping him up. All of the Ottawa, except Neolin, were wearing kitschy traditional tribal garb for the photograph. A couple of county commissioners, the local state representative, and an actual congressman also appeared in the photo.

Within a few days, the Ottawa pilgrims vacated the island, except for Neolin. The article stated that the Ottawa renegade remained on North Bass despite repeated notifications of eviction, hand delivered by sheriff's deputies—enacting a sort of *Last of the Mohicans*. (Don't blame me. I didn't write the article or the novel.)

As gloomy as she had been the previous year, as her senior year began, Shelly was bordering on ebullient and pouring most of her excess Gordon-inspired energy into the *Beacon*. Having returned to college, Augusta no longer monopolized Gordon's time and attention.

"You guys are actually dating?" I asked Gordon as I nodded to Shelly, who flitted about the media center like an ADHD butterfly.

I took Gordon's half-shrugged shoulders and half-nod as a tepid yes.

"Like, exclusive?"

"Yeah," he managed to mutter.

"I know *this*," I said. "I've never seen Shelly so happy."

Gordon ignored my observation. "Did I tell you about that chick Zoe, who I met in Greece this summer? She had a boyfriend, a good dude, named Rony. They had this—I don't know—this thing, this relationship, that was really cool. They were more than dating; they were, like, friends, partners." Gordon paused in his reflection. "Man, I wanted to bang her more than anything, and I know she liked me, but they had something stronger. Some kind of bond I couldn't penetrate."

"That's cool," I said, not really sure of the relevance of his sudden recounting or where he was headed with it.

"Then I came home, and Shelly was all geeked up about

this dude, Neolin, and it sounds exactly like what Zoe and Rony had. It kind of shook me up, you know?" He turned his head to see if I was following. "I started thinking, 'Why not me? Why can't I have this kind of relationship?' And, who better than with Shelly? We've been best friends our entire lives."

"That's great," I said, hoping he wouldn't sense the masking of my skepticism regarding this snowball's chance.

"That's just it, you see. It's not so great. I've *tried* to think of Shelly in 'that way,' but I can't. It's just not right. And have you noticed this year's freshman chicks? Dude, they're smoking!"

"Smoking? Who's smoking what?" Shelly had snuck up, and temporarily lighted behind us. "If you guys are talking about Gordon, you've got to help me break him of that nasty habit, John. It's disgusting."

I could feel Gordon's entire form tense and not relax until Shelly fluttered away. He flashed me a do-you-see-what-I-mean glance. "I've got to go," he said.

I watched Gordon capture Shelly near the door. They exchanged a few words. As he pulled away, Shelly rose on her toes, wrapped her arms around his neck, and targeted a kiss for his lips, but at the last second, Gordon turned away, and the kiss landed on his cheek.

With her feet planted back on the floor, I read Shelly's lips as she mouthed "Love you," but Gordon's remained pressed together in a half-smile. After another hug, he slipped out of the room.

Wings collapsed, Shelly stood looking out of the doorway long after he was gone—before she once again took flight.

287

I'm no psychologist, but I think it's fair to describe Shelly's obsession with Gordon as pathological. She was a "Gordon-o-holic" in desperate need of a twelve-step program. There were plenty of other addicts to help form a charter chapter, and, I'm sure, Gordon will provide a continuing stream of future members.

Given my nearly complete lack of firsthand experience in the field, I'm even less of a relationship expert, but, as I tried to warn Shelly at orientation, I think Gordon was incapable of genuinely loving anyone outside of himself—at least in the way most of us define love and love's responsibilities. What I didn't yet totally understand then was that his egotism was so substantial that it prevented Gordon from allowing Shelly to love anyone else.

But it's impossible to quantify the sustaining power of even the smallest morsel of hope, like the one Gordon had fed Shelly when he'd said "I love you" on the morning after the day of his return from Europe. With little additional encouragement since that initial declaration, Shelly clung to the possibility of recreating the experience of that first-time high. Because she wanted so badly for his love to be true, in her mind it was, and she would require a series of repudiations on a Yahweh-placing-the-smack-down-on-pharaoh level to convince her to the contrary.

Both Shelly's and Gordon's *Beacon* pieces that semester were inspired by their previous summers. Shelly's essays were hell-bent on sparking an awareness of political and social injustice in Trinity's comfortably apathetic masses. I believe she was trying to counterbalance her abandonment of Neolin and his cause. Gordon contributed a satirical travelogue of his trip to a happily secularized Europe, where he had "witnessed" kids his age legally drinking alcohol and smoking cigarettes, clothing-optional beaches, and young people clubbing until daybreak. The piece, which Shelly snuck in after Mr. Robbins's final proofreading and long after she still gave a shit, nearly cost Mr. Robbins his job at Trinity.

At that time, I thought that I wanted nothing to do with changing minds or the world—the idea of which still seems a bit pretentious. Because I'd been stamped with a fast-approaching expiration date, little of what mattered to others mattered to me: sports teams, television shows, movies, the latest cell phones and MP3 players—none of it. I had things to do. I didn't have time to waste on bullshit, and most of it was bullshit. True things, beautiful things, stuff I could wrap my soul around, were few and far between. Instead of changing the world, I had decided to try to appreciate the true and beautiful things and write about them for as long as I could.

This sense of urgency, coupled with the necessity of maintaining fresh material on my Web page, resulted in a disciplined—borderline obsessive—writing routine. I counted hits on my site like A-Rod in a contract year. As a result, other than the writing and my taking care of Tom, I had no other life, and whereas I had once looked forward to school beginning, to escaping my charnel house and returning to the classroom, where I'd always excelled, I now loathed the idea of wasting my limited time studying subjects to prepare me for a college from which I'd probably never graduate, or for careers I'd never pursue. Therefore, to the shock of my teachers and counselor, my first quarter midterm grades were uncharacteristically low (meaning Bs), and they stayed there, but what I was writing for myself and the *Beacon* seemed purposeful and invigorating, and I had an abundance of material to contribute.

It didn't take long for Gordon to return to being Gordon, for Shelly's euphoria to vanish, or for her to begin to regret her abandonment of Neolin. A month into her so-called relationship with Gordon, other than collaborating on the *Beacon* and sitting together at a few football games, there had been no real dates, few displays of affection—public or otherwise—and no discussion of love or the direction of their relationship.

Adding to Shelly's vexation, Claire's belly had ballooned and had become a reminder of Shelly's own tragic pregnancy and Gordon's most likely unalterable "player" lifestyle.

No longer feeling "cute" in her new clothes, and growing increasingly uncomfortable, Claire grew pouty. Despite having agreed, under the duress of Mr. Shelley's insistence, on the plan to lock Gordon out of their lives, Claire was having second thoughts. Contrary to any rational consideration of his behavior, she once again began to view Gordon in romantic terms, as if he were, like Leander (my allusion, not Claire's), being kept from her against his will.

Oblivious to Shelly's own Gordon-centered hell, Claire cried to her and begged Shelly to talk to Gordon for her, which Shelly would promise to do but never did. She'd give

Shelly notes to pass along to him, which Shelly insisted she'd delivered but had actually thrown away. So, on top of her breaking heart, Shelly added a conscience racked by her deceptions.

Before long, talk of Gordon's hookups reached Shelly. At first, she didn't take the talk too seriously. In time, however, she grew fidgety, nervous, and self-doubting. She squirmed in her skin as if it were lined in burlap. Shelly had never been an honor roll student, but four "In Danger of Failing" slips were mailed home at the first quarter's midterm.

Something strange was happening to Gordon also.

"Is Gordon putting on weight?" I asked Shelly one afternoon at the *Beacon*, as I watched him waddle toward the printer.

"Maybe it's sympathy weight," Shelly said. "You know, as Claire puts on the pounds, so does Gordon." (Talk of Gordon's knocking up Claire was all over school.) Her tone was bitter, more sarcastic than ironic, and betrayed a resentment uncharacteristic of the Shelly I knew. "He gets it from his mother," she added.

I looked at Gordon once more, and for the first time saw the resemblance between him and the woman I had encountered at the swim meet the previous year.

"I've only seen it once before," Shelly said, "it" being the weight gain. "After he was dumped by his first love, his cousin Annesley. When he's depressed, he eats and pouts. It's his way of coping. But as he eats, he puts on the pounds, and he hates the way he looks, which only further depresses him. A vicious narcissistic cycle."

It probably didn't help that, having already won two state

291

championships, Gordon seemed complacent and unmotivated to swim. I know he wasn't attending preseason morning workouts, because his Hummer was never in the parking lot when I got to school in the morning. He wasn't expending the calories that he'd typically burn in the pool, and they had begun to pad his cheeks, his chin, and his midsection. On many guys, the extra weight wouldn't have been noticed. Gordon was now far from fat, but he was equally distant from his typical "cut" figure.

"He's clearly depressed," Shelly reiterated.

"Depressed?" I asked, trying to imagine how a kid who had everything could possibly be depressed.

"It's me. It's this whole pseudo-relationship thing. It's killing him. He isn't any good at it. And Gordon can't handle not being good at anything."

"What are you going to do?" I asked.

"I don't know."

The very next day after school, as I was heading to the *Beacon* from the junior class hall of lockers, I surreptitiously overheard one of the junior varsity cheerleaders playfully comment to Gordon about his "man boobs."

I ducked into a crevice formed by a break in the row of lockers near the entrance to a classroom.

"You calling me a woman, Stacy? Is that it? I'm a woman now?" His tone and posture terrified poor Stacy Bloom.

"I'm sorry, Gordon. God, I was just kidding." She pled her case to no avail and, I imagine, tried to sidestep around him, but when I peered around the corner, I could see that he had her backed into a bank of lockers.

"If I'm a woman, Stacy, how do you explain this?" Gordon pulled his junk through his open zipper and waved it at her.

She screamed, twisted away from where he had her nearly pinned, and ran for help right past where I cowered.

I heard Gordon punch the locker. He must have split the skin of a knuckle wide open, for he left a trail of blood that I followed to the boys' locker room before making my way to the *Beacon*.

In Mr. Smith's office the next morning, I'm sure Gordon denied the indecent exposure. Since there were no known third-party witnesses, it was his word against Stacy's. Mr. Smith assigned him an essay on sexual harassment, and assigned yet more counseling with Father Fulop. For Gordon, it meant more study halls spent in Fulop's office, listening to Fulop brag about "sowing my own wild oats as a young man," and, finally, it meant kneeling in front of the priest as he prayed over him. I didn't need Gordon to describe the procedure. It was the same for every student, boy or girl, sentenced to Fulop for counseling. Every kid at Trinity knew the drill.

If nothing else, his traumatic encounter with Stacy inspired Gordon to end his pig-outs, and he returned to morning swims wearing one of those Olympic-style full bodysuits. At lunch he ate nothing but fruits and vegetables, and a gallon jug of water was his constant companion.

Before long, he had shifted his shape back into its model physique.

*   *   *

Mid-October. Shelly and I were in the office debating final selections for the first semester's issue. Gordon sat across the room at a computer station, surfing the Net and oblivious to our conversation.

Out of nowhere and in a suddenly somber tone, Shelly said, "We did it."

"Did what?" I asked, sincerely afraid that the "it" was the "it" usually meant when a teenager tells another teenager that she did "it."

"We broke up."

"Oh. Good."

Naturally, she looked hurt.

"I thought you meant . . . I mean . . . It's probably a good decision," I said in an attempt to recover.

Shelly said, "I just couldn't stand it any longer."

"What are you going to do now?" I asked.

"Not sure. I'm thinking about trying to find Neolin. If it's not too late."

I was about to suggest that she stay single for a while. Maybe focus on the *Beacon*, get back involved in a club or two—you know, just try to enjoy her senior year—when we heard "Well, fuck me!" I turned to see Gordon leaning in close to the screen. "Hey, Shelly. Come here." He was already his old self, acting as if nothing out of the ordinary had ever occurred between them.

Shelly made an unconvincing show of being put out, then rose and walked over to Gordon so that she stood staring at the screen over his shoulder, blocking any chance I had of cheesing in on what they were reading.

I watched Shelly's profile as she read. At first she seemed mystified, but, slowly, a look of recognition dawned over her face. She exchanged a knowing look with Gordon but didn't say a word. After Shelly backed away and returned to the table we shared, he closed the browser, rose from his chair, gathered his things, and exited the room. Shelly, no longer able to focus, soon called it a day herself.

Left alone, I reopened the browser and searched its history. The last page visited was an online English version of the *Athens News*. The lead article reported an explosion inside a small warehouse in Pireas that killed several people. The explosion had rendered the victims unrecognizable. The police were waiting on forensics reports to aid in their identification of the bodies. Based on the high concentration of ammonium nitrate and evidence of other "bomb-making materials," police suspected that the detonation was accidental and that the dead were members of the Struggle, the terrorist organization responsible for the murder of two members of Athens's riot police during an ambush the previous August.

At that time, the story was meaningless to me, but that was about to change.

None of us attended the Halloween dance. By then, an anti-Gordon vibe had begun to pulsate through the halls. He explained away his sudden social marginalization as jealousy, and to a certain extent, it was. But, to be fair to Trinity's

blockheads, it wasn't sudden. From the string of his discon-
nected hookups, to his ruination of Hogg, to being Claire's
rumored "baby daddy," to exposing himself to Stacy Bloom,
it was an accumulation of offenses. And, prudish or not, the
cold shoulders were more than justified.

But most damaging to his status was a tidbit of gossip of
the most pernicious sort that reached the high school and
the Ogontz community. Remember, the god Rumor was the
most conniving and unmanageable of all the Greek deities.
Around the same time that Gordon was growing chunky,
Augusta was also mysteriously packing on pounds and under-
going the throes of what would eventually be diagnosed as
morning sickness. Word was that she had withdrawn from
college and was in hiding with her East Coast relatives.

It was Shelly's turn to be nauseous.

On the afternoon of the dance, clearly stung by the talk
of Gordon and Augusta, Shelly asked if she could spend the
night at my house. An odd request, but I didn't need anyone's permission, and, for reasons I didn't yet know, it was
obvious that Shelly desperately didn't want to be at home
that night of all nights in the year.

"I tried to call Neolin," she said, "but either he no longer
has his cell or he doesn't want to talk to me. Maybe he's gone
home."

"I don't think so," I said.

"How do you know?" she asked in a tone tinged with hope.

"Do you remember that article in the *Reporter* that I tried
to show you, but you wouldn't look at?"

"That was nearly two months ago."

"I know. But it said that Neolin had refused to leave the

island. The reporter called him a renegade. He *may* be gone. He probably *is* gone. But for all we know, he's still there. Maybe it's worth a shot."

Shelly didn't respond to my advice, but a plan was being hatched inside her head. "I'll see you tonight, John."

That evening, with a six-pack of hard lemonade, Shelly arrived at my door around eight o'clock, already tipsy. She started talking the second I let her in, sharing the stories of hers and Gordon's summers. She didn't stop until she had passed out dead drunk around six in the morning.

At noon, still buzzed, Shelly spoke—more like slurred—of the future—how she would graduate from high school and "leave this horseshit town," how she planned to reunite with Neolin and "make beautiful babies," how she would live on North Bass with him away from the "bullshit" of people and parents and Gordon Byron, and how she'd be happy.

Trust me, I heard it all that night (well, most of it), and I've shared it all in this book.

In school on Monday, Shelly was becoming Shelly again.

On Friday, the sixth of November, three days after the passage of the casino gambling bill by the voters of the state of Ohio, a wicked nor'easter, bringing wind-whipped rain and dark skies at noon, blew down across the lake from Buffalo and beyond. Shelly and I had taken to eating lunch together in the *Beacon*'s office. Glancing at the front-page headlines of the *Ogontz Reporter*, I read, "Island Tragedy." A wave of portent nausea washed through me.

"Shelly?" I said. "Have you talked to Neolin like you said you were going to?"

"Not yet. I've tried, but he doesn't answer his cell. I'm taking the Whaler up there tomorrow. It's my last chance before it's placed in storage for the winter. Why?"

"Just wondered," I said.

As casually as possible, so as not to excite Shelly's curiosity further, I gathered the newspaper and excused myself to the restroom. Instead, I detoured into the darkroom, where in the—appropriate for the occasion—blood-red light I scanned the article. According to the reporter, whose only source was the Ottawa County sheriff, while attempting to evict a trespasser from state-owned property on North Bass Island, a contingent of deputies had been fired upon. Following a brief standoff, the officers went all Navy SEALs (that's my interpretation), and after a round of tear gas was fired, a sniper's bullet brought the incident "to a tragic but unavoidable end." At the conclusion of an autopsy, the article said, the body of Gabriel Smith would be returned to his mother and people in the Ottawa Nation of Oklahoma.

That's as far as I read before the glare from fluorescent overhead bulbs flooded the no longer dark room. Squinting into the gaudy light and guiltily hiding the newspaper behind my back, I turned and leaned against the rusted sink baths.

Shelly stood with one hand still on the doorknob. "What you doing in here, John? I thought you were going to the bathroom. What's that?" She indicated the newspaper in my hand with a thrust of her chin.

"Nothing. I . . . I . . . I just . . ."

Witchlike in her speed, Shelly closed the distance

between us. She reached around me—all the time staring accusingly into my eyes—grabbed the paper from my hand, read all of the article she needed to read, dropped the newspaper, and turned and walked out of the darkroom, the classroom, and Trinity for the final time. After Shelly was reported absent by her afternoon teachers, Principal Smith eventually charged her truant and placed her on suspension.

It didn't matter. She wasn't coming back anyway.

That night, she penned her "The Necessity of Atheism" essay and emailed it to *Newsweek*. Not long after, the article appeared in the magazine. By her birthday in December, with little resistance from Shelly's family and none from Shelly herself, she was permanently expelled from Trinity (the essay being the final nail in her cross).

I know it seems pretty shitty of me, but I never even tried to contact Shelly after that. I planned to, and I kept telling myself I would, but it's funny how seconds become minutes become hours become weeks become months become years become lifetimes without us doing the many things we promise ourselves we will.

I spoke with Gordon on only one occasion in the weeks following Shelly's expulsion. I was alone in the media center, cleaning up after a staff (myself, Mr. Robbins, and the two remaining Gordonettes who had discovered an actual interest in publishing) Christmas party. With his hair still damp from swim practice, Gordon appeared in the doorway wearing a brand-new red letterman's jacket with white leathery sleeves. I think it was part of some kind of image restoration campaign he'd begun in the attempt to clean up his toxic reputation. It included divorcing himself from all things Shelly, like the *Beacon*. He tensely held a just-released issue like a baton, as if prepared to defend himself from a rioting rabble.

"S'up, Keats?" Gordon said by way of reunion.

"Hi, Gordon. Where've you been?"

He pointed to his wet head. "Swimming mostly. And working on *Asmodeus*. My publisher wants a draft ASA fucking P. You?"

"You're looking at it. Put in a lot of hours here, and I've been working on some things of my own."

"Oh, yeah? What kind of things?" he asked, but his eyes were busy surveying the room. I imagined them landing on and highlighting little hyperlinked icons in his memory that replayed past moments.

"I got this Web—"

"That's cool," Gordon interrupted. "Hey, nice job." He raised the rolled-up *Beacon* to qualify his compliment.

"Thanks." I ignored his rudeness. "I just finished what Shelly started."

"Yeah, but you're the new editor in chief."

"For now," I said. "It's no big deal."

"Bullshit. I'm sure Shelly's proud."

With the mention of her name, a funereal pallor fell over the room. The very space, which she had filled so often, and the atmosphere, which she had charged with such energy, mourned her absence.

"Have you talked to her?" he asked.

"No." For all that I criticize Gordon for his self-absorption, I didn't prove to be such a good friend to Shelly either. "Have you?"

"No. I'm not exactly welcome at the Shelley home."

"Did you see her essay in *Newsweek?*"

"Yeah. Very cool."

"Did you hear about"—I hesitated to say the name, not sure of the degree of sensitivity Gordon felt regarding Shelly's other love—"Neolin?"

"Yeah. It sucks. I've tried texting her a few times, but she never texts me back. She probably blames me. I guess I would too, if I were her."

"She just needs some time. You know, to sort some of this out."

"You're probably right, Keats."

That was it. Neither one of us had anything more to offer regarding Shelly, or to one another.

"Guess I'll see you around," Gordon said, and he was gone.

In late December, Claire gave birth to her daughter and named her Allegra. Within six weeks, she was back at Trinity, haunting Gordon.

I saw Shelly alive only one more time; it was on a beautiful Saturday in late May with weather that can make you forget the crappy winter you just endured and how much you hate living in Ohio. The kind of day that makes you long for the summer in the offing. From my upstairs room, I heard a heavy, purposeful knocking on the front door. It was Shelly. She looked good, like her old self, with her hair long and undone, falling over a black T-shirt with the likeness of Jim

Morrison screened in white on its front. She was in flip-flops and a pair of cutoff jeans, and she was holding a box half-full of books, mostly poetry. On a quick glance I recognized several names on the spines: Plath (of course), Sexton, Dickinson, Angelou, and Ryan.

"Hey, John," she said as I gladly opened the door.

I invited her inside, but she declined.

"I was cleaning my room and"—she paused as if rethinking her decision to part with the books—"I'd like you to have these."

"Thanks," I said, "but . . ."

She stopped me before I could ask why.

"I saw last semester's *Beacon* online; you did a great job finishing that issue." She was changing the subject, making small talk.

"Thanks," I said.

"Thanks for keeping my stuff in. You must have gotten some grief for that."

"A little," I said. "I'm nearly finished editing this semester's edition."

"That's great. How's Gordon?" It took only that long for her to get to what she'd come to ask.

"Don't you live next door?" I asked.

"Yeah," she said, looking away and watching a boat-sized Cadillac, riding low, cruise by with speakers blasting some rap song. "But it's surprising how far away next door can be."

"I know that better than most," I said, watching the Caddy continue down the street.

Shelly said, "I've tried to text him, call him, Facebook

him, but he won't respond. I kind of avoided him after all the shit of last fall. I've probably hurt his feelings."

"It isn't you, Shelly. It's Gordon. That's just how he is. You should know that by now."

"I do. I finally do," she insisted. "But I need to talk to him. I have a favor to ask him. Could you maybe pass that on to him at school?"

"Well," I began. "Since you . . . um . . . left, Gordon doesn't come around the *Beacon* much. During swim season, we talked once, but I haven't talked to him since. But I'm sure I can catch him in the hall sometime."

"I'd really appreciate it if you could do it soon," she said. "Oh! Here." She reached into a back pocket of her jean shorts and held out a copy of her R.E.M. mix. "I made one for you. Keep it. I'm going to want to listen to it with you someday."

I absentmindedly started to open the case, but she stopped me with her hands. "Not now, John. Listen to it later. You'll know when," she added cryptically.

"Okay." I laughed at her earnestness. "You can trust me; I'll take good care of it."

Then, weirdly, she placed her hands on my shoulders, sprung to her tiptoes, and kissed me on the cheek. "Thanks for everything, John. Don't forget to tell Gordon that I *really* need to see him. Okay?"

"Sure," I said, still a little stunned by the kiss.

Shelly backed off the porch, down the steps, and into the MINI Cooper, with the baby car seat in the back, that she'd borrowed from Claire. It's ironic, now, thinking of the manner in which she would return to that same driveway on the day of her wake.

I stood in the doorway for several minutes, trying to make sense of what had taken place, but soon I resumed my life, after throwing Shelly's disc onto the top of my dresser.

Tom's debilitation made it impossible for him to work, so I took a dishwashing job at Tom's old restaurant and planned to increase my hours once school let out in a few weeks.

A few months earlier, the counselors at Trinity had gotten nosy and contacted Erie County Social Services. It was probably my smelly clothes that had tipped them off, or the weight I'd lost because the only real meals I'd eaten in months were school lunches. The social worker assigned to our case helped us to apply for every kind of government aid imaginable. It was humiliating, and my father was probably doing somersaults in his grave, but the aid was instrumental in providing for Tom's doctors, medicines, therapy, and the increasing number of apparatuses required to keep him even marginally mobile or able to sit or stand upright.

With the Shelly-Gordon drama out of my life, I was better able to concentrate at school and to return my grades to normal, without sacrificing the time I still needed to devote to my writing and Web page updates. Although my readership had plateaued, and the only advertiser I had attracted was for a vanity publishing company out of Cleveland, my writing was improving, thanks to the feedback from my readers and from an online writers group I had joined.

19

Shelly's father didn't set a course for the marina as Gordon had suggested he would. Instead, he idled his boat and mirrored our path through the woods from the water. His cherry-red cigarette boat was visible through occasional breaks in the trees. Tired, hungry, emotionally spent, scratched by branches and brambles, I stopped.

"Gordon, wait. I need a break."

"What you need is to start working out. We haven't gone a hundred yards."

"Just give me a minute to rest and catch my breath," I said, panting, and I bent over with my hands braced heavily against my knees.

He looked out toward the lake, where, scanning the woods with binoculars pressed to his eyes, Shelly's father bobbed in his boat.

"We need to get to this beach up ahead and spread these ashes," Gordon said. "You know, I didn't think she had the balls to go through with it," he said as he commenced blazing the trail.

"Go through with what?" I asked, sincerely clueless.

"This!" He stopped and nodded toward the urn upraised in his hands, then spun slowly around, indicating the entire island.

"What do you mean?" I asked, as a really bad feeling began to gurgle up from the well of my ignored gut feelings.

"Killing herself."

"You mean . . . I thought you said . . ."

"Yeah, I knew about it. She told me her plan."

"Wait . . . What? 'Killing herself'? You knew about it? And you didn't do anything to stop her!" I was incredulous. I was an accomplice. I was the one who'd passed on Shelly's message of needing to speak with him. This was the result.

"What'd you want me to do, Keats? Sit with her twenty-four/seven?"

"Gee, I don't know, talk her out of it, maybe? Christ, at least tell somebody!"

"She made me promise not to. Her father would have put her in a nuthouse, which would have killed her anyway. Besides, I didn't think she was serious. You know how she was."

"Oh, that explains it. She made you promise not to. What? Did you pinkie swear?"

"Look. It's what she wanted. Who was I to tell her what to do with her life anyway? If she was so unhappy that dying seemed a relief, then why should I deny her that? We have no choice in when or to what asshole parents we come into this world. At least, shouldn't we be able to decide for ourselves when to leave it?"

"You were supposed to be her friend, you selfish prick!" I shouted as I gave him the most ineffectual shove in the history of chivalry.

"*I'm* selfish?" He'd grabbed my arm at the wrist and twisted until I was bent over again and, this time, in excruciating pain. "You think I should have convinced her to go on living miserably so that *your* feelings wouldn't be hurt? Don't give me that bullshit about the selfishness of suicide. What's selfish is insisting that she continue in her misery so *you* won't have to feel sad or guilty."

"Guilty? Why should I feel guilty?"

"She told me about the poetry books, dude. What'd you think she was doing? Organizing for a garage sale?"

He released me from the submission hold and sent me reeling, as if on drunken legs, until I stumbled off the path and fell onto the razor-sharp leaves of the now pissed-off plant growing in the sandy soil. The boom box catapulted from my hand.

"I . . . I didn't think . . . ," I said, still planted on my ass.

"Yeah, that's right. You didn't think. Because, just maybe, deep down you knew what she was doing too, and you didn't want to interfere either, because in that deep-down place you understood that it was what she wanted. So keep your self-righteous bullshit to yourself. I don't need it."

Gordon tore off down the path, leaving me scrambling on my hands and knees, patting the brush in search of the boom box batteries, which had flown from their compartment when I'd fallen.

"Gordon, wait," I said, but he ignored my call.

When I burst into the small cove with the sand beach,

where Neolin had kissed Shelly last August and where she had chosen forever to mingle her atoms with those of the universe, I saw the cigarette boat anchored just offshore, and Gordon standing frozen at the gunpoint of Shelly's father's double-barrel. Mr. Shelley's blue canvas boating sneakers were soaked, as were his pants up to his knees.

"Who are you?" her old man asked me.

"Nobody. A friend of your daughter's."

I glanced at Gordon for, I don't know, direction? Reassurance? But he just stared coldly past the gun barrel into Shelly's father's eyes.

"How'd you know where to find us?" Gordon asked.

"When I got home from the wake, my stepdaughter Frances met me on her way to wherever it is she goes. 'Here,' she says, 'that girl,' meaning Shelly, 'asked me to give this to you.' And she hands me a disc."

"What kind of disc?" Gordon asked.

"A DVD. It was Shelly. She talks a bit about you, but most of it's personal." He looked directly at Gordon. "Family stuff. And she tells about this here." He pointed with the gun barrel at the urn. "Her final wishes. I guess she thought I might forgive you if I knew it was what she wanted."

"I'm not the one who needs forgiveness," Gordon said.

"Are you sure about that?" Shelly's father replied.

I jumped in front of the urn, as if willing to take a bullet. "You can't have her," I said.

"Don't want her. If this is what she wants, I can at least give her that."

"Then why'd you track us down?" Gordon asked as he brushed me aside.

"I'm afraid she may have shared a copy of that disc with you. If you do have one . . ." He paused. "What's on that disc . . ." He paused again. "I can't take the chance of anybody else seeing it. So, why don't you hand it over. Then you can go and do whatever she asked you to."

"What if I don't?"

"Well, son, I know—and I mean *know*—things about you too. Not just rumors, but things that could ruin that all-American boy image you use to sell so many books."

"You don't know anything," Gordon said.

"Oh, no? I've lived next door to you for a lot of years. I may not be the smartest man in the world, but I do pay attention, and over the years that mama of yours, on more than one occasion, talked a blue streak while sharing a nip or two over the fence, so to speak. Where should I start? The nanny? Your cousin? The fag roommate? That stripper girl? The secretary? Claire? Or maybe, your sister?"

The litany of his indiscretions did nothing to shame Gordon, nor do I think he really gave a shit who knew about them. But Gordon's innate business sense recognized the damage that could be done to his marketability.

"So, all you want is the disc?"

"That's it. Give it to me, and I'll be on my way."

Gordon hesitated, as if he were actually considering his options. "All right," he said. "Give the man his disc, Keats."

I looked at him in confusion. I didn't have it; he did, but the suggestion drew Shelly's father's attention to me while Gordon extracted the disc from his back pocket and removed from the case Shelly's R.E.M. mix CD, which he quickly tucked down the front of his pants.

"Oh, shit. Here it is," Gordon said, holding out the DVD inside the case toward Shelly's father, who snatched it from Gordon's hand.

Mr. Shelley didn't look happy or victorious—just sad and, maybe, a little relieved.

"Now, if you boys follow me out and give me a shove into deeper water, I'll leave you alone." Of course, his request for help came at the convincing end of a shotgun.

Once at the steering console, Shelly's father pressed the button to automatically withdraw the anchor from its bite in the mucky bottom. Shoeless and with pants rolled over our knees, we pushed from the bow until the boat had enough draw to start its massive engines. At their roar, we backed away, turned, and waded to the beach.

"What do you think he'll do when he realizes he has a copy of *Harold and Maude*?" I asked Gordon.

"Beats me. He'll probably drop it in the middle of the lake anyway. I can't believe that whatever is on the disc Shelly gave him is something he wants to see again."

"You mean, you *don't* have one?"

"Nope. Shelly didn't give me any discs. But you know that abortion you told me about earlier?"

He waited for me to make the unspeakable link.

"No!"

"He's got to be the one," Gordon said, "but you can't tell anyone."

"Can't tell anyone! You've got to be kidding me! Why do you want to protect him?" Still disbelieving, I stammered, "But—but how do you know? Did Shelly tell you?"

"Not exactly, but I'm pretty good at math. You can

believe me or not. Suit yourself, but it's the only thing that makes sense. Shelly must have talked about it on that disc she left him."

"How about Brandon Sullivan? There were a lot of rumors last year."

"Nope. Not according to Shelly."

"Okay. Still," I said, "why do you want to keep his secret? He should be in jail!"

"Think about it, Keats. Who's it going to help by revealing it? Shelly? I don't think so. And if that was what she wanted, she could have done it herself. Besides, he's right about my reputation. If even half of the shit I've done got out to my fans, I'd be done. Now let's finish this. I'm hungry, I need a shower, and"—he glanced at his watch—"I graduate in exactly six hours."

I wanted to throw up.

"Is this the spot?" I asked.

"You mean where they found her body? Yeah, this is it."

"How did she . . ."

"Do it?"

"Yeah."

"Keats, have you ever been attracted to and repulsed by the same thing? Kind of like watching a horror film through your fingers?"

I couldn't believe an ironist like Gordon could say such a thing with a straight face.

"Shelly was that way with drowning. I mean, obviously, the idea scared the hell out of her, but she also thought it would be a romantic way to die."

"There's nothing romantic about dying," I said.

311

"Well, Keats, that's where you lack vision. Considering your little death fetish, I'd expect you to have more appreciation for the aesthetic of this sort of thing. Don't look so surprised. Shelly told me. Your mistake is that you've concluded life is short, so you treat it as if it's precious, like a pretty little princess. Bullshit! Everyone's life is short. Quit feeling sorry for yourself. Fuck it. Treat it like a cheap hooker. Ask crazy shit from it, and you'll get more out of life than you could have ever wanted, imagined, or deserved. We all die young, Keats. It's time you stop feeling sorry for yourself and worrying about everyone else."

"That might be true for you, Gordon, but—"

He interrupted my defense. "She waited for the right day. A rough day. Almost exactly a year from when she'd first sailed to North Bass. Winds out of the east kicking up four-to-six-footers. *Ariel* was an old boat, barely seaworthy, really. When she got offshore here, I'll bet she punched a hole somehow in the bottom with a sledgehammer or something heavy like that, which she then probably hugged to her chest as the boat filled and sank. Just imagine it. That's a righteous death. Beats the shit out of old age."

"How'd she manage to come ashore right here? Right where she wanted to?"

"For once, I'd like to think, Shelly caught a break."

"But the Coast Guard ruled it an accident."

"Yeah, but give *me* a break. They haven't even bothered to search for and salvage the boat. Seems to me that everyone's happy, including Shelly."

"But, how can you *know*? I mean, for sure? Maybe she changed her mind, and her drowning *was* an accident. You can't know for sure." I was grasping for any port in a storm of rising emotions. If he wanted, if for one moment he could have stopped being Gordon, he could have provided that safe harbor.

Instead, he said, "Easy. When they found her, she wasn't wearing a life jacket. Dude, Shelly never went out on the water in a boat without a life jacket."

For a moment, trying to imagine her final minutes, I looked out over the surface of the water, until Gordon interrupted my musing.

"Let's go," he said.

We trudged up the beach to where I had set the boom box. Gordon handed me the disc to insert into the player while he picked up Shelly and removed the stopper from the urn.

"Now what?" I asked.

"Press play."

We waited for the opening measures of "Shiny Happy People," but we'd forgotten about the extra track that had bumped every other one back.

It was Shelly's voice that burst from the speakers. "Hey, guys. I threw in *Harold and Maude*. Watch it sometime; it kind of sums it all up, you know? Maude and I, we kind of share a soul. I just happened to feel eighty at eighteen. Anyway, I want to thank you guys for bringing me here. Isn't it beautiful? Romantic? It's a good place to end, don't you think? With any luck, I'm sitting in the light somewhere, talking in rhymes."

Silence from the speakers. Gordon stared at me, perplexed.

Finally, Gordon said, "That made a lot of sense."

"She got that a lot," I said. After a few moments, the violins began to play and, for one last time, R.E.M. lifted Shelly's lingering soul.

"Hold out your hands," Gordon said with the urn positioned to pour.

"What?" I instinctively pulled my hands back behind me.

"C'mon. It's what she said she wanted. It's just Shelly. Now. While the song's playing." Gordon's urgency and my memories of Shelly compelled my cupped hands forward, which Gordon filled to brimming.

When he had a handful of his own, we threw Shelly into the air, and she alighted softly on the sands and in the water. Somehow, perhaps giddy from exhaustion, we found ourselves laughing and singing and dancing like the biggest dorks in the world as we continued to empty the urn, one handful at a time.

When the song ended, we washed our hands in the lake.

"There's one more thing," Gordon said as he took out his wallet and removed a slip of paper. It was inscribed with what Gordon informed me were Maude's final words to Harold, and the words were written in what I could tell was Shelly's handwriting: "Go and love some more," it read.

Gordon rolled the note into a scroll and stuffed it inside the urn. He then secured the stopper back into its mouth as tightly as he could before gently setting the urn into the water at our feet. Slowly, the lapping of the waves drew the urn out into the lake.

That's when it hit me. "This is it," I said.

"This is what?" Gordon replied.

"Her last wish. This. Not the ashes; not the message in a

bottle. It's you and me together. That was her real last wish. This whole adventure was Shelly's way of forcing you and me to be together. Don't you see, she gave each of us pieces of the puzzle. I knew of the abortion, but she told you about her father. She told you where to spread the ashes, but she gave me the disc to play. We couldn't have done this without each other."

Gordon contemplated my theory for a second, then said, "Keats, you just may be right. It would be . . ."

"So Shelly," I finished.

20

Now that she is gone, Shelly has entrusted her most prized possession—George Gordon Byron—to me. Gordon and I have started to hang out now and then. On the last Saturday of June, Gordon threw me on the back of his Jet Ski, and we spent two hours jumping the wakes of ferries, freighters, and powerboats as they crisscrossed Ogontz Bay. In July, I convinced Gordon to come with me to Planned Parenthood, where I've begun volunteering. Sha'niqua had the two of us stuffing envelopes until our fingertips bled. And, just this past weekend, we took the Corsair back to North Bass and visited with Shelly.

With high school behind him, Gordon's second novel in the Manfred series has been completed and targeted for release next summer. He's taking a year off from school to "get his shit together" and "to chill," but Gordon with time on his hands sounds like a bad situation to me. He says that eventually he'd like to attend college back East, somewhere near his father's relatives. I haven't asked about it, but in a post on his website, Gordon congratulated his sister, Augusta, on her marriage to the son of a prominent family in Virginia, and on the birth of their baby girl, Elizabeth, who was born the very day of Shelly's drowning.

I spent most of this past summer writing this manuscript and watching a mother and her three children slowly renovating and moving into the house next door. The oldest girl is stunningly pretty and around my age. I've heard the others call her Fanny.

In other news, the Disease has begun a surge, and Tom is sicker than ever. I've also picked up the guitar and have found that I am a quick study. I've begun to convert some of my poems to lyrics, having resigned myself to the regrettable reality that in the dismal condition of today's poetry market, if I want my voice to be heard, I'd better put it to music. I've even got a few tracks posted to my page, and I'm putting together a webcam video for YouTube. Who knows? Maybe that's my way to defeat this dying thing: my voice, my words, my music, even my unremarkable face forever inhabiting cyberspace.

Which brings me back to the beginning: love and death.

In the course of the three years during which my life had intertwined with Shelly's, I'd pretty much come to accept the Trinity community's final view of Gordon as a real asshole: oversexed, arrogant, and self-absorbed. What Shelly gave me, in sharing the story of their lives, was a more open-minded way of considering him—hell, a more open-minded way of considering everything and everyone. What Shelly gave me, in asking me to share the spreading of her ashes alongside Gordon, was a friend.

318

For his part, Gordon showed me that choosing *not* to burden another with an impossible love may be the most selfless act of love of all. He knew that he could never love Shelly the way she deserved to be loved. So he never came on to her, never seduced her. And, except for their onetime overreaching, they both understood and accepted that reality. She'd once told me in reference to Gordon, "He ignores me because he loves me." It didn't make much sense to me then. Now it is crystal.

Together they have shown me the selflessness required when choosing to love or not to love, and because of Gordon's insistence on a life of his own defining, and Shelly's identical insistence on her death, I'm a little less afraid of both.

Sometimes, if I find myself thinking about Shelly or the events of that day, I play the R.E.M. disc, and if I close my eyes, I swear I can feel the kiss she left on my cheek the last time I saw her, and I can smell the sea and the sand of the tiny strand where she lives forever.

So, what I said at the beginning, I'll repeat at the end: learn to deal with the truth of dying, and you'll experience the awesomeness of living. Death and love are real. That's all I know on earth, and all I need to know.

AFTERWORD

Just as it would be a mistake to study Shakespeare's history plays for an understanding of the succession of English monarchs from the thirteenth through much of the sixteenth century, one should not read *So Shelly* for its dogged adherence to historical accuracy. Like Shakespeare, I would never let historical facts get in the way of telling a good story. I hope that the transposition of Shelley, Byron, and Keats two centuries into the future demonstrates my faith in the reader's willingness to suspend disbelief.

Admittedly, my inclination throughout the storytelling process was to emphasize each of the poets' "better angels," for it is indisputable that they all possessed off-putting character flaws of differing degrees. On the relatively minor end of the spectrum, John Keats could be intensely self-absorbed and aloof. Percy Shelley, despite his heartfelt sympathy for victims of the wide variety of social injustices of the early nineteenth century, could be brutally insensitive to the emotional well-being of his most intimate friends and family members. Worst of all, in his egomania, George Gordon, Lord Byron, was often completely oblivious, if not downright cruel, in the treatment of his family and social intimates.

So, what of *So Shelly* is grounded in historical truth? To begin with, it is important to understand that the character of Shelly is actually a blending of the life and personality of **Percy Shelley** with that of his wife, **Mary,** the author of the classic novel *Frankenstein*. Both Percy and Mary had strained relationships with their fathers and distant, at best, relationships with their mothers or stepmothers. Percy's father was fabulously wealthy. As a child, Percy was a bright and inquisitive boy who loved the outdoors, where his imagination ran wild. But in formal educational settings, he was a distracted student, peeved by being made to learn subjects in which he had little interest. During his university days, Percy had a falling-out with his father after he penned an essay titled "The Necessity of Atheism." Their relationship never recovered, and the publication of the essay resulted in Percy's expulsion from school and, ultimately, Percy's status as a pariah.

Mary Shelley's controversial feminist mother, Mary Wollstonecraft, died soon after giving birth to Mary. Her father, the radical social philosopher William Godwin, soon remarried. Mary's new stepmother was **Mary Jane Clairmont,** with whom Mary's father had a daughter, **Claire.** Mary nurtured a strong dislike for her stepmother, who showed great favoritism for her own daughter and acted as a wedge between Mary and her father. **Frances** (Fanny) was actually Mary Wollstonecraft's illegitimate daughter from a previous relationship—unlike in the novel, where I've made her Shelly's stepsister along with Claire. Claire would later travel with Mary and Percy in a sort of threesome that inspired many scandalous rumors. During one such trip, on which Byron accompanied them, Claire became pregnant with his child, and she eventually bore him an illegitimate daughter, **Allegra.** Claire developed a stalkerlike obsession with Byron, which inspired in him great anguish and loathing.

George Gordon, Lord Byron, was the son of a sea captain, **John Byron,** nicknamed "Mad Jack." John was absent for his son's birth and abandoned Byron; his wife, **Catherine;** and his daughter from a previous marriage, **Augusta,** by the time Byron was three years old. John Byron had married Catherine only for her inheritance, which he managed to drain in the few remaining years of his dissolute life. Catherine had a weak-willed and cloying personality, but she was indulgent of her ungrateful son. Together, they lived in a country estate that had seen better days, but she couldn't afford the necessary renovations.

Byron was born with a clubfoot, which mortified him his entire life. He took great pains to mask his handicap and to prove that he was a physical match for any "normal" boy. As a child, he was sexually abused by his nanny, **May Gray.** He also had a tendency toward chubbiness. As he was incredibly vain regarding his appearance, in order to combat the weight gain, he undertook periods of a strict regimen of exercise and extreme dieting.

During his time in prep school, Byron was a big man on campus—a prankster, a gifted athlete, and a big spender. Not completely atypical of students in the English single-sex prep schools of the period, he also had, most likely, homosexual relationships with, or at least homoerotic feelings for, various boys, typically underclassmen. One of the most intense of these relationships was with **William Harness.**

Despite his clubfoot, Byron became a champion boxer and swimmer. During a tour of Turkey and Greece, he re-created Leander's legendary swimming of the Hellespont. His traveling companion was **John Hobhouse.** On that trip, Byron also managed to deface the Temple of Poseidon by carving his initials in a pillar; they can still be seen today. *Childe Harold's Pilgrimage,* published when he was but twenty-four years old, was an overnight bestseller. Byron commented on its success, saying, "I awoke one morning and found myself famous." *Manfred* is a highly autobiographical verse drama, in which the title character expresses both in-cestuous longing for his sister and a deeply humanistic phi-losophy of living.

Byron had a tendency to fall in love with female relatives, among them a cousin, Margaret Parker; another cousin, Mary **Chaworth** (renamed Annesley in the novel); and, most scandalously, his half sister, **Augusta.** It is generally accepted that he and Augusta had an incestuous affair dur-ing which Augusta's daughter, **Elizabeth,** was most likely conceived.

Two of Byron's other most noted lovers were married women: Teresa **Guiccioli** and **Caroline Lamb.** Though ob-viously adulterous, his four-year affair with Guiccioli was one of the most stable romantic relationships of his life. His affair with Lamb, however, was as tempestuous as his affair with Guiccioli had been steady. After initially describing Byron as "mad, bad and dangerous to know," Lamb began a summer affair with him. After his inevitable rejection of her, she became his stalker.

The last years of Byron's life were spent supporting, both financially and by his own participation, the Greek war of independence from the Turks.

Although his poverty is often exaggerated, **John Keats** came from the lower middle class, at best, and he was much the social inferior of Shelley and Byron. Diminutive of stature, he shared Byron's need to prove his worth. Unlike Byron, however, Keats avoided debauched pursuits and took a longer view. He was determined to leave an immortal impression before what he always knew would be his early demise. His fear of a premature death was the result of his seeing both of his parents die young. In addition, he had to nurse his dying brother, **Tom,** who succumbed to tuberculosis, like their mother.

Of the three second-generation Romantics, Keats died first and at the youngest age. Although he had a relationship—more of a long-distance mutual admiration society—with Shelley, he had virtually no contact with Byron. Unlike Shelley and, to some extent, Byron, Keats did not believe poetry should be used as a tool for social improvement. He believed it should exist as a monument to beauty.

He wrote of the poet's experience of "negative capability," which is a blending in and becoming invisible, yet remaining sympathetically sentient, within any environment. This talent is what makes Keats the ideal narrator of *So Shelly* and accounts for his relative absence from the story as compared to the overwhelming presence of Gordon.

In their lives and in their poetry, Byron, the Shelleys, and Keats crystallized what has proven to be the indomitable spirit of Romanticism. Its emphasis on energy, emotion, optimism, freedom, individual and social betterment, nonconformity, and righteous revolution continues to inspire new generations of young people who starve for a better way than that perpetually offered by the status quo.

BIBLIOGRAPHY

Andronik, Catherine, M. *Wildly Romantic: The English Romantic Poets: The Mad, the Bad,and the Dangerous*. New York: Henry Holt and Company, 2007.

Eisler, Benita. *Byron: Child of Passion, Fool of Fame*. New York: Knopf, 1999.

Grosskurth, Phyllis. *Byron: The Flawed Angel*. New York: Houghton Mifflin, 1997.

Motion, Andrew. *Keats: A Biography*. New York: Farrar, Straus and Giroux, 1997.

Seymour, Miranda. *Mary Shelley*. New York: Grove Press, 2000.

Wroe, Ann. *Being Shelley: The Poet's Search for Himself*. New York: Pantheon Books, 2008.

ACKNOWLEDGMENTS

I'd like to thank the following people, without whom *So Shelly* would have never come to fruition:

My wife, Julie, who, for nearly twenty-five years, has tolerated my solitary nature and frequent disappearances into my dark places, yet has managed to be waiting for me upon my return every time.

My sons, Taylor, Travis, and Tanner, whose resilience, goodness, and courage in the face of their own adversities inspire me to adhere to my own credo: Work hard and believe in yourself, and good things will happen.

My parents, Tom and Barb, and my brothers and sisters: Kevin, Lori, Amy, J, Aaron, Troy, and Yon. Whatever I am, I am because of you.

My in-laws, Tony and Peggy Guerra, who not once, despite my lack of real-world skills, questioned my worthiness for their daughter.

My agent, Katherine Boyle, and all at Veritas Literary Agency, for spotting the potential in what proved to be a very rough draft.

My editor at Delacorte Press, Michelle Poploff, and her assistant, Rebecca Short. Their artistry turned a story with not much more than an interesting premise into a real novel, and turned a writer with an occasionally clever turn of phrase into an author.

My friend, Kelly Croy, whose relentless words of optimism and encouragement through four years of rejection continually drew me back to my laptop to eke out a few more words.

My twelfth-grade Modern Novel teacher, later a colleague and friend, Gary Kelley, who woke me to the power of the novel form and sparked a lifelong addiction to the genre. My students, past and present, who consistently prove that young people are beautiful and far more capable than that for which they are given credit.

R.E.M. and Better Than Ezra, whose music and lyrics, I believe, best capture the manic period of young adulthood and played an instrumental role in the production of *So Shelly*.

Each of you is among the countless atoms that form the pages of this book.

ABOUT THE AUTHOR

Ty Roth teaches literature and English composition at both the high school and university levels. He has studied Romantic poets and enjoys teaching his students about them. He holds a sociology degree from Xavier University and a master's degree in English literature from the University of Toledo. He lives with his family in Sandusky, Ohio, on the shore of his much-loved Lake Erie.